I0768510

A RUSTON FESTIVAL NOVEL

THE *Spite* BEFORE *Christmas*

BY JESSICA BOOTH

First edition: November 2024

Identifiers: ISBN 979-8-9870116-6-9 (trade paperback), 979-8-9870116-7-6 (ebook)

Author's Note

Dear Reader:

The Spite Before Christmas contains themes of grief, childhood illness, domestic and verbal abuse, parental abandonment, and cancer. There are open door sex scenes.

The childhood illness depicted in this book comes directly from my experience as a mother of a child who suffers from an autoimmune disease. As rheumatologists were quick to tell me, these diseases are diverse, evolving, and manifest differently in every child. They are also treated differently based on the child's health and needs. I did my best to stay authentic to both the illness and how children and adults respond to it. I recognize that not every experience is like ours, but I hope that you can relate to little Julia and unite your hope and suffering with hers.

While this does have a happily ever after for everyone, I encourage you to read carefully and protect your mental health.

XOXO, Jessica

Chapter 1

MARGIE

PRESENT DAY: NOVEMBER

The shiny, black Tesla parked in my next-door neighbor's driveway is as suspicious as a suddenly quiet toddler. Out here in the North Louisiana woods off of Farmerville Highway, an electric car might as well be a UFO. I try to make out who it belongs to from where I peer through the window over my kitchen sink. But at fifty-two, my eyesight isn't what it once was.

My neighbor, Annie Mae Hill, has been homebound for the past year. The only cars that ever stop by her house are the Meals on Wheels van and her daughter's white Suburban full of children. And unless Meals On Wheels suddenly received a charitable windfall, that Tesla belongs to a stranger—and strangers are rarely a good thing around here.

Worry slides between my shoulder blades. I hope Annie Mae is okay. I've made a point of stopping by her house a couple of times a week to make sure she's still alive and kickin'. The thought of dying alone in a house with no one to find her hits a little too close to home.

The strings of premonition pluck along my spine, and I decide it won't hurt to go check on my longtime neighbor. I grab my tall, black rubber boots and slide them onto my feet. We're in a rural area, and the walk between our spacious yards usually means dodging mole hills and kicking now-dormant fire ant hills along the way—not to mention the mud. And, my, how it's been raining this year.

As I squelch across the yard, a man in a charcoal suit steps out of Annie Mae's front doorway and bends down to fiddle with the door knob. Now, *that* definitely isn't right. No point in being shy about it, so I walk right up to the man.

"Hi there. Everything okay with Annie Mae?"

The man startles from where his focus was locked onto the object now dangling from the door knob.

"Oh, hi there. I'm Zachary Acosta," he says, extending his hand. I fold my arms and study him. He's tall and thin, maybe in his early thirties. His hair is slicked back, and he wears slacks and a button-up shirt. He clears his throat. "I'm, um, Ms. Hill's real estate agent."

That does surprise me. "Is Annie Mae dead?" I ask, never one to be delicate.

Zachary coughs, startled. "No, ma'am. She's moving into The Willows Assisted Living and selling the house now that she no longer needs it."

"Oh," I say, at a loss for words for perhaps the first time in my life. "Well, okay. I'll call up to The Willows and get her room number then." I hesitate, studying the young man who is fidgeting awkwardly before me. "Anyone looking at buying the place?"

"Not yet," he says. "But we just listed it yesterday, and I'm about to put the For Sale sign in the yard. If you know of anyone who might be interested, send them my way." He hands me a business card that I tuck into my pocket without taking the time to study it.

"Sure thing." When he fidgets again, I realize that he's trying to be polite and waiting for me to leave. So, I spin on my heel and squelch back to my house.

Assisted living. And right before the holidays. I'm sure it's for the best, but the whole situation doesn't sit right with me. Annie Mae has been my neighbor for fifteen years. Yes, she's been increasingly frail, but assisted living? Loneliness cleaves through my heart as I trudge. It's an emotion I've become well acquainted with through the years, though I'd never admit to it.

I kick my boots off on my front porch and push open the door into my aged, well-kept house. Empty mason jars are lined up on the kitchen table, ready to be filled with my now-famous peach jam. My house smells delicious from long days of cooking fruit, sugar, cinnamon, and cloves. Somehow, I, a woman in her fifties with graying, frizzy, auburn hair and an attitude that would scare the hair off a rat, has managed to become a YouTube sensation.

I glance at the ring light and the phone tripod sitting on the table. I still can't believe my channel has gained so much traction over the past few years, but it's a blessing. The YouTube ad revenue and jam and jelly sales provide for me financially and give me a reason to keep getting out of the house and going to farmer's markets and festivals. Well, that and my niece's insistence.

I smile, thinking of Amelia, or Lia, as those close to her call her. She's my niece and the light of my life. She has continually pushed me to grow my little business. And Amelia is as sweet as peach pie, but a dose of my stubborn streak rubbed off on her over the years. Hard not to when I raised her as my own. Even though she moved out of my house years ago, I swear I can still hear her laughter on the days that are just a little too quiet.

Amelia's spidey sense must be tingling because my phone rings, and I look down to see her beautiful face flash across the screen. *Amelia Hebert.* I slide it open.

"Hey, Lia."

"Aunt Margie, how are you?"

"Oh, just fine. Nothing too special going on."

"Good, because I have something for you to do," she coaxes.

"I don't know if I like the sound of that."

"You haven't even heard what I'm going to ask yet," she scolds. She really is starting to sound more and more like me.

"Fine, spill it," I demand.

"So, you know how I kind of resurrected the Fall Fest from the brink of extinction?" Amelia begins.

"I don't think that's something any of us will soon forget," I deadpan, remembering the festival that, with her tenacity and guidance, not only reinvigorated local commerce, but also became Ground Zero for solving a cold case a few years ago.

"Right, well, it turns out that when you do a good job at planning something—you get more assignments," Amelia says, exhaustion lighting her voice.

"You know what they say," I tell her. "You want something done? Ask the busiest person you know."

"Seems unfair, but that's beside the point," she admits.

"And what is the point, exactly?" I ask, already beginning to suspect what she's about to say. I rub my thumb over the worn hole in my jeans, bracing for it.

"You know the big Christmas Market at the Civic Center? Well, I have been assigned to the public relations committee for this year. I need to lock down some key vendors who are willing to also help sponsor the event. And I thought that since your business is the hottest thing this side of the Mississippi, you would be perfect," she says with false brightness.

I close my eyes, picturing her wide, whisky eyes and overly bright smile that she's used on me to get her way since she was just a girl.

"No one in their right mind would ask me to do this," I say.

"Aunt Margie, you are an ideal fit for this and have more determination than any other person I've ever met. And we could use the support of your enthusiastic fan base," Amelia pleads.

"You just want my money."

"Well, yes, we do need sponsorship money to make this year's Christmas Market successful, but you won't have to do it alone. You can be one of the lead sponsors, and I will get an additional business to co-sponsor. That will take the pressure off of all of us. And then, of course, you can talk about the event on your YouTube channel and draw in more shoppers," Amelia says brightly.

I sigh and rub my eyes, knowing I've already lost this argument. I would do anything for my girl, even if she is thirty-one now. Her tone reminds me of Amelia at twelve, dragging wild animals into my house and doing her best not to get caught.

"Fine," I say, resigned.

Amelia squeals with delight. "You won't regret this, Aunt Margie! I'll get the contract together and let my boss know you're on board. Beth and I can help you with any graphic design work for sponsorship signs."

"Yes, yes, fine," I say, waving her off even though she can't see me.

"I love you, Aunt Margie," she says, sincerity coloring her tone. My heart melts just a smidge.

"I love you too, Lia."

I end the call and, as I linger in my kitchen, overpowering quiet fills my house and sits on my chest like a mischievous cat. I stare at the rows of empty mason jars in front of me. At least the work keeps me busy and chases the loneliness away. Mostly.

Though I suppose that if I'm going to co-sponsor and be a vendor at this event in just five or so weeks, I have a lot of prep work to do. And since Amelia is in charge of vendors, I want to make extra sure that everything I produce is the best it can be. I'll need to restock all of my canning supplies, get more "Margie's Machinations" labels, and drive outside the city limits so I can legally purchase a new bottle of bourbon to get me through it all.

I look over at the worn fox stuffed animal that holds a permanent place on my shelf, and I can almost hear the little girl version of Amelia begging me to teach her how to cook. I wish she were still at my side, helping me fill these empty jars and silent rooms. But getting caught up in the past won't help me now. With a sigh, I tune the radio to a classic rock station and pull out my saucepans.

Chapter 2

FRANK

NOVEMBER, PRESENT DAY

"Dad, you really should go look at this house. It's nice, has a big yard, and you don't have to maintain acres of land just to exist," my son, Jason, pleads.

"I've lived in this house forever. I raised you and your brother here. It's not that easy to just up and leave it all," I say softly, nostalgia tugging at my heart.

But he hears the words I don't say. *This is the house I lived in with your mom. If I leave this house, I'm abandoning a piece of her, and I'm not sure my heart can take it. It's hard enough just being alive when she isn't sometimes.*

"Dad," Jason says gently, grasping my shoulder.

I look into his green eyes, the same emerald shade as his mother's. My shoulders slump. He's always been so like her, both in looks and disposition. Drew, my youngest, is the one who favors me with his pale blue eyes, dark hair, and stubborn pursuits.

"It's okay, Dad. Mom would understand," Jason continues. "She wouldn't want you to kill yourself trying to take care of this place. It's too big. Too much house, too much yard, too many utilities, and too many animals."

"But where will you and your family hang out when you come to visit me?"

"It's not like you would be moving into a one-bedroom apartment, Dad. It's just a smaller house with a smaller yard. And..." he says mischievously, "it will be easier to decorate for the holidays."

My mouth kicks up at that. I've had a special place in my heart for Christmas since my wife, Cheryl, converted me from a Grinch to a bonafide Clark Griswold. I didn't think that kind of transformation was possible, but Christmas decorations delighted her. And then my children—and now grandchild—began to seek out the new things I added to my yard each year. Picturing their delighted faces instantly turns the tide of my mood.

"Just think about it," Jason says, handing me a flier.

I roll it open and study the house for sale, noting that it's off Farmerville Highway, still kind of out in the country. I run my hand through my cropped, salt-and-pepper hair and seriously consider my son's suggestion. A smaller house would mean less to care for, sure. But, more importantly, it might do me some good to stop expecting to see my late wife in every corner of our family home. My heart tugs at the thought. It's been three years since she died from cancer, but I still sometimes expect to find her in her favorite chair or sitting in the garden, nurturing lavender to life despite the oppressive Louisiana sun. Maybe this would be good for me, good for all of us.

I turn the flier over to study the house's specs and notice that there is a shed in the backyard, perfect for Christmas decoration storage. And the oversized garage can house my woodworking tools. There's a swing out back too, and I know my granddaughter, Julia, would like that. Already, I can picture her dancing along the rock path leading from the house's back patio to the shed. I resolve to call the real estate agent today before I can talk myself out of it.

IT DOESN'T TAKE LONG to schedule an appointment to look at the house. The agent meets me there, a brilliant smile plastered across his eager face. He walks me through the place. And while it's worn and will need some fixing up, the size is good and the backyard is even bigger and better in person. It's only two bedrooms to my current four, but that's the point, I suppose.

I would have a couple of neighbors here, but the yards are spacious and spread apart. And, I know Jason would never say this to me, but he will sleep better at night knowing I have someone next door. I'm fifty-three and healthy from the consistent farm work and outdoor labor I've done over the years. But my sons constantly check on me since Cheryl died. I'm not blind to their concerns, but I appreciate them all the same. Who knows? Maybe I'll make friends with my neighbors, show my boys that I am just fine, and convince Jason he can focus more on his own family, especially with Julia's health concerns.

When I walk into the backyard and open the shed, I expect to find it full of wasp nests and spider webs, but it seems to have been cleaned out recently. It smells of sawdust and a hint of gasoline. It's empty—except for a lone, vintage Santa figure standing in the back corner. His color has faded, but his cheeks still hold a hint of rosiness. An unexpected sign.

Alright, Cheryl. I see you. I'm listening.

I turn to the real estate agent with a hesitant smile. "I'll take it, but the Santa stays."

IT'S STILL EARLY NOVEMBER, but I want to settle into my new house before Thanksgiving. I know that moving out of my longtime home will only get more difficult with the nostalgia and rose-tinted memories the holidays bring. Since the new house is unoccupied, we're able to expedite the inspection and close on it within a couple of weeks.

But moving out of my house is proving to be more emotionally challenging than I expected.

I stand outside and stare at the faded red front door I've opened a thousand times: the door I walked through as a newly married man; the door through which I first carried my wife, then both of our sons; the door I carried Julia through. I know every dip of the floor and chip in the wall, all the spots where my basset hound, Biscuit, prefers to hide.

A tear escapes down my cheek, and I reach up to brush it away, my hand skimming the new beard growth I haven't bothered to shave in days. I decided that when I sold this house, I'd also sell my horses. I don't have the time or energy to care for them like I used to. So many endings all at once, and the memories of them drape like chains across my shoulders.

But then I remember my silver lining.

I haven't told Jason yet, but I plan to use the money I'm making from downsizing my house and selling the horses to help pay off Julia's substantial hospital debts. My son works multiple jobs while his wife, Emma, stays home to care for their chronically ill daughter. I want to, and will do, anything to help them.

That thought finally allows me to turn my back and walk away from the first and only home I've ever owned.

That is until today.

Chapter 3

MARGIE

NOVEMBER, PRESENT DAY

The bright red SOLD sign catches my eye as soon as I pull into my driveway. A mixture of curiosity and fear beat through my calloused heart. Annie Mae was a known entity. I could count on her occasional greeting and quiet ways. She was safe.

But the SOLD sign could mean anything. My new neighbor could be Annie Mae the Second, or, I shudder, it could be Louisiana Tech's new off-campus frat house. With my luck, it will be the latter.

As I carry yet another load of empty mason jars into my home, I crane to see if my new neighbor is at the house, but all seems quiet. I decide the best course forward is to make a welcome basket full of Margie's Machinations and present myself after they move in. It's a convenient reason to snoop and discover exactly who I've been saddled with.

WHEN I SPY A MOVING TRUCK backing into the neighboring house's driveway, I decide it's the perfect time to set up my canning supplies on the kitchen table with a bay window view that looks directly out onto the scene. Despite my best efforts, I've been unable to ascertain who this mystery person, or people, might be.

There are two young men and a young woman in their twenties hauling stuff out of the moving truck and into the house. A little girl, who looks to be about seven or so, runs around the yard. A young family, I decide. That's not so bad. It might be nice to have some youth around here, and the little girl, with her warm brown hair, reminds me of my niece at that age. My mouth ticks up at the memory of young Amelia prowling around my yard and having conversations with wild animals. Yes, a young family will do just fine. Maybe I'll bake a batch of chocolate chip cookies for the little girl to add to my welcome basket.

I turn back to my work, content in the knowledge that not all changes have to be bad.

A LAWN MOWER GROWLS TO LIFE outside my house at 7 a.m.

And it's not just any mower. This one sounds like it wouldn't be out of place at a monster truck rally. I lie in bed and stare at the ceiling, half-convinced that this is all just some terrible nightmare. But when the sounds grow louder, I know that I am distressingly awake. I throw my bed covers off and sit up, anger rising within me like the mercury in an old thermometer.

I slide my feet into a pair of well-worn moccasins and nab my flannel robe off its hook on the back of my closet door. I briefly consider putting on a bra, but my fury is in the driver's seat now, and she is telling me to put a stop to the revving engine outside my bedroom window at all costs.

Distantly, a nagging, little Amelia-shaped voice in the back of my mind urges me to stop and take a breath. She tells me that perhaps charging over to my new neighbor's house in nothing but a nightgown, a threadbare robe, no bra, and an award-winning case of bedhead might not be the best first impression. But I snuff that voice out like a candle and charge forward.

After all, my new neighbor hasn't made the best first impression on me either.

When I throw open my front door, I squint into the morning light and can just make out a riding lawnmower cruising through my new neighbor's front yard. Just as I suspected, this isn't one of those fuel-efficient machines that can be purchased at any home supply store; no, this looks like it was purchased to level a commercial-sized cornfield. Just who does this person think they are? Someone with too much money and not enough damn sense is who.

I march over, gathering my indignation about me as I go. Dew from the morning grass clings to my slippers, and the smell of fresh-cut grass stirs to life around me. It's chilly, but I barely notice the temperature, as heated as I am by my wrath. By the time I'm within a few feet of the thing, I can make out a few of the mower riding demon's features. The demon, it turns out, is a man. *Well, no surprise there.* He's wearing protective ear coverings and most certainly does not see me. So when he makes the turn in his yard, I step a few feet in front of where he's headed.

When he spots me, he yells out what I can only imagine is a string of obscenities. But I can't hear them over the lawnmower engine that sounds like a bunch of pots and pans were tossed into a garbage disposal. He swerves the wheel and falls out of his seat in the process, hitting the ground hard. Serves him right. I don't move a single inch to help him. If he wants to wake everyone within a mile radius up at 7 a.m. on a Saturday morning, then he can damn well haul his own ass up off the ground. The lawnmower must have a safety switch because it shuts off as soon as its driver is out of the seat. Good to know for future reference.

I fold my arms over my boobs, now slightly regretting not putting on a bra as the man, clad in flannel and wearing safety glasses, stares up at me from a swirling cloud of dirt and grass trimmings.

"What the hell?" he yells, lowering his ear protection.

His deep voice rattles through me, but I am not easily intimidated. I square my shoulders and stare down at him imperiously.

"That's exactly what I would like to know," I demand.

He glares at me and I can practically see the steam rolling off him. "Did I miss something here? Why are you in my yard, throwing yourself in front of my lawnmower like you're playing chicken with the devil?"

"You are obviously missing the part of your brain that houses common sense. Why are you up at dawn mowing your lawn on a Saturday and waking the whole neighborhood?"

"The whole neighborhood? There are only a few houses out here. I'd hardly call it a neighborhood," he says, scoffing.

"I'm your neighbor, and you are the closest thing I have to being part of a neighborhood. I don't need you to mansplain it to me. And, more importantly, you are not practicing common courtesy. I repeat, who gets up at 7 a.m. to mow their lawn with a machine that sounds like a chainsaw attached to speakers on a Saturday?"

He finally pushes up from the ground and towers over me by at least four inches. His cheeks are flushed with anger and dusted with gray and brown stubble. A blade of grass clings to his forehead. His salt and pepper hair puts him somewhere close to my age: early fifties. And despite the intense anger pumping through my blood, a primal part of me is screaming about how handsome he is. I quickly kick dirt over that part of my brain. Men are nothing but unreliable trouble. They break your heart and leave you behind to pick up the pieces, or they obsess over you and hurt you. And no set of piercing blue eyes will convince me otherwise. Not even his, framed by thick eyebrows and a strong jawline. I dig into myself and hold my ground.

We are in a silent standoff, face to face, arms folded across our chests, breathing heavily. I watch his pale eyes study my face, taking in my chaotically awoken appearance. Finally, he stands down, shoulders sinking slightly. Victory sears through my chest as I prepare for him to admit he was wrong and apologize.

"You look familiar," he finally says. His anger sounds leashed, like he's trying to force the tension down a notch.

I lift an eyebrow.

"I'm Frank. Your new neighbor. Not how I planned on introducing myself." He stares, waiting for me to reply.

I huff. "I'm Margie. And if we are going to live next to each other, we should make an effort to respect each other."

His eyebrows raise. "Respect is a two-way street, Margie. And I don't think coming here and scaring me off my lawnmower falls into that category."

I bristle. I can just hear my niece telling me that he's right, that I should back down and smooth this over. But my pride won't let me. Instead, I turn on my heel and stomp back to my house. Within minutes, the lawnmower has fired back up, and I swear Frank is pumping extra gas into the engine as he rage mows his giant lawn.

Chapter 4

FRANK

NOVEMBER, PRESENT DAY

So much for a quieter, less busy life. It took me a while to remember where I knew my new neighbor from, but it finally hit me when I was lying in bed last night. That was the woman who stormed up to my previous house and blamed me for letting my horses into the fall festival barn a couple of years ago. She kept calling me "Fred." Seems about right. I finally stepped away from the house my heart had refused to let go of for three years, only to be landed with a harpy for a neighbor.

If Margie thinks she can bully me out of my new home, though, she has another thing coming. I actually love my new house. Yes, I'll need to take down some flowery wallpaper and replace old carpet, but it feels right. There's a cavernous fireplace that makes the main living room feel cozy. And the back patio is covered, making it the perfect place to sit and enjoy morning coffee and a spring rainstorm. And today, I finally get to welcome my dog to his new home.

Biscuit has been staying with Jason while I get everything settled. Julia loves him so much that I knew he would be in good hands for a few days. My old basset hound is beginning to show his age in his snow-kissed muzzle, but I love the guy and can't wait to see what he thinks of our new home.

Jason and Emma really should get Julia a dog. Maybe I'll say something to them. Or maybe they could just leave my granddaughter with me for a week while they take a break and get away. Lord knows they need to. Julia's autoimmune disease means that she has good days and bad days with her flare-ups. But the bad days can get really bad. Efforts to get her well mean medically suppressing her immune system—and that means she gets sick constantly and for much longer than other kids her age. And it also means they have to take a lot of drives over to Children's Hospital in Dallas, four hours away. Jason doesn't talk about it with me much, but I know the medical and travel expenses are chipping away at my son and daughter-in-law. I'm not wealthy, but I do what I can to help—when they will let me.

Thoughts of my beautiful granddaughter race through my mind. She loves Christmas just as much as my wife did, and with Thanksgiving only a couple of weeks away, I can't wait to pull out all the stops and bring a smile to her face.

I flip through the stack of mail sitting on my kitchen table and notice a flier. I start to cast it aside when something catches my eye. In bold, red type, it says: "Vendors wanted for this year's Christmas Market. Interested? Contact Amelia Hebert."

I slowly lower the paper to the table as my mind sifts through the pile of woodworking supplies and tools sitting in my new garage. My sons have pushed me to sell my wood cutouts and carvings for years. Is it a coincidence that this Christmas Market found me at the same time I was thinking of ways to help my son's family?

Fate seems to tap me on the shoulder and whisper that maybe it's time to finally do something useful with my hobby. And maybe, just maybe, Christmas, my late wife's and my granddaughter's favorite holiday, is the time to do it. And, if I spin this just right, I think I can get Jason and Emma to accept the proceeds of my work to pay off their ever-expanding medical bills.

Plan forming in my mind, I reach for my phone and dial the number on the flier.

MUFFLED, HOARSE BARKS SOUND through my closed front door. The noise tickles the piece of my soul reserved for the kindness that only animals can bring to our lives. I open the door and see the drooping eyes of Biscuit. His tail makes a sad attempt to wag, but I know that he's happy to see me.

"Hey Papa!" Julia says, cheerily, her round, pink cheeks dimpling in greeting. She holds Biscuit's leash. I silently chuckle at the thought of my old hound attempting to run away. He'd trip over his own ears if he could muster the energy to run more than a few feet.

"Hey, Dad," Jason calls, walking up to my house carrying Biscuit's dog food and bowls.

I usher them inside, and Biscuit immediately puts his nose to the ground, using his best asset to assess his new territory.

"It looks like your house now that you have your stuff out of boxes, Papa!" Julia says. At six years old, her voice still holds the innocence of childhood.

"Why don't you go check it out with Biscuit?" I encourage. "Let me talk to your daddy for a bit."

She takes off, intent on finding an unsuspecting cockroach or lizard, I'm sure.

I look at my son, studying the dark circles under his eyes. He's only twenty-nine, but life's difficulties have begun to age him prematurely. I reach over and clap his shoulder.

"Thanks for watching Biscuit for me while I settle in," I tell him.

"Of course, Dad, no problem. You know Julia loves him, and he's a low-maintenance dog."

"Sit down. I'll fix you a cup of coffee," I tell him. He eases into the wooden chair, foot tapping the ground as he waits. "How is Julia doing?" I ask quietly, not wanting my granddaughter to overhear our conversation.

Jason exhales a long, heavy sigh and leans back, considering. "Okay, right now," he says. "But you know how it goes. She will seem fine for weeks, months, even. And then a flare-up will come out of nowhere and take her down."

"Any updates from the doctors on what it is?" I ask, taking a sip of decaf.

"Her immune system is still attacking her body. The immune suppressant she's on now isn't doing enough to halt it, and the shot we give her at home isn't as effective as they would like it to be. Plus, it's giving her anxiety. Last time Emma gave it to her, Julia started panicking and threw up. We will go back to Dallas next weekend. Her doctor wants her to start IV infusions for medication, but getting insurance to approve them has been a nightmare. We're looking at four hundred dollars a piece every two weeks," he halts immediately, and I can tell he's afraid he's said too much.

"Jason," I start, hesitating. "I want to help."

"Dad, we've been over this," he defends immediately. "You need your money for retirement."

"And I won't be happy in my retirement if I see my son and his family hurting," I say gently. I rub at my graying scruff. "I just sold the house and downsized. Sold the horses. I have some extra money."

"No, that's not fair to you—" he tries again.

"And I'm starting a business," I continue, cutting him off. "It's for fun, really. But I want the proceeds to pay for Julia's medical care. That way, your work can pay for all the other things your family needs."

"You're going to continue to do farm work *and* run a side business? That's too much, Dad."

"It's woodworking. More like a hobby, not a business," I say simply and shrug. I take a sip of my coffee and wait.

"I've been trying to get you to pick woodworking back up since Mom died," Jason says incredulously.

"And now I'm going to. You can't tell me I need to pick it back up in one breath then tell me I'm not allowed to in another. It's fun for me. Let me use it to help my granddaughter. I can't promise it will be much, but it will be for her."

His shoulders slump in acceptance. "Fine, but pay the hospital directly. I feel weird about you giving me money."

"Papa! I found a moth!" Julia cheers as she skips into the kitchen and breaks the tension. She opens her palms to reveal brown fluttering wings.

"Good job, Jules. Let it outside and come back. I'll fix you a hot chocolate, and then I have something exciting to share with you."

Chapter 5

MARGIE

NOVEMBER, PRESENT DAY

I inhale, close my eyes, and slide my headphones over my ears. Prince sings to me about doves crying while I gather my canning supplies. This is comfortable, the rhythm of boiling sugar and peaches, adding just the right amount of bourbon, and sealing the cans. The smells twine together in the air, transforming my house into the ultimate cozy sanctuary. My mother taught me how to can as a girl, and even in the most difficult moments of my life, I have found comfort in the activity.

Those first days after David left were the hardest. No, that's not true. The day I took my sister, Josephine, and her daughter, Amelia, into my home was earth-shattering. Jo was falling apart, abused by her worthless husband, and she couldn't protect and care for their daughter on her own. She tried once, briefly moving the two of them to an apartment, but she couldn't sustain it. They needed me, and nothing this side of heaven could keep me from caring for them. Not even David's request that I choose him over them, choose *us* over them.

The simple syrup starts to bubble, and the smell and color thread through time, drawing me back. This could easily have become an activity I hated, one inextricably linked to sad memories and sleepless nights. Instead my lips tick up at the thought of Amelia's small hands on the wooden spoon as I encouraged her to keep stirring so the sugar wouldn't burn. I can still see the pride shining in her earth-colored eyes when she canned her first jar of peach jelly. And even though her entire world was falling apart—and mine too—we had this activity we did together.

When Stevie Nicks sings "Rhiannon" in my headphones, I sway to her husky voice and carry the freshly boiled jelly to the waiting jars. As I pour, I force myself to shut down the memories of all the men who have disappointed me and focus instead on how I've made myself successful. And, even better, how my niece has become a force to be reckoned within the local community. Women always get shit done.

Just as Stevie croons, "Would you stay if she promised you heaven," I hear a crash outside. I pause, hoping it is just the rotting branch finally giving up its hold on the giant pine tree in my backyard. But then I hear… my God, *is that "Jingle Bells?"*

Slowly, I set the pot back down on the stove and take steadying breaths. Maybe I was just lost in a memory. There is no way someone is playing Christmas music more than a week before Thanksgiving at high volume outside my house. I take my headphones off and strain to listen. Nothing. I breathe out a sigh of relief. And that's when "Grandma Got Ran Over by a Reindeer" roars to life. *You have got to be kidding me.*

I throw the front door open, ready to give Frank a piece of my mind. But just as I step outside, my foot bumps into something that bellows at me, and I go down hard, landing on my ass. Pain shoots down my leg and into my hip.

When I roll to the side, a large, pink tongue covers my face. At first, I panicked, thinking my neighborhood coyote had finally stopped threatening me from a distance and made its way to my front door. But then I realize that this particular tongue is attached to something small and stumpy.

I sit up and peer down into the drooping eyes of a basset hound.

"Where did you come from?" I ask as if he came over for a bit of conversation on my front porch. He seems to have the same idea because he sits on his squatty little back legs and looks at me expectantly. "Well, fella, what do you have to say for yourself?" I demand.

He woofs. Then the Christmas music blares to life again, reminding me of my quest. I slowly push to my feet—and that's when I see the atrocious display.

Frank, it seems, is one of those people who times his Christmas lights to music and decorates for the holiday before Thanksgiving. I could probably deal with this tacky display if the lights and music were all I had to encounter over the next six weeks, but they are only the beginning. Because as I watch, Frank is assembling what appears to be a life-sized Santa in a sleigh being pulled by eight life-sized, alligator replicas. Rarely am I taken aback by gaudy displays, especially in the great state of the Mardi Gras float, but this is enough to unsettle me.

I walk in dazed horror towards the decor, if it can be called that. My new dog friend trots along behind me, and I wonder what he thinks about all this. If I were on the same level as a life-sized alligator, I'd probably run in the opposite direction.

As I approach, Frank glances up and sees me. A smile lights his face, cheeks dimpling beneath the graying scruff that's quickly becoming a beard. The phrase "silver fox" crosses my mind, but I shut it down immediately. Men are never worth my time, especially not one building an homage to Père Noël in his front yard.

"Like it?" Frank asks. And it seems he fully expects me to praise his tacky Cajun creation.

"Like is a strong word."

His face falls. "I think it's nice," he insists. And I'm not sure if he's trying to convince me or himself. "It says 'Christmas in Louisiana,' and no one else around here has anything like it."

"There's a reason for that."

"Just wait until you see it with the lights. I've timed them to blink to 'Grandma Got Ran Over by a Reindeer,'" he says with pride.

"Quite possibly the worst song in existence. And those are not reindeer. They are gators."

His brows furrow. "I don't know, I think it's kind of funny."

"Yeah, killing grandma at Christmas is hilarious. Thanks for the laugh." I know I'm being snippy, but I can't seem to stop myself. Something about this man crawls under my skin and scrapes at my nerves.

He clears his throat, and I can see emotion color his cheeks. But instead of lashing out at me, he closes his eyes, breathes, opens them again, and his smile reemerges. Well, I'll be damned, he's not easily cowed then.

"I can't please everyone, I suppose, but I'm sure you'll like one of my other Christmas displays that will go up later this week."

I blink once. Twice. "How can there possibly be more?"

Frank laughs. "Oh Margie, you ain't seen nothin' yet. This yard and house have so much potential for Christmas decorations. I can't wait to pull out all the stops. I'm happy to lend you some if you'd like."

"I'm good, thanks," I snap.

His sincerity in the face of my ire makes me feel like a bully, and I don't like it, not at all. "It's not even Thanksgiving, and the music is too loud. You might consider your neighbor when you're doing all this."

"Oh, right. Well, I'll keep it down. I was just testing it out. Thanks for telling me, Margie."

My cheeks heat, but in anger or embarrassment, I'm not sure which. I decide that now is the time to make a dignified retreat and get back to canning, submerging myself into my happy place. I nod, then turn and start walking back to my house.

"And thanks for bringing Biscuit back to me," Frank calls out.

I turn to see him kneeling and petting the old basset hound's head. Swathed in flannel and faded blue jeans with a dog, Frank looks like he belongs in one of those sexy lumberjack calendars. I swallow, turn, and keep walking, refusing to let Frank get the upper hand on me. I've seen too many men use charm as a weapon to be taken in by it.

But even as I storm away, I can't stop thinking about his clear blue eyes and dimpled smile.

Chapter 6

FRANK

THANKSGIVING, PRESENT DAY

I stare at the rough sketch in front of me with a mix of pride and indecision. My yard map for this year's Christmas decorations is one of my best yet. I've made sure every square inch is covered, and the way I have it planned out, I'll have it all done before the first day of December. Julia is going to love it.

My mind drifts to my neighbor, and my shoulders sink. Margie, however, will absolutely hate it. Do I want to stir up her ire? I imagine it will be a bit like dumping gasoline on a bonfire. Though she's awfully pretty when her cheeks flare and match her fiery hair. Maybe I should feel bad about pissing her off, but she certainly hasn't taken into consideration what I want. Instead, she makes a point of tearing me to shreds at every opportunity.

Perhaps I need to better consider my decorating timeline. I talked to Amelia Hebert and told her I'd like to co-sponsor the Christmas event. In order to make that happen, though, I need to dedicate time outside of my regular work hours to creating wooden signs, cutting boards, and other wooden figures that I can sell at the

Christmas Market. After all, any profit I make is going to support Julia's healthcare bills.

And then, of course, Thanksgiving is in a week. I've invited both of my sons, Emma, and Julia over for the holiday. It will be good to fill this new space with happy memories. Already, Julia has asked me if she can explore the woods behind the house when she visits.

My phone rings, and I look down to see Amelia's name flash across the screen.

"Hello?"

"Hi, Mr. Campbell. How are you today?"

"Doin' all right."

"Great! I just wanted to check in with you about your co-sponsorship. Thank you for agreeing to that, by the way," Amelia says sincerely.

"Christmas is kind of my thing," I demure. "Plus, my son has been encouraging me to sell my woodworking. Figured this is a great way to get my name out there."

"Oh, it will be," she says cheerily. "The Christmas Market is in three weeks, so I want to make sure that I have all of your information correct for the promotional materials we are going to publish. And because you're a co-sponsor, it would be great if you'd be willing to schedule an interview with *The Ruston Daily Leader* newspaper with our other co-sponsor. It will be great press for the event. I'll be there to guide you through the whole thing."

"Oh, um, well. Now I don't know about all that. I don't think anyone wants to hear about my work," I hedge.

"Now, don't be bashful, Mr. Campbell. In our conversation, you mentioned that the proceeds will go to benefit your granddaughter. If you're not comfortable talking about yourself, you can share how you're doing this for her. I'm sure people would love to come out and buy one of your beautiful pieces and support her at the same time."

Guilt tugs at me. *Right, Julia.*

"I want to keep that part of things quiet, about my granddaughter, I mean," I say.

"No problem. I'll keep it between us."

"I won't have to do this alone, right?" I ask.

"Nope. Both myself and our other co-sponsor will be there. I know her well, and I can vouch that she doesn't mind being on camera. Between the two of you, it will be nice and easy. You have nothing to worry about," Amelia reassures.

"Okay, that will be fine then," I agree.

"Great! We will schedule it for the week after Thanksgiving. I'll be in touch with more details."

I hang up the phone and push my Christmas decoration plan aside with a sigh. It's time to get some pieces ready to sell. I'll save the decorating for when my family is here at Thanksgiving.

THE SMELL OF CAJUN-FRIED TURKEY fills my house, making it feel more like home than ever.

"When do we get to eat, Papa?" Julia asks, hand reaching for the rolls tucked in a covered basket.

"Not yet, Juju Bug," I tell her. "We have to wait until everything is ready."

She visibly wilts, only to immediately perk back up again. "Can I get out the Christmas ornaments and sort them by color?"

"Hm," I pretend to consider. But she already knows I won't tell her no.

"Pleeeease, Papa?"

"Oh, all right. There's a big box in my bedroom already pulled out and waiting for you. Go start sorting while I get this turkey out of the fryer and sliced up for us. And then, after lunch, I have a big surprise for you!"

With a cheer, she takes off to my room, ready to help me get started on my decorating.

Chapter 7

MARGIE

PRESENT DAY: THANKSGIVING

My house isn't big, but it's the house I raised Amelia in, and it's the house she wants to return to on the holidays. It will be a tight fit with my niece's extended family accompanying her, but I've added a card table to accommodate the overflow of people visiting for Thanksgiving lunch.

Amelia and her husband, Rhett, will be here. And Rhett's family refuses to have Thanksgiving without him, so all of the Heberts will be here, too. So I'll need four extra chairs for his parents, Ben and Kathy, as well as his sister, Katie, and her fiancé, Jacob.

It's a cobbled-together setup with folding chairs, but it warms my heart to see seven people fill the space that once only held two. And while most men in my life have been nothing but trouble, Amelia managed to find one of the best there is in Rhett. That boy dotes on her like she hung the moon.

Just as I pull an apple pie out of the oven, I hear voices outside my front door.

"Aunt Margie! We're here!" Amelia calls. My house seems to recognize her soul and settles, knowing our girl is back within its walls.

I put the pie down on the counter and walk over to her, pulling her into a hug. Her familiar weight sinks into me, steadying my soul. She smells like apple cider and pumpkin spice, and those scents tug at joyful memories tucked in close to my heart. Amelia pulls away and I greet Rhett with a hug, too. It's a relief every day of my life knowing these two are taking care of one another.

"Now, now, you're hogging my hugs!" a male voice calls out.

I turn and see Jacob, Katie's fiance, grinning at me. He's always a delightful bundle of mischief, and I'm glad these two drove in from Dallas for the holidays.

Soon, my kitchen is filled with laughter and conversation. The nostalgic smells of a traditional Thanksgiving fill the space. I pull the cornbread dressing out of the oven as Amelia sets the tables. Rhett slices up the turkey and Katie pours glasses of wine for everyone. We gather around the table.

I tap the side of my glass, getting everyone's attention. "I'd like to thank y'all for coming to my place today. I'm grateful that Lia has brought you into my life and helped us form our own little family together. This house has seen a lot of things over the years, but these are some of the best memories yet."

"Cheers!" Amelia calls out. We clink our glasses together. And, in that moment, everything feels absolutely perfect.

And then Christmas music blares to life outside my window. *Again.*

I wince and try to convince myself to ignore it. *Frank is just really into the spirit of the season.* Nothing to get upset about, I insist. Maybe I'll just, I don't know, ask Rhett if I can borrow his amp and electric guitar for a while and grind out my own obnoxious musical response. Better yet, Jacob can bring over his drum set, too.

"My, that is quite loud," Kathy says, walking to the window over my kitchen sink to peer out at the yard next to mine.

I clear my throat. "Not exactly what I was hoping for in a new neighbor," I mumble.

Amelia joins her at the window and peers out. "Well, that's certainly a choice," she says.

"Are you talking about Santa and his eight ferocious rein-gators?" I ask dryly.

"Well, yes, that. But also, I can't say I've ever seen a full-sized, Christmas-themed Mardi Gras float in someone's yard before. That definitely wasn't there when we arrived. I wonder where it came from," she says, her tone hovering somewhere between horror and awe.

"Please, for the love of all that is holy, tell me that you are joking," I say, strolling over to the window.

But, alas, she was not joking. There is an honest-to-God Christmas Mardi Gras float in Frank's front yard. And not just any float. It appears to be themed around Christmas in July. There are faux palm trees with string lights and bubblegum pink lawn flamingos adorning its sides. An inflatable Santa stands on its prow, and he looks ready for the beach in his swim trunks and dolphin floaty around his waist. Lights flash in erratic patterns around the whole structure.

"What in the mele kalikimaka is happening over there?" Jacob asks delightedly. Clearly, this is his brand of chaos.

And as if summoned by his words, Bing Crosby and The Andrews Sisters croon "The Hawaiian Christmas Song" at top volume from a speaker attached to the side of the monstrosity.

"That does it," I huff. I have had enough. I let the gators go. I let the life-sized Santa before Thanksgiving go. But Frank will not ruin my Thanksgiving with this Mardi Gras and Christmas love child in his front yard.

I set down my glass of wine and charge out the front door. I don't stop to think about what I'm doing or even who is around me. I lock in on my target: Frank, dressed in jeans and flannel, with flashing reindeer antlers on his head. Distantly, I notice that there are other people there, but I don't let them distract me from taking care of business.

Frank looks up at me charging toward him from where he leans over the float's speaker.

"Oh, hey, Margie. Sorry about the noise. I'm working on the volume so it won't be so loud."

"What in the hell is happening here?" I ask, rage bubbling beneath my words.

Frank chuckles, trying to soften the growing tension as he casts his gaze around. "It's nice, isn't it? My son, Drew, is a member of the Highland Parade in Shreveport and told me I could use his float for my Christmas decorations this year. I thought it would be something different to bring a boost of Christmas cheer to my new home."

"Could you, for just one second in your life, stop and think about someone else?" I demand. Rage is fully at the helm now as the words come spewing out of my mouth. "Ever since you've moved in here, all you've done is operate everything at top volume without thought for anyone else. You mow your lawn at an ungodly hour. You blast music so loudly they can hear it in New Orleans. And you let your dog roam free and crush my garden."

The words are scathing, but no part of me feels remorse.

"Aunt Margie," Amelia tries to soothe. I feel her hand on my shoulder. Brave of her, really.

"This is *my* Thanksgiving with *my* family. And you are out here doing your damn best to make sure that gets interrupted. Well, I've been patient, and I'm done with it."

"And are you done talking now?" he asks irritably.

His words ratchet up my anger. "You," I shove my finger into his chest. "Need to stop being so damn selfish."

"And you," he says, his mood shifting to fury and charging his voice, "Need to stop being a *Grinch*."

"Oh no, Papa, don't call her a Grinch! That's mean!" a little girl says.

I turn and stare at the girl I've seen running around here before.

She's mousy, with chocolate brown hair and eyes. She clutches a stuffed elf and glares at me with fear in her eyes. *Well, shit.*

Frank reacts immediately, softening and stepping toward the girl. "I'm sorry, Juju Bug, I didn't mean to scare you."

"You didn't scare me," she says indignantly. "But we don't call people ugly words. Mama says so," she says matter-of-factly.

"And your mama is absolutely right," he says. That simple interaction throws a bucket of water on my fiery mood. This little girl reminds me so much of Amelia that I'm tempted to walk over and scoop her up in a hug.

"Just calm down," Amelia murmurs so only I can hear her. "No need to let this ruin Thanksgiving."

Between the girl's interruption and Amelia's plea, my rationality slowly begins to douse my rage. My shoulders slump. "I'm sorry, Lia. It's kind of a long story."

"Let's just go back home and eat, okay?" she coaxes.

"Yeah, alright," I agree.

Just as I start to turn, Frank says, "Hey, Margie." I lock up, waiting. "I'm sorry. I shouldn't have called you a Grinch." His mouth twitches, and I can tell he's making a Herculean effort to keep from laughing.

I turn to walk away when the little girl pipes up. "You have to say you're sorry, too," she encourages me. I turn and stare at her, seeing a little bit of myself reflected in the way she juts out her chin and puts her hands on her hips.

I glance at Frank, noticing his dimple flash as he continues to try and hold his laughter at bay. I scowl. "I'm sorry for yelling at you in front of your…"

"Granddaughter," he finishes for me.

I raise an eyebrow, surprised he's old enough to have a granddaughter. "In front of your granddaughter," I continue.

And then I turn and walk back home, Amelia hustling to keep up beside me.

"What was all that about?" she hisses.

"Later," I tell her. "After I've had some bourbon."

But what I won't tell her, can't tell her, is that my rage against Frank is so much more than tacky, Mardi Gras, Christmas floats, and life-sized reingators. It's the threat of ruining this perfect family moment I've been trying to cultivate for Amelia's entire life. It was almost perfect. *Almost.* But the interruptions to holidays have been par for the course her entire life, and I want to guard these perfect moments for *her*, for *me*, at all costs.

Chapter 8

MARGIE

NOVEMBER 30, 1998

The pounding fist on my door startles me, and I drop my wooden spoon into the simmering jelly on the stove. I glance up and realize the sun set over the last hour. My brows furrow. The pounding comes again. My heart flutters in warning, and I consider calling the police, and then I hear a child's voice, and my fear morphs. I'm no longer scared for myself.

I quickly slide the pot off the stovetop and turn off the burner, then rush to the door. When I throw it open, I see a pair of wide, brown eyes staring up at me. They hold a mix of emotions, a pendulum swinging between joy and sadness.

"Lia," I say, leaning down to scoop my young niece up and hold her close. "Where's your mama?"

She turns and looks back toward my driveway. I see the idling car and realize that's where my sister must be. My fear intensifies, but I steady my voice so I don't scare Amelia.

"Lia, baby. Why don't you come on in and sit down on the couch?

I'll make you a cup of apple cider in a few minutes."

"Okay," she says and then wiggles out of my embrace and darts past me and into the living room.

I stare out across my now-dark front yard, lit only by the orange glow of artificial light spreading from my front door. It's cool at the end of November, and the breeze that shudders through the trees and rustles the few remaining leaves amps up the uneasiness creeping into my bones. This isn't the first time my younger sister, Josephine, has shown up at my house unexpectedly, and things must be dire for her to be here tonight.

I reach for my rubber boots that I keep next to the door and slide them on. Then I grab a flashlight and walk toward the beat-up, faded red Pontiac in my driveway. The smell of woodsmoke drifts through the air, lingering from the leaf pile I burned earlier. It would be cozy if I weren't so worried.

"Hey, Jo, you okay?" I call. I don't want to startle her.

But when I reach her car, I shine the light on the driver's seat and see… nothing. At least not at first. But then I move the light to the back seat and gasp. Josephine is lying down in the back seat, not moving. I reach for the car handle and yank. A brief flash of relief washes over me when it opens.

"Jo, wake up!" Panic edges into my voice. I shake her. A moment passes, and I hold my breath. I shake her again. "Dammit, Josephine. Wake up!"

She groans, and I nearly collapse with relief, but it's short-lived. Because when she rolls over, the skin around her right eye is the black and blue of a stormy sky, and her cheek is cut with dried blood, gluing her hair to the side of her face.

"That motherfucker," I growl. "I'm calling the police."

"No," Jo gasps. "No, Margie, you cannot call the police. He'll kill me." I reach for her, but Josephine pushes my hand away. "Promise me."

I stare at my sister, waffling on the best way to proceed. At twenty-four, she's just eighteen months younger than me, but I feel like I'm more mature than her by nearly a decade. It wasn't always that way, though. She used to be quiet but vibrant. That is until Dale got her knocked up at eighteen and hid her away from everyone who loved her. Her piece of shit husband needs to be thrown in jail, but if I call the police on him, there is a good chance that Josephine will never come to me for support again. And Amelia… I can't let my niece get caught up in that. I nod reluctantly, and Jo sinks with relief.

Lightning cracks across the sky, and a loud clash of thunder follows behind it. I can smell the rain on the wind as it picks up. When lightning strikes again, I see the flash of pigtails and then feel the squeeze of a small hand in mine. "I'm scared, Aunt Margie," Amelia says in a low, uncertain voice.

Her words snap my sister out of her stupor. Josephine climbs out of the car and reaches for her daughter's other hand. Together we hurry into my house just as fat drops of rain begin to plop onto our shoulders.

"Are you hungry?" I ask them, even though it's nearly 9 p.m.

"I'll take a drink if you've got one," my sister says roughly. I walk over to my liquor cabinet and pull out my favorite whiskey, pouring her a finger over ice. Jack Daniels has become a friend over the last six years, and I keep it in stock, even though it means driving out of the city limits to buy it legally. I hand the glass to my sister, who promptly takes a large gulp and winces. Then she drinks another.

"Want some hot apple cider, Lia? I know it's your favorite?"

A tiny smile flickers across her pouty lips before she nods. I grab one of the instant packets out of my pantry, the ones I keep in stock just for my niece. Then I open my cabinet and select her favorite mug—it's vintage with a fall leaf on the side.

I heat the water in the microwave, then mix it up and place it on the kitchen table before her. "Here, Lia, blow on this and let it cool down. I'm going to run back to my guest bedroom and grab some extra toothbrushes."

Just as I start to walk to the back of my house, the phone rings. I stare at the ochre handset anchored to my wall. An ominous feeling sinks into my stomach, spreading like a virus through my system. I hesitate, then decide that it's best to get this over with–whatever this is.

"Hello," I answer cautiously.

"Hey M. Tried to catch you before bed," the male voice purrs over the line.

All the dread stabbing my stomach immediately dissipates as the adrenaline that's been building over the last twenty minutes finally begins to make its way out of my system.

"Hey David," I say, relaxing into the wall. "Made it to Charleston, okay?"

"Yep. Weather was perfect. Just wish you were here with me."

I smile to myself, picturing his deep dimples and night-black hair; the way his pale green eyes devour me like I'm his favorite dessert every time he sees me.

"Maybe next time," I allow. "Hey, can I call you back? I have a situation going on right now." I peer around the corner to make sure that Jo and Amelia aren't eavesdropping, but both seem preoccupied with their drinks and are having a low conversation across my kitchen table.

"What kind of situation?" David asks.

I lower my voice. "A Jo and Lia situation."

Silence crackles over the line, and I hold my breath.

"Margie, you have to be careful. I don't want that man showing up at your house and beating you, too," David says sadly. They are words he's said a dozen times since we got engaged six months ago–words that make me simultaneously love and hate him.

"We've been over this, Davy. I can't turn my sister away, and I won't leave my niece to fend for herself."

"You've got to call the police," he insists.

"Jo doesn't want me to get law enforcement involved. Begged me not to."

"Margie," his voice is pleading.

"I know. I've got to figure something out. I'm just not sure what that something is yet. I'm working on it," I tell him.

He sighs. "Just be careful. Alright? Men like that are dangerous and have no problem crossing boundaries they shouldn't. Keep the doors locked and your pistol at the ready."

"That goes without saying," I murmur. "Listen, Davy, I gotta go. Call me tomorrow?"

"Yeah, of course, Margie. I'll only be in Charleston for a few days. Let's go on a date when I get back, yeah?" he asks.

I tilt my head back, leaning against the wall. "Of course. Can't wait," I sigh.

"I love you," he says softly.

"Love you, too."

As I hang up the phone, I turn to stare at my niece and the growing bruises on Jo's face. And I know that there is no easy solution to this situation. They can't go back home, and I'm not sure where they will land, but that's a problem for another day. Tonight, at least, they are here and safe.

Chapter 9

FRANK

THE DAY AFTER THANKSGIVING,
PRESENT DAY

Black Friday. Cheryl always hated that anything associated with Christmas should be labeled as such. Christmas should be bright, cheery, and painted with broad strokes of sparkling lights and tinsel. Although I got an early start on my Christmas decorating this year, Black Friday is the day my family gathers at my house to help me decorate. Since my late wife passed, this tradition has become something of a memorial for her.

And we are still going to do it, dammit. No amount of adult temper tantrums from my neighbor will interrupt this day, I silently vow. Even if the thought of Margie all riled up makes me want to rankle her even more. It's... fun. And I don't think I've had real fun in years.

"Papa," Julia's voice squeaks from where she stands just outside the kitchen door, watching me drink my coffee.

"Hey, Juju Bug, come here."

She scurries over to me and climbs in my lap, wrapping her

thin arms around my neck. "Can we turn on Christmas music?" she whispers, acknowledging the sacredness of this day.

"Of course. I'll turn it on and make some cinnamon rolls for breakfast. What do you say?"

"I love you, Papa!"

My heart squeezes, and I hug her again, holding on a little too long. I soak up her childhood joy and innocence, letting it sink into my bones. She smells like grass and chocolate, likely a byproduct of having free reign of this place while the adults sat around and talked last night.

I tune my radio to the Christmas station, then pull out a can of cinnamon rolls. I've never been great at making them from scratch–that was Cheryl's territory–but I am good at following directions. Most of the time, anyway.

"Jingle Bell Rock" plays through the speakers, and Julia sings along as she watches me preheat the oven and pull out a pan.

Just as I'm placing the cinnamon rolls on the baking sheet, the radio cuts to a commercial. The local DJ announces: *Do you have what it takes to win this year's prize? Ivy Electronics will present a cash prize of five thousand dollars to the best-decorated Christmas yard of the year! So pull out your lights, inflate your reindeer, and go online to register. Judging begins on December Tenth.*

I look at Julia, who is dipping her fingers into the cinnamon roll frosting. I study her thinning frame, the way her cheeks are a little too sallow, her walk a little too stiff. Selling my woodworking pieces will do a lot to help pay down her bills, no doubt. But "Yard of the Year?" Now, that is something that I could do in Cheryl's honor to help her granddaughter.

The wheels in my head start turning, presenting me with a mental inventory of everything at my disposal. I have years of collected decorations, most I don't pull out every Christmas. And then I have plenty of woodworking supplies–things I could use to build more decorations. Last year, I hit up Walmart after Christmas and stocked up their leftover lights at clearance prices. My inventory is at an all-time high.

"Papa, why do you look like that?" Julia asks.

"Like what, sweetheart?"

"You look like I feel when Daddy gives me five dollars and tells me to pick out whatever candy I want to bring to the movies."

"Well, Juju Bug, that's because I feel that very same way. We are going to decorate my yard this year and make it the biggest and brightest it's ever been. What do you say to that?"

She stares at me, contemplating. "I have some ideas," Julia says solemnly.

"Oh yeah? Let's hear them."

"You know how I was sorting all your ornaments last night? Well, I thought that since you have so many, we should decorate your outside trees."

"What a brilliant girl you are," I acknowledge.

"And do them in rainbow order," she continues. "You can have a red tree, an orange tree, even a hot pink one!"

"I like the sound of that," I agree.

"We can make your whole house look like Candyland," she continues, really getting into it.

"Should I cut some pieces of candy out of plywood? Maybe you could help me paint them?"

She squeals at the suggestion. "Can I make rainbow candy?"

"With glitter," I suggest.

And then she throws herself at my legs, squeezing me with all the force her tiny body can muster.

"DAD, ARE YOU SURE ABOUT THIS?" Jason asks, staring at the hoard of sparkly things in the pile before us. "Seems like your neighbor over there wasn't too happy with the Hawaiian Santa float. This may be more trouble than it's worth."

"Son, when has a little protesting ever stopped me?"

"That's what I was afraid of," he sighs.

"I'm going to win "Yard of the Year!" You should be proud of your dear old dad."

"Well, Julia is certainly excited," he says begrudgingly.

"And we could all use a bit more of her enthusiasm."

Jason sighs but doesn't say anything more. He helps me move the ladder along the front of the house and feeds me the lights while I use my staple gun to fix them along my roof line. It's strangely quiet as we work. By now, I would have expected Margie to be over here, reading me the riot act. Frankly, I'm slightly disappointed that she's not. Fortunately, our few other neighbors, including the young woman across the street, have remained mum on the topic. Though, come to think of it, I rarely see that neighbor. From what I've gathered, she's a young, single woman in her late twenties who has a demanding job that keeps her from her house.

I've given Julia full license to decorate the naturally growing trees in my front yard. And even though a couple of the magnolia trees are too tall for her to decorate, she's informed me that we can wrap lights around their trunks. That's my girl.

By the time evening encroaches, my yard looks like a Christmas Hallmark movie threw up on it. It's perfect.

"Papa, we still have to put up the house for Baby Jesus," Julia says.

"Ah, I'm building him a new house this year, Juju Bug," I tell her.

"Will there be donkeys?" she asks, wide-eyed.

I nod. "Maybe even real ones," I tell her.

"Your neighbor really will kill you if she starts having to step over donkey poop," Jason says wryly.

"Nonsense, it's just fertilizer," I quip.

"Somehow, I don't think that explanation is going to win you any brownie points, Dad."

Chapter 10

MARGIE

THE DAY AFTER THANKSGIVING, PRESENT DAY

For some ungodly reason, I let Amelia talk me into going shopping on Black Friday, the single most miserable day of the year. She saw how riled up I was after my confrontation with Frank yesterday and thought that this would be the perfect way to cheer me up.

And I thought she knew me.

And yet, when she showed up in my driveway at 4:30 a.m. so we could get in line at Walmart to presumably fight strangers over electronics, I was dressed and ready. She doesn't need to know about the bourbon tucked in my cargo pants pocket.

It's only 8 a.m., we've already been to three stores, and Amelia's Christmas shopping is nearly done. She said that since she has to place all her focus on the Christmas Market this year, she wants to get most of her shopping squared away early.

We pause our shopping just long enough to pick up coffees from Lattes and Lagniappe before heading to our final stop of the day: the home supply store.

Amelia has been on my case about getting an artificial Christmas tree ever since she moved out of my house. When she was a kid, we would go to the small, local Christmas tree farm, where she would pick out the perfect pine for our living room. But since living solo, I just can't seem to find the Christmas magic that was there when she was around. So, I opted not to have a tree over the past several years.

Apparently, this is unacceptable. And while Amelia argued that I should have a real tree, she agreed to a compromise. Thus, here we are, running the Black Friday gauntlet alongside the shopping masses to pick out an artificial tree.

"So I have another interesting project coming up at work," Amelia says, keeping the conversation going while we wait in the checkout line.

"Another one? They keep you busy, don't they, girl? I hope they're giving you a raise."

"They are actually. A big one. It was part of the deal for me to take on yet another big event."

"Well, good for you, Lia. What do they have you doing this time?"

"A New Year's Eve event. It's going to be really fun, I think. But it's super labor-intensive. I'm organizing a city-wide race with big prizes attached, thanks to some local businesses."

"Sorry, Lia, this Christmas Market is all the participation I have in me this year."

She laughs. "Don't worry, I'm not asking you to help with this one. I'll probably pull Beth in. And then, of course, I'll recruit Katie, Jacob, and their friends, Brian and Celia, to participate as a team. I'm worried we won't have a big turnout, but it's an inaugural event, so all I can do is hope for the best."

"It won't be long before you're replacing that bitch boss of yours, mark my words," I tell her seriously.

"Yeah, right," she says, rolling her eyes. "I don't think even Godzilla could drag Janet from her pristine office, not even if he ripped the top of the building off and tried to physically remove her. She'd just stare him down, and he'd run away with his tail between his legs."

A large dolly rumbling along the concrete floors and to the front of our checkout line catches our attention. On it sits several mammoth cardboard boxes.

"What in the world?" Amelia wonders aloud. I squint, trying to make out the drawing on the side of the box. Amelia starts giggling. "Oh, I've seen those in some yards this year already, and they are ridiculous. Giant balls! Didn't see that trend coming."

"Excuse me?" I ask her. "You can't be serious."

"Oh, I am. I mean, officially, they are ornaments. Big, giant, shiny, red, and pink balls that come in pairs. But sure, ornaments."

"No one in their right mind would spend money on that," I mumble under my breath.

"Probably some Louisiana Tech frat boys," she giggles.

"Can someone help me load these in my truck?" the mysterious purchaser says.

The voice sounds familiar. It pings around in my mind like a ball trapped in a pinball machine until it finally clicks.

"No," I say simply.

"Hmm?" Amelia asks.

Amelia and I lean around the line of people in front of us to confirm what I already know. Tall, graying beard, flannel.

"That asshole," I grind out, just as Frank walks outside with his dolly full of giant balls.

"AUNT MARGIE, JUST TAKE A BREATH. It's not worth it. Christmas will be over in a month and all of that, erm, stuff will be tucked away out of sight," Amelia says, trying for casualness and coming up short.

"Only to be dragged out again next November. Lia, this has to fall under 'Disturbing the peace.' I'm going to call the police," I tell her.

"You're going to call the police? For Christmas decorations?" And my gosh, if her sarcastic tone doesn't sound just like me.

"Fine. Suggestions?"

"I don't know. Have you considered just letting it go? I mean, yes, it's a lot. But it brings him joy and makes his cute little granddaughter happy. Plus, surely the giant balls were the final touch, right? I mean, there can't be much space left in that yard. Just be glad you're not the one who has to clean it all up after Christmas is over."

I sigh in defeat. I never back down from a fight, but Amelia mentioning Frank's granddaughter is enough to make me back down. At least, I thought it was. But now that I'm home and preparing dinner for the two of us, I look out my window and see cars lining up along the street in front of my house. I step outside to take in the scene and notice that the line flows all the way down my usually quiet street. I wonder if Frank is having a party—and then realize that they aren't parked. No, these cars are moving slowly, windows rolled down, to take in the nightmare before Christmas happening in my neighbor's yard.

"Look at Santa in his swimsuit!" a child cries out from the back seat of a slowly moving car.

"Couldn't get worse, huh? Well, have fun getting out of my driveway, Lia. Should I make up your bedroom for you, for old time's sake? Because there is no way either of us is going to be able to leave my house any time soon."

I say the words calmly and carefully. But all I can think is that there's yet another man ruining my Christmas. And there is no way I'm going to let him get the upper hand on me.

Chapter 11

FRANK

NOVEMBER 30 , PRESENT DAY

Every muscle in my body aches. I had an unprecedented amount of traffic driving past my house last night, and I felt the need to sit in my window and keep an eye on things. Between staying up to midnight and recovering from a full day of yard decorating and shopping, my body is screaming at me to take ibuprofen and a nap.

I'm still surprised, and disappointed, that Margie didn't show up to protest my yard last night. I wonder if she finally realized that she's lost this battle. A sense of satisfaction creeps through me at the thought. I love a challenge; it makes it even sweeter when I win.

But as I walk into my kitchen to fix a cup of coffee, a flash of red catches my eye outside my window. Probably just my new lawn ornaments I got from the store yesterday. But something just doesn't sit right with me, so I go out and look around.

There, poised on the prow of my Mardi Gras Christmas float, Hawaiian Santa is wearing a Bama football jersey. My breath hitches in my lungs at the blasphemy. I nearly drop my coffee mug on the table and reach for my shoes, anxious to strip Santa down before an LSU fan decides to egg my house.

I yank my slippers on and hustle outside, then climb up the side of the float. I start to yank the Bama wear off of my inflatable Santa, but feel my foot start to slide. I move it to get better traction, and then my other foot slides. I adjust, but find that I'm now imitating a cartoon character stuck in an oil slick, my slippers flapping as I curl my toes in a desperate attempt to keep them on my feet. Whoever defaced Santa left something slippery behind. My arms pinwheel and I fall face first into inflatable Santa, bending him at the waist.

"Well, well," a voice calls out across my yard. "I've heard of mommy kissing Santa Claus, but bending him over and taking him from behind in your front yard really takes it to an inappropriate level, Mr. Campbell."

Margie. Of course.

I try to stand, but my feet continue to take on a life of their own. Gravity finally wins as Santa and I pitch forward. My slippers fly off my feet as I scramble for a foothold. But I only manage to slam my hand into the speaker system. And just as Santa and I hit the floor of the float, "All I Want for Christmas is You" booms from the speakers.

I hear Margie begin to honest-to-God cackle as if this is the most delightful, diabolical thing she's ever witnessed in her life. I grab the side of the float and pull myself up to a stand. Something glistening coats the front of my favorite flannel shirt. Indignation and anger flare to life inside me.

"You," I growl out and jab my finger in her direction.

Margie's hands go to her hips and she lifts one eyebrow in challenge. "What about me?"

"You did this," I hiss.

"I have no idea what you're talking about, Frank. But it looks like you could use some help. Need me to go fetch a ladder? Or an ambulance, perhaps?"

"You wicked, terrible woman," I grumble.

"Oh honey, I've been called much worse than that by men far more charming. You're going to have to think–and stand–better on your feet to get one over on me."

She turns and begins to walk back to her house, leaving me seething. Then she pivots and glances to where the giant ornaments sit on my lawn.

"Nice balls by the way," she quips.

And that's when I notice that my life-sized Santa, who formerly led my reingators, is now suggestively perched atop the giant things making them look like, well, his balls. I want to be angry, and I am. Really I am. But that's also hilarious. And the laugh that escapes me is only stifled by my socked-feet slipping out from beneath me again.

GAME ON. The thought drums through my head as I think about Margie sneaking out to my yard in the wee hours of the morning to sabotage my Christmas decorations. She thinks she's so funny trying to turn my yard into *Home Alone*. I'll show her. I'll just add more stuff. Though, at this point, I'm not sure where.

And then I get an idea. I head into my makeshift wood shop in my garage and pull out the plywood. I need to get started early if I'm going to finish this project before the weekend is up. Afterall, tomorrow I have that newspaper interview for the Christmas Market, then I need to make some more items to sell. But first, payback.

BY THE TIME I MAKE IT to the convention center to meet up with Amelia for the newspaper interview, I'm feeling much better. I've nearly completed my surprise, additional Christmas decoration and I'm ready to help promote the event that will help get my granddaughter's medical care back on track.

Amelia told me over the phone that she'd be wearing a yellow shirt and dark wash jeans so I would be able to recognize her. I spot the sunshine-colored blouse as soon as I walk into the large space and make my way over to her.

"Hi! Mr. Campbell I presume?" she asks cheerily.

But as we get closer, her smile falters and her eyes grow wide. She looks familiar, but I can't place where I know her from. So I aim for levity.

"Not who you were expecting?" I ask lightly.

"Um, well. I just didn't realize that you were *you*."

I frown. *What's that supposed to mean?*

She stumbles over her words as she continues. "That came out wrong. I'm sorry. I just mean that this is really going to be awkward. My aunt is going to kill me."

"I'm sorry Mrs. Hebert, but did I do something wrong? This is where I'm supposed to meet you for the newspaper interview about the Christmas Market right? I didn't get the day wrong?"

"Oh, it's not that. You're at the right place, the right time," she says, then mumbles, "Or wrong place at the wrong time."

"Hey Lia, sorry I'm late!" a woman calls from the door.

I whip my head around and see… *Margie*. What is *she* doing here?

"What in the hell is *he* doing here?" she says, echoing my thoughts. And then I realize where I know Amelia from. She was with Margie on Thanksgiving when she stormed into my yard. She's the one who got her to back down.

"Well, this is awkward," Amelia murmurs. Then louder, "Aunt Margie, come here for a minute. Let's all just sit down and have a little chat before the reporter arrives for the story. She's a new hire at the paper and Rhett has been mentoring her. We don't want one of her first solo pieces to turn from human interest into police investigation."

Margie is staring at me like she's going to whip out throwing knives any second and use me for target practice. Amelia gestures to folding chairs she's pulled out for this interview.

"Amelia Louise Hebert, sweet niece who I raised as my own dear child, why do you have my troublesome neighbor here when you promised me an easy interview? Hmmm?"

"Well, it's kind of a funny story," Amelia starts, glancing at me and then back to Margie. "You know how I mentioned that this Christmas Market would have co-sponsors?" She glances back and forth between us again. A feeling of uneasiness washes through me. "Well, you see, I didn't quite realize that Mr. Campbell here was Frank Campbell. Your neighbor." She says quickly, then winces.

"Well that's an unfortunate coincidence," Margie snipes. And then she levels her glare at me. "Are you really so hellbent on ruining my peace and quiet, ruining my Christmas, that you would sign up to do this just to take me down? Because, I'm going to tell you right now that there is not a damn thing that you could do to make me withdraw from sponsoring this event. I'm not only doing this to support my niece, I'm doing it to help grow my business. And if one more man thinks he is going to stop me from pursuing my dream, then you have another thing coming."

I sit in stunned silence for a beat. "You can't honestly think I signed up to do this because I'm out to get you?" I say in disbelief.

"Oh yes, I do," she asserts.

"I had no idea you were the co-sponsor of this event," I tell her with as much sincerity as I can muster.

"Didn't know my ass," she asserts. Color flares in her cheeks, setting off her brown eyes and flaming hair. The sight stirs my heart to life, causing it to beat faster with indignation and... something else.

"I swear to you, Margie. When I called Mrs. Hebert, she told me there was a co-sponsor, but not who it was."

We both turn to look at Amelia for confirmation. She shrinks into her seat. "I, um, didn't think that was relevant."

"Lia, you can't be serious," Margie says.

"Come on, Aunt Margie. This isn't a big deal. It's not like the two of you are going to hold each other while you sculpt pottery on a wheel."

My cheeks flush at her words, and I notice with satisfaction that Margie's do too.

"Listen, I just need you both to be adults about this. I have a reporter who is going to be here any moment. So put smiles on your faces, and pretend like today is the best day of your lives and that you want everyone in a hundred mile radius to come here in two weeks. Aunt Margie, speak to your audience. Mr. Campbell, you can be charming. Use it."

Amelia's phone buzzes. She glances at it. "Okay, the reporter is here. Be nice. And please don't get into a wrestling match while I go get her."

She gets up and walks toward the door, leaving Margie and me behind in tense silence. Margie folds her arms and sighs. I notice the color is still high on her cheeks, saturating all of her features. She seems to glow, or maybe sizzle is a better word for it.

I fold my arms and sink back into my chair. We are both staring mutinously ahead as Amelia and a curvy, young, blonde woman walk into the room. Margie stands and plasters a smile across her face, extending her hand.

"Hi there, I'm Margie Murphy."

"Oh I know who you are," the girl practically cheers. Her eyes go all dewy. "I follow you on YouTube! My mom and I love watching you work. You always make us laugh. We keep your bourbon peach jam stocked in our pantry year round. Oh, and I'm Bailey, by the way."

"Well this will make this interview fun," Margie says, and I can tell her smile is real. Who knew Margie had a YouTube channel? I make a mental note to check it out when I get home tonight. She's inadvertently given me a surreptitious way to learn more about her.

"And this is Frank Campbell," Amelia says, gesturing at me.

"Hi there, nice to meet you," I say, shaking her hand.

"Amelia says you do woodworking?" she asks hesitantly. All of Bailey's enthusiasm from meeting Margie has ebbed, and she slips into professional mode.

The four of us sit down and the reporter pulls out her recorder. "Okay if I record this? I want to make sure I get all of your quotes correct for my article."

Chapter 12

MARGIE

DECEMBER 1, PRESENT DAY

Bailey is cute, blonde, young, and bubbly. And her sunshiney, eager personality only highlights how much I am none of those things. This rarely bothers me, but right now, it casts my dour mood in an even darker shadow.

Amelia, I remind myself. *I'm doing this for Amelia.*

"Great, so I've already chatted with Amelia about how the event will function, attending vendors, and the potential boost to our local economy. I want to talk to the two of you about what you bring to the table, quite literally," Bailey enthuses.

She's proud of herself for that last line.

"So, Margie, you've made a name for yourself with your jams, jellies, and your viral YouTube channel. What do you think makes you so popular?"

I shuffle in my seat again. I can brag about everyone I care about without stuttering, but when it comes to boasting about myself, I have to fake it 'til I make it.

"Well, I've been cooking them up since my mama taught me how to when I was about eight years old or so. Over time, experimenting with flavors and ingredients became my favorite way to pass the time. And it turns out that other people seem to like what I make, too."

There. I even answered in full sentences, just like Amelia asked me to.

"Yes, everything you make is delicious, but your personality has lured in fans as well. Can you tell me a little bit about that?"

"Well, you'll have to thank my niece, Amelia, for insisting I film what I'm doing. She used to help me in the kitchen when she was just a girl, and apparently, she thought her experience was worth sharing with a wider audience. As far as my personality? It's kind of hard to comment on that. But I guess I'm no-nonsense, and people find it entertaining."

I glance over at Frank and see that he's staring at me intently. My cheeks heat.

"Anyway, I'm glad people seem to enjoy it. I certainly do, and it's nice not to have to go into an office every day. I think I have the same kind of charm as those judges on *The Great British Baking Show*, and for some reason, people like it. I'm not going to pretend and say something just to be pleasant. Life is too short, and there's no point in wasting it trying to make everyone else happy. If I tell you something is delicious, it is. If I tell you I fuc–, um, *messed* something up, and it's terrible, then that's the truth too. Social media sugarcoats things, and I think people get tired of it. They just want something real. At least that's what I think."

I take a breath. I need to calm my racing heart. Stuff like this doesn't usually get to me. I glance at Frank again; his icy eyes are still locked onto me. *Is it hot in here?* I resist the urge to fan myself. Probably just a hot flash. Damn, getting older sucks.

I realize that Frank and I are still staring at each other when

Bailey chirps, "I think you're onto something there, Margie." I snap out of it and turn back to her. "And what will you have at the market this year?" she continues.

I give her a list of my lineup, including a couple of new flavor combinations. This part of the interview is easy. I give this spiel all the time.

Finally, she turns to Frank. I watch with interest as Bailey seems to melt in front of him. Frank has to be more than twice her age, there's no way she's flirting with him, is there? I've heard the term "silver fox" before, and apparently Bailey has too, because she seems to have no problem with their age gap. Bailey reaches out and touches Frank on the arm. Something flares to life in my chest, scorching and angry. I choose not to look at it too closely. Men are only trouble. I repeat that mantra to myself over and over. This, after all, is just a prime example of why women need to stick together. I should not be fantasizing about lecturing Bailey about keeping her hands to herself.

I realize that I've been stuck inside my head on this unfortunate thought pattern when Frank says my name and snaps me out of it. I blink, frantically searching for clues about their topic of conversation.

"Sorry, I missed that. Could you repeat the question?"

Frank smirks and I want to punch him.

Bailey perks up. "I was just asking Frank about the role the two of you will have in this event. Will you be working together?"

"And I told her that I am honored to work alongside the famous Margie Murphy," Frank supplies, the sarcasm practically dripping from his tongue.

I fight the urge to roll my eyes. "I'm not sure that we will have to work together, per se, but I'll do whatever it takes to make the event a success."

"That's great to hear! Because I have a little surprise for you both," Bailey says.

Dread curls up in my belly, a snake ready to strike.

"A little friendly competition," she continues. "To help support the Ruston community, Oakley Community Bank has agreed to match the sales of whoever sells the most at the event for a charity of the winner's choice! So Margie, if you sell more items at the Christmas Market, your selected charity will receive the prize. And Frank, if you sell more, your charity wins."

I swear I see a light flicker in his eyes, one born of a frightening ambition. The spark in my chest rises to meet his.

"Oh, this will be fun," I say.

"It will indeed," Frank agrees.

Once the interview wraps up and Bailey leaves, Amelia gives me a hug and thanks me for being part of this. She turns to Frank and shakes his hand, thanking him as well. He's all charm and easy conversation with my niece. Trying to win her to his side already. Well, he's got another thing coming if he thinks that's going to work on my Lia.

"We will begin set up for the market in a week," Amelia says. "You two will have the main vendor spaces near the stage, right next to each other. Once the newspaper announces the charity competition, I hope it will bolster enthusiasm for both the Market and the two of you specifically. Maybe we can figure out a way to show your sales in real-time during the event to get the community involved. Also, both of you need to think carefully about the charities you choose."

"I already know mine," Frank says immediately.

"I have some forms you will both need to fill out for Oakley Community Bank so they will be able to create one of those giant checks for the winner's charity," Amelia says, heading to her backpack to get the information.

My sneaky little niece knew about this. Of course, she did. While she grabs her things, Frank leans down to me, his warm breath tickling my ear. "I think only one of us has the balls to win this thing."

I whip my head around to face him and gape. Wicked delight

dances in his eyes.

Amelia returns, hands us the paperwork, and then tells us about event table set-up times. "And remember, you two, this is all for charity. Let's play nice, yes?"

"When am I ever not nice, Lia?" She lifts an eyebrow.

"You got it," Frank says amiably like he didn't just issue a quiet challenge to me.

"See you around, Margie," Frank says, and then heads out the door without a backwards glance and, presumably, back to his house.

"Well, this is certainly going to be interesting," I murmur.

"Come on, let's go get a coffee and talk about how you're going to win this thing," Amelia says, grabbing her backpack.

ALREADY ANTICIPATING THE CROWD that's going to line up on the street outside my house tonight to see Frank's yard garbage, I hurry home. But it seems that I still didn't correctly anticipate the amount of growing attention his yard is creating in the local community. Because as soon as I turn onto my street, I'm met with a line of cars. I'm stuck in a traffic queue to get to my own damn driveway. My anger, which seems to be my constant companion since Frank moved in, swells until I'm vibrating with the intensity of it.

I consider swerving into the oncoming traffic lane to go around all these gawkers, but a quick glance shows that side of the street is clogged, too. I turn on the radio, ready to find the classic rock station and rage sing AC/DC, but when I flip on the radio and hit scan, "Up on the Rooftop" blasts through my speakers. I swear that Santa is mocking me. Then I glance up to Frank's flashing yard in the distance and realize that his lights are synched to the music now booming through my car.

I am going to *Home Alone* him. Tar, feathers, nails, swinging buckets. Nothing is off the table.

In a fit of rage, I pull off the road into the grass beside me. Screw this. I'm walking home. And Frank can come collect my car in the morning. We live near the woods, and I am grateful that it's winter, although a balmy one. Otherwise, I'd also be battling mosquitoes and ticks, and then Frank would need to watch his bed for bugs at night. My limit for revenge does not exist at the moment.

I know the people in the line of cars are staring at the mad woman stomping across the field beside them, and I do not give one flying fuck. I dare someone to say something to me. For a brief moment, my conscience in the form of Amelia pops up and reminds me to be nice, but I yell at her to leave me alone and keep charging forward.

By the time I finally get to my house fifteen minutes later, I have scratches on my arms from the overgrown grass, and God knows what's tangled in my hair. It's a good thing I never wear dresses, or my legs would be destroyed. As I walk up my long driveway, I briefly consider changing my trajectory for Frank's house and pounding my fist on his door. I eye the line of cars, and reason takes over just long enough to remind me that I'm representing Amelia with this Christmas Market and a front-page story about me murdering my next-door neighbor might put a damper on the event. Growling, I march up to my front door, muttering that Amelia has no idea how much I love her.

And that's when I see it.

There is a giant wooden cutout of the Grinch right on the edge of my yard. He's carrying a strand of lights like he just removed them all from my dark house. That asshole. As if it's not hard enough that he has blocked the entrance to my own damn house and created enough lights to rival the surface of the sun outside my bedroom window while blasting Christmas music. No, now he's going to insult me by indicating that *I'm the Grinch*.

I don't stop to think. I just act. I storm over to Frank's house, but I don't go to his front door. No, that would be too easy, too kind. I look for the extension cords and follow them to their source. I find a complicated system of cords connected to a timer and surge protector.

Bingo.

Cold calculation settles over me. I'm livid, but I don't want to be electrocuted. I find the main power button, and I punch it. The North Pole in Frank's front yard immediately goes dark. All the music cuts off, and the frogs begin to sing, just as thankful as I am for some peace and quiet.

And then, using the flashlight on my phone, I steadily unplug every single cord and timer. I know that Frank will likely emerge any moment now that it's clear that the circus in his yard has shut down. If I'm lucky, he will go to his breaker box first and buy me a little time. I consider my options. I eye the water hose on the side of his house, but decide that I'm not even that mean. Instead, I grab Frank's ridiculously large surge protector, tuck it under my arm, and march back over to my house, guided by the flashlight on my phone.

Maybe I'll return it tomorrow. But tonight, at least, I will sleep in peace.

Chapter 13

MARGIE

DECEMBER 1, 1998

Small icicles press into my calves. I yelp and roll over in my bed to see a pair of whisky-brown eyes looking at me with warmth and mischief.

"Aunt Margie," the little voice whispers. "I brought you a present."

Amelia's eyes grow wider, begging me to ask her what she's got.

"Is it a cookie?" I ask.

She shakes her head determinedly, her brown flyaways clinging to my pillowcase with static electricity.

"Hmmmm. A flower?" I try.

She shakes her head no again and fidgets, glancing down to where she has her small hands clasped in front of her.

"I know. It's a button."

"Aunt Margie, no!" Amelia giggles.

Then she eases her hands open and invites me to look inside the makeshift container she's formed with fingers. I peer inside the dark space, and, at first, I don't see anything. And then something moves. I startle and scramble out of bed; my hand flies to my chest, where my heart thrums like it just got a jolt of caffeine.

"Amelia Louise. What is that?" She giggles and snaps her hands closed again. "Is it alive?" I push.

She nods her head in agreement and whispers, "It's a toad."

My eyes flutter closed as I will my heart rate and breathing to slow down. When I open my eyes again, I see that she's crawled out of bed and is standing in front of me. My old Ruston Peach Festival t-shirt hangs off her small frame, and her sleep-mussed hair is sticking up in every direction.

"Lia, baby. I don't think that toad likes being inside. Why don't you go on outside and set it free?"

"He does like it inside. I know because I found him in your pantry," she says, like she just offered me a cupcake.

"Is that right?" I ask, silently making a note to call pest control. "Well, toads need water and--"

"I already set him up a little bowl," she says proudly. "His name is Frogbert."

"And," I continue, "Frogbert will want to eat bugs. All those are outside darlin'." She wilts in disappointment, and I suddenly feel like the worst person on earth for telling Amelia that Frogbert has to go outside. "Don't be sad, baby. I bet his family is out there looking for him," I encourage.

It was the wrong thing to say because Amelia immediately folds in on herself, appearing for all the world to have shrunk three sizes. "Do you think–" she whispers, "That my dad will be looking for me? Will Frogbert's dad hurt his mom, too?" Tears well at the corner of her eye. Shit.

"No baby, nothing like that. I'm sure Frogbert's dad is very nice and just worried about him. And you're safe here. Nothing can hurt you in Aunt Margie's house."

"Promise?"

"Promise. Now go let Frogbert hop away outside then wash your hands. I'll check on your mama and make some banana pancakes. How does that sound?"

She brightens and nods, scuffling off to my back door.

I sigh, thoughts turning to my sister in the guest room down the hall. I have no idea what version of her I'll get this morning: depressed and listless, or false, manic cheer. Regardless, David is right. She and Amelia have to find a different living situation. I can't keep watching them diminish into smaller versions of themselves.

I knock lightly and ease the door open to the guest room. My sister sits on the bed, facing away from me and staring out the window. She looks resigned. To what though, I'm not sure.

"Hey Jo," I say gently.

But she doesn't show any signs that she recognizes I'm there. I step toward her slowly. When I place my hand on her shoulder, she tenses and then turns to look at me.

"Hey Margie, sorry. Lost in thought." Her voice is rough like she hasn't spoken in weeks.

"I'm making breakfast. Why don't you come to the kitchen and eat something with Lia and me," I coax.

An expression flashes across her face, but it's there and gone before I can decipher what she's thinking.

"Yeah, okay. Sounds good," she agrees, standing to follow me.

As Jo sits down at the table with Amelia, I start the coffee brewing. I make it stronger than usual, knowing I will need all the fortification it can afford me. I glance over my shoulder to see Amelia animatedly telling her mother about the toad she found this morning. Melancholy filters into my heart at the sight. I pull the ingredients out of the pantry and begin to make banana pancakes while I eavesdrop on the mostly one-sided conversation happening at the table behind me.

"Mama," Amelia says tentatively. "Does it hurt?"

I tense, knowing she has to be referring to the swollen, mottled skin around my sister's right eye and jawline. Though the way she phrases the question makes me think that, even at age five, Amelia is asking about a much deeper pain.

"It's nothing, baby," Jo says dismissively. "Just a little bump. It will heal right up. Don't you worry."

Amelia doesn't say anything more, but as I walk over with a cup of coffee for Jo and an apple cider for Lia, I notice my niece's frown matches my own.

Chapter 14

FRANK

DECEMBER 2, PRESENT DAY

I stare at the empty space where the surge protector should be, all the wires yanked from their station lay sprawled on the ground like dropped spaghetti. I rub my throbbing temples. I saw Margie fleeing from my yard when I went to investigate everything shutting down last night. And when I discovered the missing surge protector, I was furious. But then, this morning, as I was preparing to go talk to her, I noticed her car parked a quarter mile down the road. Guilt quickly replaced my anger as I realized what must have happened.

The traffic. Margie unable to get to her home. Her fury. And I can't even blame her for it. I have to figure out a solution for this, but I'm not sure what the answer is. I want to win the Yard of the Year prize, want to pay off Julia's hospital bills.

Perhaps it's time to sit down with Margie and talk this through. I don't like sharing Julia's story without my son's permission, but maybe Margie will understand if I explain why I'm going all out for Christmas this year, well more than I usually do anyway. Though, she might think that next year will be different, and I have no plans to give up my Christmas decorating tradition.

Sighing, I climb into my truck and head to a nearby farm where I work. It's going to be a full day of charting out plans for where and what we will plant in the coming year. Though perhaps work is exactly what I need. It's good for my soul. I love digging into the land and watching as she gives back with joy.

BY THE TIME MY WORK DAY IS OVER, I've resolved to have a serious conversation with Margie. I've decided meeting at her house will be best, and I've jotted down a list of points to cover. She's got to understand why my decorations are so important. And nobody *really* hates Christmas, right? I park my truck and head into my house. After I change, I stride over to her place, ready to try and mend the fence.

I knock gently on Margie's front door and hear a voice call out for me to wait just a minute. The door swings open, and Margie says, "Lia, you're early--oh. You are not Amelia."

I shrug and shuffle on my feet a bit. "No, I'm not Amelia. Can we, uh, talk?"

"Oh, so *now* you want to talk?" she demands.

I inhale and let the breath out slowly. I try to remember why I'm here. I'm making amends.

"Yes, I'd like to talk," I say steadily.

Margie eyes me, looking me up and down. I hold my breath as I wait for her verdict. My phone starts buzzing in my pocket. I ignore it, determined to show her that our conversation is my priority.

I try again. "We are going to be seeing a lot of each other, both working on the Christmas Market and living in such close proximity. I want to come to an understanding."

She raises an eyebrow. "Is that man-speak for 'Here's why you have to accept this?'"

My phone buzzes with an incoming call again. That's weird.

"Do you need to answer that?" Margie demands.

"No, no. I need to talk to you. Work all this out," I insist.

She lets out a heavy sigh and steps aside. It's a silent invitation to come inside, and I accept, crossing the threshold into her home. The space smells like cinnamon, peaches, and bourbon, with the warm tones of sandalwood underlying everything. All around, I spy nods to a time long past. There are old crayon drawings framed on walls and pictures of Margie and Amelia together. I spy an old fox stuffed animal sitting on top of a shelf that doesn't look like it's been played within a decade. This place feels settled and brimming with love.

Homesickness takes me inexplicably by surprise and threatens to overwhelm me. Margie's house reminds me so much of the home I sold, the home that held small touches of Cheryl, our kids, and Julia all over it, that I almost choke on my grief.

"You okay?" Margie asks, concern slipping through the cracks of her anger.

I can't speak, so I just nod.

"I'll fix us some coffee. Have a seat," she says, gesturing to her kitchen table. Like the rest of her house, the small, round, wooden table is worn by thousands of plates that slid over its surface throughout the years.

I continue to study her kitchen, noting the dozens of empty mason jars waiting for her to fill them on the counter. She carries two mugs over to us and sits down.

She starts talking before I have a chance to. "Look, I shouldn't have unplugged and stolen your electrical thing. My temper got a hold of me and–"

Buzz, buzz. My phone comes to life again. I furrow my brow.

"I'm sorry, this never happens," I tell her, concern causing me to reach for my phone.

When I pull it from my pocket, I see that I have three missed calls from Jason. My stomach jumps into my throat and balloons there. On autopilot, I stand up and call him back as I walk out of Margie's house.

He picks up on the second ring. "Dad?"

"Yeah? Are you okay?" I ask, and I can hear the low current of panic in my voice.

"It's Julia. We're at Lincoln Memorial Hospital. We may need to head to Dallas and–"

"I'm on my way," I say simply and run to my truck. I climb in, fire it up, and drive off, heading straight to where my granddaughter, son, and daughter-in-law are waiting for me at the hospital.

"JULIA IS GOING TO BE OKAY," I tell Jason for what feels like the hundredth time in the past hour. "She's strong. She's fine. This is just a hiccup in her recovery."

My son paces the small hospital room while Emma holds her daughter's hand and talks to her about Christmas.

"Let's step outside," I encourage him, hyper-aware of my granddaughter's proximity to our conversation.

Together Jason and I walk a loop around the hospital parking lot. He tells me that Julia had a flare-up. She started screaming in pain, and it terrified them. When they got to the hospital, her whole body was hot to the touch. No one is really sure what's going on, nor why her current medication isn't working properly. They want her to go to Dallas and see the specialists at the hospital there.

"I have to work still. We'll make a plan to go to Dallas this week but we have to be back in town by Monday. And God, we are still paying into our ridiculously high insurance deductible and, shit," he mumbles.

I pull my son into a hug and hold him while his shoulders shake, desperately wishing I could do more to help him with this. There is nothing I wouldn't do for my family. Nothing.

"Jason, I am going to help you with this, okay? And don't you dare tell me no. I'm your father. Just like it's your job to take care of Julia, it's my job to take care of you. And I have a plan. We are going to get through this. And our little Juju Bug is going to bounce right back. She'll be giving us hell in no time," I reassure.

I don't let him see the tear that slides down my cheek as I hold my adult son in my arms, just like I did when he was Julia's age.

Chapter 15

MARGIE

PRESENT DAY, DECEMBER 3

"And then he just got up and walked out without explanation," I tell Amelia over the phone. "I don't know how that man thinks he can just come in here and tell me he wants to talk and then bolt." I'm irritated all over again. For just a moment, I thought Frank was coming over here to set things right. He even looked like he was going to be vulnerable with me.

But I should have known better. He is a man, after all.

"There's got to be more to it, don't you think?" Amelia asks. Always ready to give people the benefit of the doubt, my niece.

"Unlikely," I quip.

"Aunt Margie. You unplug the man's electrical thing. And then it is kind of your fault for making his yard go viral. Give the man a little grace," she adds, slightly exasperated.

"Wait a damn second. How is this *my* fault?"

"You have to have seen the posts," she hedges.

"What posts?" I snap.

"Aunt Margie. You mean to tell me you are on YouTube all the time and don't check Instagram or Facebook?"

"I don't have time to look at all those ill-informed political opinions on Facebook. And I do post my work on Instagram all the time. That doesn't mean I look at other people's crap," I tell her.

Amelia sighs heavily. "Aunt Margie, the stunt you pulled in Frank's yard with Santa and the ornaments and the Bama jersey was spotted by some of the local college kids. They took a ton of photos and started calling it Santa Balls. Students have been sneaking over there during the day to take photos with him and posting them with the hashtags #santaballs #illbeyourhohoho #santaclausiscomingtotown. It's a local sensation. Of course, people are lining your street to see his house."

I find myself totally and entirely flummoxed.

"Aunt Margie, are you still there?"

"You can't be serious," I finally say.

"Get online and look for yourself," Amelia insists.

I pull the phone away from my ear and navigate to Instagram. I type in the hashtags, and sure enough, images of college students sitting next to Santa on his giant ornament balls fill my feed. There's even a photo of old Birdie Jones sitting on them, arm wrapped firmly around faux Santa, red globes shining beneath her.

I raise the phone back to my ear. "Well, shit," I say.

"It seems to me like you kind of engineered your own destruction," Amelia insists.

"Do you want me to co-sponsor your Christmas Market or not? Because if so, I'd stop right there with your philosophical bullshit."

"It's not philosophical—it's just the facts, ma'am," Amelia says.

"Goodbye," I say.

"Oh, come on now. I'm just saying that it wouldn't hurt to try to re-engage Frank in a conversation. Maybe you can own up to your part in all this and help smooth things over."

"You're just saying that so both of us won't quit the Christmas Market," I sulk.

"Of course I am. But also because I love you, and both of you have to live next to each other. And, besides, I need you to swing by my office and approve your recipient for the charity competition next week."

"Where is the sweet girl I raised?"

"I'm still right here, Aunt Margie. But never say that I didn't learn a thing or two from you."

We say our goodbyes. I turn and stare out my window at Frank's mess of a yard. And as I watch, a car pulls up, and two teens jump out and make a run for Santa Balls. They chuckle as they take turns snapping phone pics of each other.

THAT NIGHT, FRANK'S CHRISTMAS LIGHTS are all back on. I sigh and hang my head trying and failing to reconcile myself to many more weeks of this. Already, a line of cars stretches down the street, blockading me into my house. Not that I have any plans, but if I did, I certainly wouldn't be able to go to them.

I stare at the line of mason jars on my counter, waiting to be filled for both my online orders and the upcoming Christmas Market. I decide to invest my involuntary house arrest time wisely.

I get to work cooking, pouring, and canning. About halfway through my planned work for the night, I glance up at the window to see a TV news crew marching across my yard. I panic for a brief moment, guilt making me think they are coming to ask me why I sabotaged my neighbor's nauseating light display. But, as I watch, they keep going over to Frank's yard.

Curiosity gets the better of me. I turn off my burners and grab my boots to see for myself what's going down. *Maybe there's been enough noise and night pollution complaints to get him shut down? I should be so lucky.* I walk outside across my dark yard, stand on the periphery of

Frank's glowing nightmare, and watch.

The camera crew starts filming B-roll shots of the lights and figures in the yard. They take their time zooming in on Santa Balls I notice wryly. One of them goes up to the front door and knocks. The door opens, and the reporter seems to talk to the person inside for a moment, then the door closes again. I furrow my brows, my mind whirling through and discarding possible explanations.

"Okay, he's ready. Let's set up for the shot," the cameraman calls out to his crew.

And then I watch as Frank's front door is thrown open, and out walks–well, Santa Claus. But this isn't just any Santa, I realize almost immediately. This Santa is svelte with a trim body–he must have missed the memo that said St. Nick has a belly that shakes like a bowl full of jelly. He struts out to the middle of his front lawn with a bag tossed casually over his shoulder. He looks at the camera, winks, then kneels in the middle of his yard.

It should have been obvious, but it's not until he looks up, casting his gaze around his yard. That's when I realize that *Santa is Frank.* And Frank didn't bother with a false beard, no. He dons his salt and pepper close-cropped beard like a Santa who is better suited to an Axe Body Spray commercial than the man who spends his nights eating cookies from every house across the globe.

Suddenly, I'm very, very warm. Never in my life did I think a man in a Santa suit would make me hot under the collar, but damn. Most Santas don't wear form-fitting suits that show off their tight asses and rub their hands over their strong jawlines, either, I suppose.

And just when I don't think the man before me could get any more attractive, Frank calls out. "Santa is here, kids! Come and get it!"

And, as if on cue, children pour from the cars lined up along the street and run to where he kneels on the ground. The cameramen move in as Santa Frank hands out candy and small trinkets to each of the children who approach him. They giggle and ask for more as they shove candy canes into their mouths and run in and out of his yard displays. They are utterly, horribly, delighted.

As the kids dissipate, either roaming his yard for a closer look at the items there or returning to their parents, a reporter begins his interview with Sexy Claus. I mean Frank, the asshole, Campbell. Yes, that's it.

I can't hear what they say, but I make a mental note to watch the ten o'clock news to find out what he could possibly have to say for himself.

THAT NIGHT AS I CLEAN UP my canning space, I turn on the news. When the Santa Frank segment finally airs, I gape. You have got to be kidding me.

"That's right, James," Frank says into the camera, eyes twinkling like he's the centuries-old St. Nick himself. "I'll be at the Christmas Market selling some of my very own, hand-carved wooden pieces made in the North Pole!"

James, the reporter, chuckles. "Is that right? And will one of your elves be there selling them for you?"

"Oh no, I wouldn't want to disappoint anyone. I'll be there, myself. And for every piece sold, you can get a photo with me, Santa Claus!"

That conniving asshole. That whole stunt with the kids tonight was Frank's first move on the chessboard of our charity competition. And he just hard launched it publicly to the whole city.

Santa Frank turns to the camera and says, "I'll see you there," and winks. And I'm not sure if the heat that courses through my body is anger or desire.

I shut the TV off and rage-clean the rest of my kitchen. By the time I finally sit down and open my laptop, I've got the first inklings of a plan to best him in our competition.

Chapter 16

MARGIE

DECEMBER 3, 1998

It's been nearly a week, and Jo hasn't said a word about leaving my house. The three of us are walking along a razor's edge—one slip and the police will get involved. The threat is unspoken, but it looms with the weight of an incoming storm on the horizon.

In silent agreement, Jo and I work overtime to keep Amelia content and distracted. She hasn't once asked about her dad or when they are going home. Instead, she spends her time following me around the yard as I prepare my flower beds for winter, bundling them up with pine straw. Living this far away from the city means that all sorts of animals wander into my yard, and Amelia is positively delighted by them. She's turned it into a game, keeping track of how many deer, armadillos, possums, and birds she sees each day. She is plodding along behind me, singing "Baby Beluga" to herself when she pauses and declares, "Aunt Margie. It's almost Christmas. Why don't you have a Christmas tree?"

I turn to face her, matching her stance with my hands on my hips. "Well, I guess because I didn't realize it was time to get one yet."

"You turned your calendar to December," she insists. "It's time for a tree. That's what Mama always says. We can get a tree once it's December.'"

My heart aches at her words, and I know that I'll do anything to keep an ounce of normalcy in Amelia's life.

"Well then, I guess you're right. I don't have a lot of Christmas decorations, but we can go get a tree, and then maybe you can help me pick out some lights and ornaments to decorate it with?" A grin spreads across Amelia's face, momentarily wiping away my worry about the future. "Alright, let's tell your mama, and then we can go pick out our tree."

Amelia dances off ahead of me to the house.

"Margie, you there?" A deep male voice calls out from my driveway. My heart stutters for a moment, thinking Jo's husband has finally shown up. But as the man's tone and cadence filter past my panic and into the folds of my brain, I relax. *David.*

Warmth spreads through me as I realize my future husband is back in town. I jog, my wild hair falling into my eyes as I turn the corner. And there he is, tall and solid. His dirty blonde hair is brushed back. He's still wearing a button-up and slacks, so I know he came straight here from his business trip. I sprint the rest of the distance and reach for him. He pulls me into an embrace and holds me tight. He smells like the airplane he flew home on and the soft hint of spearmint. His lips brush the top of my head and when I pull back, his mouth finds mine.

"I missed you," he whispers into my lips.

"I missed you too."

"I'm ready, Aunt Margie!" Amelia calls, interrupting our reunion.

I feel David tense, but his smile never wavers. "Good to see you again, Amelia," he says gently.

"Hi, Mr. David. Aunt Margie and I are going to get a Christmas tree. Want to come with us?"

I look at David and study his expression. I know he isn't comfortable with my sister and Amelia staying at my house because he believes they make me a target. But he knows how much I love them, how much this wide-eyed child with big dimples and an even bigger heart means to me.

"Yeah, I'd love that," he finally says.

"Yay! Let's go!" Amelia cheers.

"Just a second, let me tell Jo and see if she wants to come," I tell them.

I go inside, grab my wallet, and look for my sister. I find her still sitting in the guest bedroom, staring out the window. If I didn't know better, I'd think she was a ghost, trapped here and looking for a way to move on to the afterlife.

I clear my throat. "Hey Jo, I'm taking Lia to get a Christmas tree. David is here and going with us. Want to come?"

She glances at me, then back to the window. "No, I think I'll stay here and enjoy the quiet if that's okay?"

"Yeah, of course. We'll be back in a couple of hours. Make yourself at home."

She nods, so I leave her be, and head out the door.

OUR TRIP TO THE ONLY small Christmas tree farm in town is short but fun. David and I follow along behind Amelia as she looks at trees and tries to decide which one is best. I suspect she's the kind of kid who will empathize with Charlie Brown's brand of Christmas tree, and I am therefore unsurprised when she picks out the smallest one in the lot.

"It's just a baby and needs some love," she declares. My heart pinches with guilt seeing Amelia in her own words. "Of course," I say gruffly. David squeezes my hand, then goes with my niece to find someone to help us load it into the car.

Afterwards, we drive around town and I tune the radio to the Christmas station. I allow myself to enjoy this small slice of domestic life with my niece in the backseat and my fiancé beside me. At this moment, at least, everything feels good.

When we get back to my place, I half-expect Jo to be gone, but her car is still there. And when I walk in, I discover that she is back in bed and sleeping. I'm not sure what to do about it. I want to encourage her to join us, but I suspect she hasn't slept well in years and who am I to rob her of a moment of peace? I gently close the door to her room and return to my living room.

Amelia, David, and I spend the rest of the evening setting up the small Christmas tree, drinking apple cider, and cooking dinner. Pine, cinnamon, and freshly baked bread mingle in the air, and I wish I could store the holiday smell in a jar and crack it open anytime I feel down. After we eat, I pull out playing cards. Amelia seems content to play Go Fish the entire evening, but when I see her eyes get heavy, and yawns drown out her words, I suggest turning on a Christmas movie.

We settle into the couch around the TV with the lights off, save for the small white strands on the petite tree. And as "The Island of Misfit Toys" plays in the background, I notice Amelia has dozed off on the couch. I study her as she sleeps peacefully, eyes twitching occasionally while she's lost in dreamland.

David slides his hand over mine and presses his forehead into my temple. "She's a good kid," he whispers.

"The best," I agree.

"What are they going to do?" he asks gently.

I sigh, tilt my head back on the couch, and close my eyes. "I don't know. I've thought about a million different possibilities, each more unlikely than the next. Their best bet would be to move far from here, somewhere that man can't find them. Get a restraining order. But I don't think Jo has the courage to do it. This is the longest I've ever seen her stay away from him, and I don't imagine it will last much longer."

"And the girl?" David asks, looking at where she wiggles in her sleep.

"I can't let her become his next target. And I'm scared that Jo isn't in the right state of mind to take care of her."

"So she's going to what? Stay here with you?" he asks, not unkindly.

I shrug. "Would that be such a bad thing?"

He pulls away and leans back against the couch with a heavy sigh. "Margie, there's something I wanted to talk to you about."

My shoulders tense, and my mental hackles raise. Those words never lead to anything good.

"It's just that I'm doing really well at my job. They want to give me a promotion." But the way he says it doesn't make it sound like a good thing.

"Congratulations, honey. That's great," I whisper, careful not to wake Amelia up. He looks at her, thinking the same.

"Let's go outside so we don't wake her," David says.

We get up and step out onto the dark front porch. The leaves that still manage to cling to the trees rustle, and the temperature has dropped into the fifties. I shiver.

"The thing is," David continues, "If I accept the promotion, I've got to move."

"Okay," I hedge. "Like to Baton Rouge or something?"

He rubs his hand through his hair. "No, to South Carolina."

The words clang into me, a hammer on a reverberating gong.

"Oh," is all I can manage.

"And since we're planning to get married, I was hoping you would move with me. If not immediately, then after a few months," he continues. "This past year with you has been hectic with my work travel and the trouble with your sister and niece. Despite that, you and me? We're good together. We get each other's sense of humor and enjoy doing stuff together. We are the real deal."

His words buzz around in my mind like flies on roadkill. Move? To South Carolina?

"Margie, say something," he encourages.

"I need a minute."

I close my eyes and allow myself to picture that future: the one where I go with David to South Carolina. Maybe we live on the Atlantic coast, and I get to breathe in the sea air–my favorite thing– every morning. I can work on the cookbook I've dreamt of writing and make myself and my husband my top priorities. Maybe there's even a dog and children of my own in the future.

"Aunt Margie!" a troubled voice cries from inside the house.

And just as quickly as the dream painted itself in front of me, it's washed away into a swirling stream of paint and water. The doorknob wiggles, and I open it to see Amelia, tears sliding down her rounded cheeks. I reach for her, scooping her into my arms and letting her rest on my hip.

"It's okay, Lia. Aunt Margie is here," I soothe.

I glance up and notice David staring at us with pain and acceptance in his eyes. I haven't given him an answer, but he seems to know already what I will say.

"Davy, I–"

"No, it's okay," he interrupts. "You don't need to answer me now. We've got a few weeks to sort things out. Take care of your girl, and I'll see you tomorrow." He kisses my temple, then walks to his car, starts it up, and backs out of the driveway.

I'm being pulled in different directions as I stare at the two paths stretching out before me. The tug of war on my heart burns and stretches. Amelia snuggles her tear-stained face into my shoulder. As her sobs begin to ease, I finally register what David said as he left: "Take care of *your* girl."

I squeeze Amelia tightly and carry her back into my house,

bringing her to my bed. After we crawl under the covers, she snuggles in tightly to me, her cold toes pressing into my legs. And together, we drift off to sleep.

Chapter 17

FRANK

PRESENT DAY, DECEMBER 4

She probably thought she was being sneaky, but I saw Margie watching me from the edge of my yard last night. And I saw her scurry off back to her house after the TV interview. I still need to talk to her, but after abandoning her without a word to check on Julia, I'm not sure she will hear me out anyway.

And, besides, right now, I have more important things to do. Julia is home from the hospital, and she's coming to stay with me for a week while her parents go to Dallas. They are going to look for short-term housing so Julia can undergo a trial immune system treatment. But she will have to be there, in person, for eight weeks. Jason will commute back and forth to work as he's able, but that kind of travel is too much for Julia's already stressed body.

Even now she's still recovering from her latest flare-up, thus I offered to keep her here with me. I have enough sick time built up that taking a week off from work is nothing, plus I need to put in some time in my makeshift woodshop to build up my stock of items for the Christmas Market.

Julia is ecstatic to stay at Papa's Christmas house. You'd never even know the kiddo just spent time in the hospital with the way she's buzzing around my house like an inquisitive little bee. I'll think I have her settled with lunch. Then I'll go out to my garage shop for thirty minutes, come back to the kitchen, and she's inexplicably gone.

All attempts to convince her to tell me where she's darting off to have been met with giggles and "I'm just exploring Papa," alongside doe eyes. I'm a sucker and let her get away with far more than her parents would.

"As long as you stay on my property, Juju Bug. Don't go wandering off down Farmerville Highway. It's dangerous along the street."

And despite her intrepid explorations, she abides by my rules. I continually find her digging in the pine straw beneath my bushes, wandering the tree line along my backyard, or snooping in my woodworking space. But Julia is well-behaved, just curious.

After two days of our explorations, she waltzes up to me, hands on hips. "Papa, why don't you have a Christmas tree inside your house?"

I study her determined expression, noting the knots forming in her dark hair. I should probably help her untangle those before my son and daughter-in-law get back in town. "Well, Juju Bug, I guess I was so fixated on doing the outside decorating that I forgot about the inside."

"Can we go get a tree, Papa? Pleeeeeease?"

"Of course, baby. Let Papa just finish cutting out this sign and we'll go to the Christmas tree farm and pick something out."

She claps and darts out of my shop. I shake my head and chuckle, wishing for that level of energy again. I turn off my saw and flip the light switch as I head out. I fully expect to see her already sitting in my truck, bouncing up and down in the seat. So I'm surprised when I walk out to my driveway and don't see Julia anywhere. I duck into the house and call for her, but she's not there. I wander back outside and walk the property, concern starting to ratchet up in my chest. And then I hear Julia's distinctive giggles. I follow the sound to find her standing on Margie's front porch. Margie stares down at her, hands on hips, and the two seem to be engaged in an important conversation. I sigh and walk over to collect my granddaughter, already forming an apology in my mind.

"Sorry about that," I say in greeting.

"For once, you don't have anything to apologize for," Margie quips. "Julia here was just telling me that you, somehow, don't have a Christmas tree in that holiday-soaked house of yours. Seems like a real shame there, Frank."

I don't miss her sarcasm, but Julia does. "I know. That's what I told him, too, Miss Margie. And that's why we are going to get a Christmas tree. He told me he would take me. You should come with us." Julia says this as if it's a foregone conclusion.

"Oh, I wouldn't want to intrude on your time with your Papa," Margie hedges.

"You wouldn't be intruding," I say too quickly. I don't know why I say it. Margie gave me an easy out. But, surprisingly, I want her with us for this. I want to show her that Christmas doesn't have to be terrible despite the tension between us.

"I don't know…" she tries again.

"Oh please, Miss Margie! Come with us to get a tree. Papa says that if I'm well-behaved, he will buy me a hot chocolate. I bet he will get one for you if you behave, too."

A chuckle slips out of me before I can help it. Margie snaps her head up at me and glares. But I can see the laughter that threatens the corners of her mouth.

"Surely you can behave yourself for an hour or two?" I coax.

"I don't think I'm the one who has a behavior problem," she says, folding her arms. "What about your Papa, Julia? Does he have to behave, too?"

"Oh yes. You'll be good, won't you, Papa?" My heart melts like a snowman in the Louisiana sun.

"I'm always good, Juju Bug." I look up in time to see Marige's expression transform into one of awe. She's just as wrapped up in my granddaughter as I am at the moment.

"Well, if you insist, I'll tag along," Margie says to Julia. "Just let me grab my jacket."

My heart begins to thunder. It's ridiculous. I know we will hold our unspoken truce in front of Julia. There will be no ugliness between us over the next couple of hours, just two adults who want to give a six-year-old a happy Christmas memory. But as Margie steps outside again, a beanie cap tugged down over her wavy locks, and smiles widely at Julia, I realize suddenly and shockingly that perhaps the uptick in my heart rate is more than just nerves.

"Right, then. Let's take my truck," I say, coughing to clear out the rasp that clings to my words.

THE TEN-MINUTE DRIVE to the Christmas tree farm is dominated by Julia's excited ramblings. Thank goodness.

Margie and I focus entirely on her. I love the way Margie asks her serious questions and really pays attention to Julia's answers. I think back to the photos I saw all over her house of just Margie and Amelia and wonder at it. Margie treats Amelia more like a daughter than a niece, and instinct tells me that their relationship is closer than that of a typical aunt and niece. I want to ask about it, but Margie and I don't have that kind of friendship.

We park at the Christmas tree farm, and Julia practically leaps out of the back seat of my extended cab. "Look at them all, Papa! Just look at them! How are we going to decide which one to take home?"

"I'm going to leave that to you, Juju Bug. It just has to fit inside my house, so nothing too big."

She skips along ahead of Margie and me, a litany of "Oh, maybe this one?" and "I like the branches of this one!" spilling out of her mouth.

I glance at Margie just as she looks at me. Smiles still linger on our lips at witnessing Julia's delight. The space between us pulls taut for just a beat as something unspoken passes between us. It's there and gone as soon as it appears, but I feel it move through my body and into my chest, shocking my heart back to life.

I look away, confusion and guilt churning inside me. *Is this wrong?* I haven't so much as looked at another woman with interest since I met Cheryl decades ago. Now she's gone, and here I am smiling and looking at another woman with interest. My good mood evaporates on the wind as I turn inward and continue to berate myself silently. My hand flutters to where my wedding ring sat on my finger for thirty years. I just stopped wearing it a few months ago, and now look at me. I loved Cheryl, hell I still love her even three years after her death. *What am I doing?*

"Papa, I found the one I want!" Julia's voice snaps me out of my guilt spiral and back into the here and now.

God, I wish Cheryl could see her granddaughter and be here with us at the Christmas tree farm. She would be vibrating with joy at the very sight of her granddaughter loving Christmas as much as she did. But she's not and never will be. My heart slides into my gut and stays there.

I watch as Margie walks to where Julia looks excitedly at her chosen tree. I keep watching as Margie pauses, her eyes going wide. "Why did you choose this one, Julia?" she asks quietly.

"Because it's just a baby and needs a home," she declares.

And I swear Margie swipes a tear from her cheek. My traitorous heart thuds in my stomach. I want to go to her, hug her, even though I have no idea why she's trying to hide her tears.

Cheater. My brain screams. I take a step backward instead.

"I'll just go get someone to help us buy it," I say, darting off. My brain is reeling. I'm feeling a hundred emotions at once. Love, guilt, fear, devotion, nostalgia. Attraction. Dammit.

I get one of the workers to follow me out to where Julia stands next to her chosen tree, talking to it and telling it how much it's going to love its new home.

"That's the perfect tree for you, kiddo," the farmer says. And soon, it's wrapped and resting in the back of my pickup truck.

"I've had good behavior, and so has Miss Margie!" Julia declares. "That means we get some hot chocolate," she sings and dances in a circle.

"I could never deny you that," I agree.

The three of us walk to the little hot chocolate stand. I start to order one for each of us, but Margie intervenes and tells the worker that she'd prefer an apple cider. We crowd around one of the small tables, sipping our hot beverages. The piney smell of the Christmas trees mix with the chocolate and cinnamon of the cider.

"What's your favorite Christmas song, Miss Margie?" Julia asks.

Margie hesitates, looks down, then back up again. "I don't know that I have one. Christmas songs always make me a bit sad, so I don't really listen to them."

"Why do they make you sad?" she asks in that unfiltered way that children have.

I start to intervene, but Margie answers her. "Because they remind me of a time in my life that wasn't very happy. So I guess it's not the songs themselves, but what they remind me of."

"Oh, that makes sense," Julia declares.

"Maybe we should figure out a way to make them happy for you again," I say before I can stop myself.

Margie glances at me, hints of emotion lining her features.

"Good idea, Papa!" Julia cheers. "Let's sing them on the way home, and then the three of us can decorate the Christmas tree!"

"Miss Margie is probably tired of hanging out with us," I say, trying to save her from having to say yes to all of Julia's demands, especially when I can tell she's hurting.

But when she glances at me, emotion still glittering in her eyes, I don't see gratitude. No, I see hurt. "I mean, uh, unless you want to?"

"No," she cuts me off. "I've invaded enough of your evening. I'll just go on home before all the traffic on our street blocks me out of my driveway again." She says it coldly, chopping me off at the knees with her words. "I'm going to find the restroom and then we can be on our way." She stands quickly, collects our now-empty cups, and strides away.

Chapter 18

MARGIE

DECEMBER 4, PRESENT DAY

I'm still not sure why I agreed to join Frank and Julia on this outing. No, that's not true. I know exactly why I did. When Julia showed up on my front doorstep, she reminded me so much of Amelia at that age that it made my heart ache. I wanted to pick her up, wrap her in my arms, and make her a mug of hot apple cider. Saying no to her was never an option.

And the Christmas tree she picked out? I'm not sure if fate is trying to take aim at my heart, but the fact that she picked out a small tree just like Amelia used to nearly unraveled me.

And then there was Frank. Lord help me. The way the man looks at his granddaughter like she hung the moon and all the stars in the sky did something to me. It woke up a part of my heart I thought long dead and buried inside a Christmas more than twenty years ago. Just thinking about the Christmas that changed everything was enough to unearth memories I've tried to bury deep, deep down. I loathe thinking about the year that changed my life. Yes, it was the year that Amelia became my all, but it was also the year I lost two slices of my heart and burned down the bridge to a hoped-for future.

Now here I am, thoughts of the past churning with strange and unexpected feelings of the present, and I don't know what to do with myself. I thought, for just a moment, that Frank felt it too. That heated look we exchanged, the way he almost reached out to hug me. And then he shut down completely. His handsome smile retreated and was replaced with a solemn glare. Like a switch, he just turned off.

As I finish up in the restroom, I give myself a pep talk, reassuring myself that I read into Frank's glance. That the sight of the man in a form-fitting Santa suit addled my brain. And by the time I walk back out to Frank and Julia, I've pulled myself together, and my dignity is back in place where it belongs.

EVEN THOUGH THE DRIVE BACK to our houses is short, Julia falls asleep in the back seat almost immediately. And as she dreams, she leaves behind an awkward silence between Frank and me.

"Margie, we still need to talk," Frank says.

Just like that, his words remind me that he offered and snatched away an olive branch just a few, short days ago. All the affection I built toward him over the course of this day crashes down around me like a matchstick house. The cold mask of anger descends over me.

"I thought we did already," I snap. "You showed up uninvited on my doorstep, started to say your peace, then bailed before I could get a word out. Sound familiar?" I watch as the words land like daggers into him.

"I'm sorry about that. I had a family emergency."

I don't miss the way he glances in his rearview mirror to look at the little girl sleeping there. Anger morphs into concern as I turn to look at where Julia rests, then back at Frank. "I should have come back over to your house once things settled, though. I'm sorry for that. I was distracted."

"But not too distracted to host a whole TV crew at your house a couple of days later," I insist. And, God, part of me knows I'm being a bitch, but I can't seem to stop myself. The man gets under my skin.

He winces. "Yeah, well. It's all kind of connected."

I raise an eyebrow. "Was the family emergency you having a meltdown because you needed more attention?"

He lets out a long, exasperated sigh. "If only," he pauses. "Look, I'm trying to apologize and make things okay between us. I'm not always the best with words, but we're neighbors, Margie. And, more than that, we're both going to be part of this Christmas Market. Can't we just call a truce?"

"And what about that nightmare of a yard you've got going on that keeps me awake at night? The same one that keeps me from getting in and out of my driveway? And let's not forget the Grinch stunt you pulled. That was low, even for you," I snipe.

"And Santa Balls and a Bama shirt were perfectly mature," he says dryly. I blush. Dammit. "And we haven't even mentioned the whole stealing the surge protector–"

"Okay, I think I've heard enough," I say, cutting him off, embarrassment fueling my rage and indignation. "You obviously don't want to actually talk. You just want to lay the blame for everything at my feet."

"Now that's not fair," he protests. "I apologized."

"You did not. You said you were trying to apologize and then laid all the blame on me. And then, to top it all off, you went on camera and made an unfair plug for the Christmas Market charity prize. Not only was that cheating, it was mean."

"I wasn't aware there were rules for this," Frank says dryly.

"The competition doesn't start until the Christmas Market starts."

"Says who?"

"Says anyone who has ever competed. There's always a clear

starting line and a clear finish line and you jumped the gun. You should be disqualified."

"There is no rule. You're just making this up because you're mad that I'm going to win."

"I have no doubt that I'm going to win. I'm just pointing out that you're cheating."

"Is everything okay, Papa?" Julia rasps from the back seat.

Guilt slams into me, and I answer her before Frank can. "Yes, your Papa and I are just having a little argument. But don't worry, Julia. We're at your Papa's house now. I'm going to go home. I hope you have a good evening." I reach back and give her arm a gentle squeeze as Frank parks his truck.

And then I turn and glare at Frank. Hurt clings to my final declaration as I try to squash the quaver in my voice. "And make sure your Papa doesn't get any more hot chocolate because he has had terrible behavior."

And with my final words thrown at him like a grenade, I climb out of his truck and march back to my house.

ONCE INSIDE MY HOUSE, I decide it's time to put the charity marketing plan I've been plotting into action. I grab my ring light and place it on my kitchen table. I work methodically, setting up the shot and trying to settle my mind.

As I work, a narrative spins out in my head. *Frank trying to soften me up by taking me with him and Julia to look at Christmas trees. Frank getting me locked into his truck and dumping blame on me. How could I have ever thought I felt attraction for that man? Yes, his granddaughter Julia is a doll, and she's clearly not faking anything, but what lengths is Frank willing to go to best me?*

I mount my phone to the tripod, sit down, and take a breath.

I hit record, then stare into the camera lens.

"Hi there, friends. Thanks for stopping by my channel. I've got some exciting news for you tonight. I'm going to be part of a Christmas Market coming up here in Ruston, and I need your help to make it a success. You have helped me build this channel, and now I need your help to support a cause near and dear to my heart."

DECEMBER 7, PRESENT DAY

Amelia studies the paperwork we completed for our charity competitions.

"So, to be clear," she says, eyeing me and looking back down at the papers. "Frank is raising money for Ronald McDonald House. And you are raising money for," Amelia pauses and raises an eyebrow. "Ruston's Yard Beautification Foundation?"

I nod proudly. "Yes, they are dedicated to helping clear out dilapidated properties and eliminate house and yard eyesores around the community. I thought raising money for a local cause would go over well."

I can feel Frank's gaze tunneling into the side of my head.

"Okay, well, the charity choice is up to you, of course. May the best seller win. Now, let's talk logistics. The Christmas Market is in ten days. We will have the venue open the day before so you can start setting up. Other vendors will be in and out that day, too. You two will have the largest tables near the stage. Behind you, we'll have visual guides for the amounts sold so people will know where you both stand in the charity race. To take things up a notch, we will have separate boxes for each of you where people can make donations. But there's a catch. Every time someone donates to Margie's fund, it will be deducted from Frank's total and vice versa. So if someone really wants you to win, they can love bomb you with donations."

Already, I'm calculating a list of locals and my YouTube followers who I can count on for those donations. I make a mental note of all who want to support local beautification projects. I'm going to get the whole Junior League on board and Frank is going to rue the day he entered into a competition with me.

"Regardless, everyone wins because the funds raised will be matched by our bank sponsor for your charity of choice. So this is all in good fun, you two," Amelia gently admonishes.

"Of course," Frank says dryly.

I can feel him staring at me again, willing me to meet his gaze. But I ignore him and continue to focus on my niece.

"I'd love for you both to begin promoting your charities as soon as possible. Frank, I loved what you did with the TV station. That was brilliant."

I stare daggers at my traitorous niece.

"I have a plan, too," I insist.

Amelia beams. "That's wonderful. Feel free to reach out to me with any questions."

Frank and I turn to leave at the same time and bump into each other. Heat singes my cheeks. I finally look at him, and his pale blue eyes find mine immediately. We freeze, a long conversation passing between us in a moment. There's mutual anger, shared irritation, and something hungry.

Frank breaks our stare and, without saying a word, marches out of the convention center.

I was ready for a fight, ready for us to hurl insults and blame at one another. I was not prepared for him to give me the cold shoulder and walk away. That somehow hurts far worse than angry words and yard pranks. At least those things were communication, a commitment to dig down and stay right where we are. *But this?* This feels like giving up, like walking away from trying to fix things.

Like all the men in my past.

Hurt creeps up and around my heart, burrowing in deeply. I know I'm not blameless in this mutual hatred that has festered between us, but I don't know if I can trust Frank enough to make an effort to hash it out.

I consider running after him. Consider pulling on my metaphorical boxing gloves and having it out with him in the parking lot. But right now, I think he would just turn the other cheek. With hurt in my heart and determination in my soul, I move forward with my single-minded plan to dominate this charity competition.

Chapter 19

FRANK

DECEMBER 8, PRESENT DAY,

Over the next few days, I throw myself into woodworking, channeling all my anger and irritation with the infuriating woman next door into crafting beautiful pieces for the Christmas Market. Julia hovers around my house, darting in periodically with her safety glasses on to ask what I'm making, giving me a thumbs up or thumbs down for every sign, cutting board, and small bench I make. She's taken a particular shine to the tall, carved black bear holding a welcome sign and has named him Todd. I don't think I'll be able to sell him after this, which means I need to make a Todd Junior.

Cars continue to line up in front of my house every night. To Julia's delight, I put on my Santa costume and make an appearance outside a few evenings. She insists on being my elf, so we go to Walmart to get supplies and assemble a costume for her that consists of green leggings and a t-shirt, along with a green Santa hat. Together, we meet and greet the people of Ruston. And through it all, I leave Santa perched on his ornamental balls because I relish the fact that

Margie's failed attempt to sabotage me turned my yard into an even more popular Christmas attraction.

Despite the ever-increasing traffic, Margie has gone ominously silent. I've seen her walk to and from her shed from time to time, but she never bothers to look up. And as irritated as I am with her about refusing to have a conversation with me in my truck the other night, I also miss our banter. The back and forth has given me something to look forward to. I'd be lying if I said I didn't glance over at her house every time I add one more small decoration to my yard to see if it will be the thing that has her stomping back over over, ready to go toe to toe with me again.

"Papa, where's Biscuit?" Julia asks.

At her words, I realize I haven't seen my canine companion, who is usually always underfoot, since I first got up this morning. I turn my table saw off and remove my safety glasses. The clean smell of lumber fills my lungs as I brush sawdust off my jeans and take my granddaughter's hand.

"He's probably just hiding under my bed," I reassure her. "Let's go find him."

"I already looked there," she insists.

And sure enough, Biscuit is not only not under my bed, he doesn't appear to be anywhere inside the house. Together, we call for him, and I strain my ears to hear the shuffle of stubbly legs and ground-dragging ears. But there's nothing. Panic flares to life in my chest. Biscuit is nine, not exactly a young pup. It should be too cold for snakes, but my thoughts wander to wild coyotes, and I begin to secretly fear that I'm going to discover that my old friend has crossed the rainbow bridge.

Julia and I search outside for him, calling his name and promising him treats.

"We should go ask Miss Margie if she's seen him," Julia insists.

A protest rises to my lips. Our quiet standoff has both granted me peace and eaten me alive. But I can't not ask her. What if Biscuit wandered into her enclosed patio or crawled under her car? Plus, I have Julia as a buffer, so the conversation won't get too hostile.

We go to Margie's front door and knock. We wait a couple of beats and no one comes to the door. *Is she ignoring me on purpose?* I hate the feeling of rejection that stirs inside my heart. Her truck is in the driveway. I knock again, harder this time, but there is still no answer.

"What about there?" Julia asks, pointing to the large shed I've seen Margie disappearing into over the past several days. The door is cracked, and lights are on inside.

We walk over to it and peek inside. At first I'm overwhelmed by the sheer aesthetic of this thing. Margie has made this oversized shed into a bonafide bar. There are couches, a large TV, and even a full offering of various bourbons, whiskeys, and beers next to a sink. There are mason jars on every counter and surface. Some are filled with jams and jellies, topped with bows, twine, and labels. Others sit empty, awaiting their contents.

"Papa, look," Julia whispers and points to one of the couches.

I missed it at first glance, too distracted by the sheer volume of mason jars everywhere. But when I look more closely, I see that Margie is asleep on the oversized couch—and Biscuit is curled up on her legs. He must have used the cardboard box of mason jars next to the couch as a step-up. As if sensing our attention, my dog blinks awake and raises his head. He doesn't look the least bit ashamed of scaring me half to death. And why here, of all places? Margie doesn't even seem to like him very much.

Julia trots over to where Biscuit lays across Margie's legs and pats his head. "Come on, boy. You need to come home and let Miss Margie get some sleep. She's pretty strong. I don't think she needs you to protect her."

My chest flutters at the sight and Julia's words. *Does Margie need someone to protect her?* Ruston is a pretty safe place, and nothing much happens around here. But she lives alone and is always pushing people away. I wonder, for the first time, why Margie seems to keep everyone but her niece, and possibly Julia, at arm's length.

With a groan, Biscuit rises from his impromptu nest and flops off the couch. He follows Julia to the door. I consider turning off the overhead lights so Margie can get some sleep, but I don't want her to wake up and fear that someone invaded her bourbon-lined sanctuary. So I leave them on. Biscuit, Julia, and I head back to my house.

I try to shift my focus back to the work at hand. I outline, saw, and carve, but my mind keeps drifting back to Margie. In sleep, all the anger that sneaks into the time-worn lines of her face is smoothed out. She looked, well, *beautiful*. Content. My mind drifts to how she treats her niece, the fierceness with which she talks to and loves her. And even with Julia the other day, I know I saw a tear slip down her cheek at the Christmas tree farm. My guess is that it is exceptionally difficult to get through Margie's case-hardened exterior, but once you do, she will fight for you with her last dying breath. Even now, I notice how she takes care of Amelia and even feeds her whole extended family on holidays.

I have to wonder: *who takes care of Margie?*

I shake my head, irritated with myself for fixating on my competition in such a compassionate manner. Because that is all Margie is to me, all she wants to be. I stand and go to the radio I keep in my workshop. I flip it on and tune it to the Christmas station. I move back to my workspace, singing along to "Hark! The Herald Angels Sing." The radio station pauses its music marathon with the "News on the Hour."

I listen to updates about road work and construction, the buying and selling of local businesses, and the announcement of a New Year's race that will take place locally this year.

"And finally," the DJ says, "Now is the time to get your generators ready and firewood stocked. Meteorologist Jeff Stevens is here with your weather report. Jeff?"

"Thank you, Brett. This week is shaping up for a major weather shift as a cold front begins to make its way across Northern Louisiana." I stop my saw so I can listen more closely.

"The front promises to knock out our usual temperatures in the upper-fifties with an arctic blast. Although rare for this area, this storm system is expected to bring rain that will likely turn into sleet and ice overnight, with some accumulation as the temperatures drop quickly into the upper twenties. This system is expected to hit the Ruston area in four days. Now's the time to stock up on flashlights, extra batteries, firewood, and gasoline. The Louisiana governor has issued a state of emergency, allowing him to call in backup electricity personnel in case of power outages."

I roll my eyes. This type of dire warning seems to happen at least three times a year. Schools shut down, businesses close, and we get nothing but a cold, rainy mist. I think our meteorologists just get tired of saying "sunny and fifty-five" every day in December and look for a reason to spice things up.

I return to my table saw and get back to work. But I can't shake the ominous feeling that climbs up my spine and taps on my shoulder. I think of Julia. She's my responsibility while her parents are out of town, and I'd never forgive myself if the electricity went out, especially with freezing temperatures and no firewood.

Grumbling, I turn off my table saw and scan the garage. When I spot my chainsaw, I pick it up and head to the woods behind my house. Julia is outside playing with Biscuit, trying in vain to get him to fetch a ball. But my derpy dog is utterly uninterested. His nose is to the ground, sniffing out holes and burrows.

"Whatcha doing, Papa?" she asks, noticing me.

"What do you think about having a fire in the fireplace?"

"Can we roast marshmallows and make s'mores?" she squeaks.

"I suppose we could do that. I'm going to chop some wood for us. Want to help me carry it into the garage so it will stay dry? And then we can go to the store to get s'mores supplies before all the people come to look at my house lights and we have to change into our Santa and elf outfits."

With an enthusiastic "hooray," Julia trots along behind me. She points out trees that look old and dry. I don't have all the equipment to take down large trees, so I pick out branches and trunks that have already fallen. Julia delights in the game, collecting her own small stack of branches to help start a fire.

I lost a lot of woodworking time to this firewood collecting endeavor today, but it was worth it for peace of mind and to see Julia's sense of accomplishment as she carries twigs to my shop, Biscuit trailing behind her. Soon, we have a small stack of wood and a large pile of branches ready for our fire.

THAT EVENING, JASON AND EMMA FACETIME to check on us. Julia tells them all about our wood-gathering expedition and Biscuit's great escape to Margie's bar shed. When Julia darts off to go to the restroom, Jason and Emma turn serious.

"We are still in the process of securing a place for Emma and Julia to stay," Jason says earnestly. "But we are worried about the bad weather they are predicting for Ruston. We are considering coming back early just in case."

I can tell he's troubled by the idea. He wants to stay and use his time off to get everything they need set up.

"There's no need for that," I reassure. "Julia and I are just fine. You know they predict bad weather for us all the time. And how often does it actually come true? Maybe once every fifty times?"

Jason and Emma chuckle knowingly. "Those meteorologists do get a bit overexcited," Emma admits.

"Julia and I are fine. And if you come get her early, she's going to be furious that she didn't get to make s'mores in the fireplace with me."

"Well, we wouldn't want that," Jason says with a laugh.

"No, we certainly wouldn't," I agree.

"Mama, Daddy, look!" Julia says, bounding back into the room. She runs up to the phone camera with a turtle shell. "I found this in the woods today while we were gathering branches. Isn't it pretty?"

"Julia, make sure you wash your hands," Emma frets. "You know your immune system isn't great. We don't need you to get sick right now."

I feel guilt wash over me at her words. I should have thought about that. Sometimes, I forget, with all her immune-suppressing medications, Julia gets sick far more easily, more often, and for longer than other children.

"Sorry about that," I mumble. "We will get it cleaned up and sterilized for you, Juju Bug. Now give that shell to Papa and go scrub your hands. Nice and thorough. Sing the Happy Birthday song while you do it."

She pouts but hands the shell over and does as I ask. I turn back to my phone screen.

"Seriously, don't worry. We will be fine. She has been helping me decide which pieces to sell at the Christmas Market and entertaining Biscuit. And, God forbid something actually does happen with the weather, we now have plenty of dry firewood, lighters, and a full pantry. You two should make sure you have enough as well."

Jason rolls his eyes, echoing the teenage version of himself. Julia darts back in to tell them both goodnight, and we end the call.

"Papa, can we decorate our Christmas tree now?"

"Of course, Juju Bug. I have your grandma's ornaments from when she was a little girl out in the shed. Let's go get them."

She stares at me, starry-eyed and joyful.

"What is it?" I ask.

"I just love you so much," she whispers, then reaches for my hand.

Chapter 20

MARGIE

DECEMBER 15, 1998

Over the next few days, we fall into a rhythm. I get up to check my garden beds while Amelia follows along behind me, stopping to chase the occasional lizard. During the week, I take my niece to school and pick her up at the end of the day. I have to go to work but I don't feel comfortable leaving Amelia at my house, even if her mother is there. Fortunately, my boss at the hardware store is understanding and allows me to bring her along as long as she doesn't mess up displays or merchandise. But there's never a worry about that with Amelia. No, my little niece either sits quietly with a book or explores the shelves looking for wayward bugs that scuttled into the store.

While we're away, Jo stays in bed. She's always in bed. I coax her out for dinner, and Amelia begs her to come outside, but she rarely spends more than twenty minutes with us before retreating into her dark room. David joins us for dinner, and we play card games or watch a movie. I do my best to keep things upbeat for Amelia—and myself, if we're being honest.

Christmas is just over a week away when I realize that Jo likely hasn't gotten Amelia a single gift. I don't make much money at my job–enough to keep the lights on and take care of my basic needs without much left over. But there is no way I'm going to let Christmas pass without doing something to make it special for my niece.

"Can you watch her at my house for a couple of hours this weekend?" I ask David before he leaves for the evening. He hasn't brought up moving again, and I'm too scared to say anything. "I need to get Amelia some Christmas presents, so I have to go alone."

"Yeah, okay. No problem," he agrees, but I can see concern deepen in the lines around his eyes and mouth.

AS I BROWSE THE TOY SECTION at JCPenney, I realize that I have no idea what a five-year-old girl would want for Christmas.

"If you're trying to find a Furby, you're out of luck," the person shopping next to me says.

I turn to see a young woman with long, wavy, reddish hair. She's about my age and staring straight ahead of us at an empty shelf space.

"What is a Furby, exactly?" I ask.

She looks at me like I'm the one who has lost my mind.

"You know, that little gremlin-looking toy that talks? The one no one seems to be able to find for Christmas, but every kid in the world, including my son, Rhett, wants even though it's terrifying and talks when you've hidden it away in a dark closet?"

"I am kind of glad I don't know what that is. Sounds like the stuff of nightmares." She nods in solemn agreement. "I'm shopping for my five-year-old niece," I tell her. "I have no idea what to get her. How old is your son? Do boys and girls like the same things?" I hate how uncertain I sound.

The woman's face softens. "Does your niece like princesses? Disney movies?"

"She likes anything with animals. Not so sure about princesses." I realize I am in way over my head here.

The woman smiles knowingly, then browses the shelf for a moment and returns holding a plush, rust-colored fox cub.

"Then I bet she'll love this," she offers. "Do you need other things?"

I nod, grateful that fate has sent me this kind soul to help me figure out how to give my niece a good Christmas. "She likes anything outside," I say.

Together, we wander through the shelves and pick out an ant farm, and the board game "Guess Who."

"Thank you for your help," I say as we part ways.

"Sure. I'm Kathy Hebert, by the way. You work at the hardware store, right? I've seen you in there a few times."

"Yes, Margie Murphy," I acknowledge and shake her hand.

With promises to say hello the next time she's in the hardware store, Kathy walks through the door with her own purchases. I'm about to check out when I look up and see stockings on sale. This close to Christmas, they are trying to get rid of them. I hesitate for only a moment before picking up three. I'll need them this year, I think. And next year? Well, who knows how my family will change and grow? Never hurts to have an extra one or two.

WHEN I ARRIVE HOME, I spy David and Amelia huddling over something in the yard. The sight tugs at something deep in my soul, a yearning for a future life. I leave my purchases in the car, making a mental note to wrap them after Amelia goes to sleep tonight. I crunch through the pine straw, their scent kicking up around me and making everything smell like Christmas. They turn to look at me, knowing smiles on their faces as I approach.

"Aunt Margie!" Amelia exclaims, jumping up to wrap her thin arms around me. "Mr. David and I have been getting ready for Santa to come. We've been putting out reindeer food and clearing the yard so I can find their hoof prints."

I glance up at David and he has a sheepish grin on his face. He's enjoying this. And I can see the dad he might be one day. My chest warms and then cools.

Charleston. Right.

I walk to him and give him a lingering hug. He presses a kiss to my temple as I murmur words of thanks into his chest. Amelia's little body slams into our legs. Instinctively, I reach down and pull her into our hug. I love my niece so much, and more than anything, I wish she could have stable, nurturing parental love in her life.

"How about some apple cider, kiddo?" I ask.

"Yay! Yay! Yay!" she cheers, skipping and dancing her way into the house.

David reaches for my hand and squeezes. Together, we walk inside and watch as Amelia walks directly to the clock radio and tunes it to the Christmas station. I've never been into Christmas traditions, but as Bing Crosby croons "I'll Be Home for Christmas," while David pulls out mugs and apple cider packets and the lights twinkle on our tiny tree, I can see the appeal. It's more than just buying things and hanging up decorations. It's a feeling, a sense of belonging and coziness that wraps us up in its embrace and roots us in this time and place.

My gaze drifts down the hallway where my haunted sister is likely staring into the dark, and the warm feelings ebb. She's become a ghost, a shell of herself looming and casting a cold web around us. Amelia tries to engage with her, but my niece still sleeps in my room every night. We will have to do something about this situation soon, and I have yet to think of any option where this works out well for any of us.

Chapter 21

MARGIE

PRESENT DAY , DECEMBER 8

I knock on the door of my former archnemesis' house. And no, I'm not talking about Frank. As I wait for Greta to answer, I think about the time more than two years ago when Greta Clark threatened to have Amelia's Fall Festival shut down and was positively wretched to her. I chuckle, remembering the way this bold woman had the audacity to throw a damn chicken at me.

"Margie, haven't seen your face in a month. Finally decided to visit your old friend?" Greta says, swinging the door of her old farmhouse open with a strength that belies her small frame. With the help of her daughter, Greta has been working on fixing the once-crumbling front porch. And where a rusted, broken swing sat, there are now freshly tended flower pots, though nothing is blooming in December.

"Brought you something to make up for it," I say, offering up a jar of my apple cider jam.

"Apology accepted," she says, snatching it out of my hand.

I follow her inside, glad to see her vintage furniture hasn't changed, though the faded carpets have been replaced with vinyl wood planks.

"What brings you knocking on my door?" she asks, pouring us each a cup of coffee. She adds cream and cinnamon to mine without having to ask, knowing my coffee preferences.

I sigh, pulling out a kitchen chair and settling in. "I have a new neighbor, and I'm having some trouble with him. Since you are the expert on the topic of being a terrible neighbor, I wanted to get your thoughts," I say, sipping up the cinnamon goodness.

"Is that right?" Greta asks. She looks and sounds so much like Dorothy from The Golden Girls that I chuckle inwardly. This is what I needed. I'd talk to Amelia, but she has too much of a vested interest in the Christmas Market's success, and my girl has always been tenderhearted to others. I need to talk to someone who can shoot it to me straight.

Greta joins me at the kitchen table, ochre coffee mugs stretched out before us.

"What's she like, this new neighbor?" Greta asks.

"Not a she. He. Frank Campbell. And he is a menace," I say, irritation scratching at my words.

"Well, hell, what did you do to the poor man?" Greta asks.

I raise an eyebrow. "What did I do to *him*? Why am *I* the presumed villain in this situation?"

"Well, isn't that obvious, Margie? Don't you remember pounding your fist on my front door and demanding I get my shit together about that Fall Festival Lia was in charge of?"

"If I remember correctly, you threw a gumbo pot at my head!"

"I have the right to defend my property, and you were trespassing," Greta insists. "Did you waltz onto your neighbor's property and read him the riot act, too?"

"I–" I start to tell her no, that he started all of this mess. And then

I remember the morning I threw myself, bra free, boobs flapping in the wind, in front of Frank while he was on his riding lawn mower.

"That's what I thought," she says, looking smug. "Alright, start from the beginning." She sips her coffee and leans back into her chair, looking like she's ready for a fireside tale of adventure and violence.

And so, I tell her everything. From the mower to the front yard Christmas extravaganza and the missteps in between. And when I mention Santa Balls, Greta snorts, shooting coffee out of her nose.

"I can't breathe," she gasps through tears of laughter.

"I don't think it's *that* funny," I insist.

"Oh God, woman. Lighten up. That shit is hilarious," she says, still cackling. She stands and grabs a box of tissues, wiping her nose and patting the tears of laughter from her eyes.

I frown. "I don't think you'd be laughing if that atrocity was going up next door to your house," I insist.

"Margie. Be serious. This same thing happened to me two years ago when your spunky little niece reignited the Fall Fest on the property right next to mine. And you were so angry I wouldn't just roll over and accept it that we nearly got into a Jerry Springer-level tussle on my front lawn."

"Well, shit. I didn't think about that," I mumble.

"And I'm not saying I love that festival with all the people practically in my yard, but you helped show me that it's only once a year, and it makes a lot of people happy. Maybe it's time to take your own advice and just deal with it until Christmas is over. Yes, it's annoying as hell, but the man isn't hurting anyone. And you have to live next to him for God knows how long. Do it for yourself, not for him."

"You should not be making this much sense," I say, resigned.

"Lord, I know that's the truth," she admits.

"And what about this charity competition between us? Should I just shut my mouth and let Frank win?"

"Well, I never said that. Come now, Margie. You can let the man turn his own yard into a dumpster fire, but you don't have to lower yourself and let him *win* a real competition between the two of you. Now tell me what you're going to do to win that prize."

Finally, something Greta and I can both agree on. I pull up my YouTube channel and show her the video I made. After it stops, she turns and looks at me, eyes wide.

"You are an evil genius," she finally says and bursts into a delighted cackle.

THAT NIGHT, I BATTEN DOWN THE HATCHES. I go out to my she-shed and prepare to label the fifty new jelly and jam jars I've made for the Christmas Market. I close the door, pull down the blinds, and do my best to ignore the chaos happening at my neighbor's house. I can still hear the muffled notes of "Up on the Housetop" blasting from Frank's yard, and I decide to turn on the TV to drown it out. I flip through the channels, landing on the local news. Content to listen to the latest details on Christmas goodwill happening around the city, I start labeling my jars.

"And, after the break, join us live as we interview this year's Yard of the Year winner, Frank Campbell," the news anchor proclaims.

I pause, head slowly lifting to stare at the livestream teaser of Santa Frank waving to the camera in his front yard. I fight the impulse to sabotage him, trying to remember Greta's words of wisdom earlier today. I attempt calming breaths.

Just as I'm making headway in lowering my blood pressure, a small knock sounds at my shed door. I pause, thinking I must have imagined it, then keep labeling. Tap, tap, tap. There it is again. I stand, hesitating. Has Frank come to gloat? If I open that door, will there be a whole camera crew waiting for me to tell them, live on camera, how proud I am of my beloved neighbor? Will Frank be wearing that ass-clinging Santa suit with a smoldering twinkle in his eye?

I fling those thoughts away as I reach for the doorknob. But when I open the door, there are no camera crews, no boom mics, nor smoldering Santa looks. I don't see anyone.

Until I look down.

There I spy wide brown eyes peeking up at me from beneath a hot pink beanie cap with a pom on top.

"Julia? Everything okay?" I ask.

"I made you something," she says, offering up two mugs of what appears to be hot apple cider.

"For me?"

She nods, a grin sliding into place. And that look, right there, is so much like Amelia at her age that it nearly knocks me to the ground.

"Well, thank you so much, sweetheart. Would you like to come inside?"

She nods and turns to look behind her. "Come on, boy," she calls. Frank's basset hound emerges from behind a bush, tail wagging lazily behind him.

"Does your friend need something to drink too?" I ask Julia, nodding at the dog.

"Are you thirsty, Biscuit?" she asks him seriously. Flashbacks of the past roll over the present, and I have to swallow down the emotion that threatens to clog my throat. "Yes, I do believe he is," she says, sounding all the world like someone in her sixties.

I walk to my bar sink, fill up a coffee mug with water, and bring it back to the dog. While he laps at it, Julia sits our apple ciders down long enough to remove her sparkly, rainbow rain boots and leave them by the door. Then she scoops the cups up again and sits them down on my coffee table before settling herself on my couch.

"Thanks for letting me in. It is too loud at Papa's house tonight," she says.

"It's loud there every night," I mumble.

"I know," she says. "But it's worse tonight because there are camera people over there. It's hurting my eyes and ears. And Mama always says when I don't feel good I need to find a quiet place to lay down for a while. I don't think Papa knows that, though."

"Are you feeling sick, Julia? Should I check your temperature?" I slide easily into maternal mode. It's muscle memory, like fingers finding the keys on a piano after years of practice.

"Oh, it's not the flu or anything," she says with confidence. "I get sick all the time. I have an auto-mune disease and have to take medicine that sometimes makes me more sick. Mama and Daddy are in Dallas looking for a place for us to live so I can go to a hospital there."

At first, I'm not sure if this is a game she's playing or if she's being serious. But intuition creeps along my shoulders, rolling down my arms into the tips of my fingers. And everything points to honesty. "Do you mean an auto-immune disease?" I ask, testing the waters.

"Yes, that's what I said, auto-mune."

"Have you been sick for a long time?" I ask cautiously.

"Yes, since I was just a little baby. I got fevers all the time, and my knees and elbows would puff up like apples. Mama says that when I wouldn't walk, they got scared. We had to go to a bunch of hospitals. They still don't know what's making me sick. That's why we have to go live in Dallas for a little while."

That's when it hits me like a bolt of lightning. *Frank's charity choice.* Ronald McDonald House for sick children and their families to stay at while they get treatment. Color begins to drain from my face, and a cold sliminess sinks into my stomach. God, I am the villain.

Julia continues on without embarrassment, her childlike innocence allowing her to share her story in a way that suggests she's told it a million times. "And now Mama and I have to go live alone in Dallas while Daddy stays here and works. So they are trying to find a place for Mama and me to live for a little while. That's why I'm staying with Papa this week."

I hesitate. Do I tell this child that I'm sorry she's sick? Would she even care or just shrug her shoulders, accepting the hand life has dealt her? I consider her as she sips her apple cider and swings her legs.

"And how do you feel about all of this?" I finally ask.

She wilts. "I don't like that I have to live away from Daddy and Papa. I don't want to leave my room or my house. I want to play with Biscuit and run in Papa's yard."

"Well, that makes a lot of sense," I agree.

She looks at me in surprise. "Usually, grown-ups tell me I need to be brave so I can get healthy." Julia sounds so small that I want to pull her into my lap and hold her close to my chest. But I'm leery about touching anyone, even this small child, without her consent.

"Julia, do you want a hug?"

She nods ferociously, puts her apple cider down, and scrambles into my lap. She slides her jacketed arms around my neck and squeezes me with all the strength a kindergartner can muster. I inhale, smelling her bubble gum-scented shampoo and the remnants of apples and cinnamon.

"That really sucks," I tell her.

"Mama says sucks is a bad word," she murmurs into my shoulder.

"It is, but sometimes we need bad words to express bad feelings," I say.

I feel a cold, wet sensation bump my knee and look down to see saggy basset hound eyes staring at me in consolation. I reach out and pat the top of Biscuit's head.

"I don't want to go to Dallas. It sucks," she whispers. And, I can't help it; the little devil who lives in my conscience preens at her expressing herself with a "bad word."

"Here's the thing, Julia. It's going to suck a lot. And there will be a lot of days when you will get really angry or really sad. And it's okay to feel those things. Don't let anyone tell you that you can't. But you will have some good moments too. You will get to meet new nurses and doctors. And at children's hospitals, they have all kinds of fun things for kids. Plus, it sounds like you're a total professional at this hospital thing now. I bet you can teach the doctors and nurses some things."

She pulls back and looks at me, considering. "What can I teach them?"

"Well, I bet they don't know how to make a good cup of hot apple cider, for one," I say solemnly.

She smirks just a little. "And I bet they don't know the best branches for firewood."

"Certainly not," I agree.

"Miss Margie, I'm tired. Can we watch a Christmas movie?" Julia changes the subject effortlessly.

I break out in a light sweat, the question reminding me of Amelia's favorite comfort as a child: how we would crawl into bed together and watch hours of *Rudolph the Red-Nosed Reindeer*. I breathe in deeply. If Julia can face a hospital in a new city, then I can certainly power through my past trauma long enough to watch a Christmas movie with her.

"Sure, Jules, let's see what's on TV."

Soon, I've navigated to *Home Alone*, which has the benefit of being mostly funny, which I think we both need right now. I sip the now-cold drink while Julia lays her head in my lap and stares transfixed at the TV screen. I feel weighted warmth seep into my feet as Biscuit makes himself at home on top of them. I'm so caught up in Kevin's plight in the movie that when I finally look down again, I realize that Julia is asleep. Cautiously, I reach out and brush her hair off of her forehead, whispering prayers to whoever is listening that Julia finds her miracle cure.

A knock sounds at my shed door, but this one is much heavier and insistent. "Margie!" Frank calls through the closed door. "Margie, are you in there?"

"Come in," I call, trying not to wake Julia.

He swings the door open, half out of breath. "Margie, have you seen Julia? I can't find… oh! Thank God." He rushes to where his granddaughter sleeps in my lap and kneels down to her. He brushes her hair back from her forehead and studies the gentle ebb and flow of her chest and the REM movements of her eyes beneath her closed lids. Then he bows his head, rests it gently on her stomach, and exhales.

"I was terrified," he whispers so quietly I almost don't hear him.

"I'm sorry. I thought you knew she was here. I should have called. I didn't think–"

"No, it's not your fault," he says, still staring at his granddaughter.

Frank kneels on the concrete floor, his worn jeans the only barrier from its cold, unforgiving surface, and it's like he doesn't even feel it. His pale eyes are glassy with tears, and his piney, sawdust scent envelops us both. Despite the openness of the large shed, the way he kneels here, with Julia between us, has made the space feel small, intimate. I study the way Frank's gray and brown stubbled jaw clenches as he steadies himself.

I try to breathe slowly for the both of us, willing it to filter into this man who is bowed down before us like he'd sacrifice his own life for the sake of this small, fragile girl. All the anger and frustration I've been struggling with over the past month shatter like glass and fall like shards around us. Like defogging a windshield, I feel like I can see Frank clearly for the first time. And when he finally lifts his head, his tear-clouded eyes lock with mine like magnets. All his bravado and silliness are gone, replaced with raw vulnerability. Warmth creeps up my neck and heats my ears. Suddenly, Julia's tiny body on mine feels a little too warm.

Frank's hand slides from where it rests on his granddaughter and finds my knee beside her. It rests there gently, like a question, igniting an unsettling tingling through my body. It awakens something inside me I thought long dead and buried, never again to be resurrected. I hate it. I love it. I want to douse it with ash and flame it to life at the same time. He doesn't move his hand, and I don't push him away. We are locked in a strange standoff. My hand inches forward and finds his. I'm not sure if I'm trying to comfort Frank or keep him from leaving. His pale eyes dart around my face, taking in my nose, my eyes, my laugh lines, my frizzy hair.

"Papa?" Julia's small, raspy voice asks.

The moment between us crumbles to dust. We both look down at the sleep-mussed child between us, and I quickly pull my hand away.

"Hey, Juju Bug," Frank says. "You gave your Papa quite a scare disappearing on me like that. I didn't know what happened to you."

"I'm sorry, Papa. I was tired and needed to find a quiet place to lie down. Your house was too loud."

I watch guilt ripple across his features. "I'm sorry, Julia. You should have told me. I would have turned it all off so you could rest."

"No, Papa. The TV people were there. You couldn't do that. You won the prize. But it's quiet here and Margie let me watch a movie. Is it okay if I come over here again?"

I jump in to answer before Frank can tell her no. "Yes, as long as you ask your Papa first," I say.

Biscuit woofs, startling all three of us. "I guess he agrees," Frank says. He smiles, and it's not fake, or condescending, not challenging or flippant. It's soft, dappled with lines that show how often he has made the expression over the years.

"Come on, Juju Bug. It's past your bedtime, and I know Miss Margie is probably ready to go to bed, too."

Frank stands, lifting Julia in his arms as he does so. His biceps flex with the motion, pulling his flannel shirt tight around his arms and back. I swallow and look away. He walks to the door, calling Biscuit to follow along behind him. And just as he exits the shed, Frank glances over his shoulder.

"Thank you, Margie," he says in a way that makes me wish that I could snuggle into his chest, too.

Then he walks out the door and back to his house. I continue to stare at his retreating form, his dog meandering behind him. I allow myself to watch as he opens his front door and steps inside, and then all his Christmas lights go dark. I blink, surprised. Usually, they blaze the whole night through. And then I remember Julia's complaint about the noise and lights and an ache forms beneath my ribs.

Chapter 22

FRANK

DECEMBER 9, PRESENT DAY

I can't stop staring at Julia sleeping in her bed with Biscuit curled up next to her. I lost her because I was so consumed with celebrating my Christmas decorations, convinced that winning that ridiculous Yard of the Year prize was more important than making sure my granddaughter was comfortable and well.

I've spent the past month thinking Margie is unreasonable, determined to show her that she just needs to relax, have fun, and enjoy the Christmas season. And I got so caught up in my own need to win everything–the yard, the Christmas Market competition–that I forgot to take care of what's most important: my family.

Guilt is eating me alive. I storm outside to the pile of large branches I have been gathering. I grab my ax and begin chopping it into fireplace-sized pieces. As the wood chips fly around me, I lose myself in the movements: grabbing, chopping, tossing. When my shoulders begin to ache, and my hands start to scream, I lean into the pain, knowing I deserve it, wanting more of it.

Minutes might have passed, or maybe hours. I don't know. But when I hear my dog's familiar "woof," I turn and see Julia and Biscuit watching me.

"Hey, Juju Bug. You hungry?" my voice comes out gruff.

She nods. I walk to my garage and leave the ax there, then trail behind her inside. I go to the sink and wash my hands, shocked when I find they are bleeding and threaded with splinters. I wince as the antiseptic soap seeps into my wounds, setting my hands on fire.

A knock sounds at the front door. Julia runs to the window. "Papa, Miss Margie is here."

My heart flutters, letting me know I'm still alive beneath the self-loathing and grief I've heaped onto my soul over the past three years. It's an odd sensation, and I'm not sure if I want it there or not.

"Go ahead and open it," I tell her.

"Come in, Miss Margie. Papa hurt his hands, and he's cleaning them up in the kitchen."

Margie steps in, holding a basket. "Um, hi. Are you okay, Frank?" She looks at me skeptically. Or maybe it's concern.

"I'm fine. Just got carried away chopping wood."

Her face pales. "Oh my gosh, do you need me to call 911?" she asks, fear lighting her eyes.

"No, no. Not that kind of chopping accident. All fingers are still intact," I say, holding my hands up and wiggling my fingers to show her. "Just blisters and splinters."

She sets the basket that smells like fresh chocolate chip cookies down on my kitchen table and walks over to me. "Here, let me see," she demands, holding her hands out for mine.

"I'm fine," I insist.

"Quit trying to be brave, and just let me see them."

Julia giggles. "Yeah, Papa. Be brave like me."

Well, shit. Not like I can deny her that. With a sigh, I lay my hands in Margie's palms and wince when she scolds.

"Good Lord, Frank. Why didn't you stop chopping? This looks painful."

I just shrug.

"Do you have hydrogen peroxide?"

"There's some rubbing alcohol beneath the sink," I nod in that direction.

"Well, that will hurt like a bitch, but it will get the job done," she sighs.

"Miss Margie, you said a bad word!" Julia cries.

"Remember what I told you about using bad words?" she asks Julia.

A look passes between them, and when Julia smiles, I begin to wonder if letting these two spend time together is a good idea.

"What about tweezers?" Margie asks.

"Oh, I'll go get them," Julia says and hustles out of the room, reappearing a moment later.

We move to the kitchen table. Margie spreads out paper towels beneath my hands and gets to work. My guilt-driven adrenaline haze over the past hour has finally faded, and now I feel every splinter, every blister, as Margie pokes and prods at my damaged hands.

"Dammit, Margie. Be careful," I grouch out at her.

"Serves you right," she says and doesn't stop her single-minded pursuit.

I glance at Julia. "Sorry for the bad word, Juju Bug."

"Sometimes bad situations need bad words," she says proudly.

I glance at Margie, who is trying to stifle a laugh. She grips my right hand, steadying it so she can nab another splinter. Her focus allows me to study her up close. I notice the way her brows furrow in concentration, the way she bites the side of her full bottom lip. Her brown eyes seek the tiny pieces of wood lodged in my fingers.

Laugh lines frame the sides of her eyes. She smells of cooked jams and peaches, with a hint of chocolate chip cookies. She smells like cozy rooms and fireplaces. Like… *home*. I blink and look away.

But even as I study the floor instead of her rounded cheeks, I can still feel her warm, callused hands grasping my own. Every place we touch is an electric circuit coursing between our bodies. I try to shut those thoughts off, feeling like I'm betraying Cheryl. But when Margie's hand slides up to grip my wrist, her thumb rubbing over my pulse point, all my attempts at distraction fail. I'm fixated on that point of touch, and my sensitive skin lights up as her callused finger rolls against it.

And then she yanks out another splinter. *Fucking hell, woman.* I force myself just to think the words and not say them aloud. I already feel bad enough that Julia is going to return to her parents with a new, colorful vocabulary and stories of me losing her.

"Alright, all done," Margie declares. I sigh with relief and start to lean back in my chair.

"With that hand," she adds, then gestures with a "gimme" motion to my other hand. I grumble and reluctantly hand it over.

"Be brave, Papa!" Julia cheers.

And I settle into another round of painful splinter extraction. I hiss as Margie gets to work, but don't complain further. When she reaches for the rubbing alcohol, though, my whole body tenses, preparing for the onslaught of pain that's about to come my way. Margie looks me dead in the eyes and then, like a practiced villain, pours it over my blisters and cuts.

"Mother fucking shit!" I scream out, jumping back and flailing my hands, desperate to get the alcohol to dry and stop tunneling its way through my flesh like hydrochloric acid.

"Well, Julia is certainly getting a vocabulary lesson today," she says dryly. I don't even care. I hop and clench my jaw, desperate for the pain to stop. Biscuit seems to sense my distress because he starts howling with me, harmonizing my pain.

"Are you finished with all that yet? No? Okay, well Julia, come here, darlin', I made you something."

The smell of chocolate chip cookies fills the room as Margie unveils the contents of her basket. I walk over and look inside to see a container of cookies, multiple jars of jellies and jams, fresh bread, and even a couple of t-shirts.

"I figured my 'welcome to the neighborhood gift' was overdue," she says with mischief.

Julia reaches into the basket without hesitation, going straight for the cookies. She shoves one into her mouth, smearing chocolate over one cheek in the process. "These are yummy, Miss Margie!" She grabs another.

"What about breakfast?" I ask her.

"Oh, let the kiddo enjoy cookies for breakfast," Margie chides. "You're her grandfather, not her parent. You're supposed to spoil her."

I sigh in defeat. "Well, I guess it's too late anyway." I grab a cookie and take a bite. I groan.

"Good, right?" Margie asks. "I've been working on perfecting that recipe for years. There are some people in town who would rip the shirt right off your back to get one of them."

And I'm honestly not sure if she's joking or not.

"Anyway, I realize we have gotten off on the wrong foot with, well, just about everything," Margie says, running her hand through her hair. "And you and I are neighbors now. I thought it best to make a better effort to get along."

I stare at the way her hair sticks up where she's run her fingers through it, tracing the flowing coppery strands with hints of gray. I'm fixated on it.

"That is unless that's too much to ask," she quips dryly.

"I, uh, yeah, sorry. You just surprised me," I try to recover. "You're right, of course. I haven't been the most thoughtful, either."

"So a truce then?" she asks, sticking out her hand. I take it, and we shake.

"A truce," I agree. "I'll start by making sure I turn my Christmas lights off by eight o'clock every night." I glance at Julia when I say the words, feeling a little guilty that my concession is more for my granddaughter than for Margie. But I'll honor the truce even after Julia returns to her parents.

"Thank you for that. And I promise to stay away from your yard chaos," she says solemnly.

I chuckle, privately loving her brand of straightforwardness.

"But, I'm not going to just hand over the charity competition to you," she continues. "It's not in my nature to give up on something without seeing it to the end."

"That's fair," I allow. "And when I win, you can't come back over here and sabotage my yard."

She stares at me like I've struck her, and then a wide smile creeps up her face. The sight is so unexpected that I momentarily stop breathing. Margie is stunning.

"Want to place a little friendly wager on it?" she asks conspiratorially.

"What do you have in mind?"

"If I win, you have to mow my yard for a month," she declares.

"And if I win, you have to come over to my house for coffee every Saturday for six months," I say.

She blinks. "That sounds like a punishment for you, not a prize."

I laugh. I can't help it. "Or maybe a punishment for you. I'm a lonely old man in a quiet house. I usually just have my dog for company. You will have to sit and listen to me ramble about woodworking and horses for an hour."

"Alright then," she agrees. "It's a bet. Now, I need to go back home and get to work on my stock for the market. And you better make sure your lawn mower is working."

"By the way, since we're having a truce and all. Would you mind returning those Christmas decorations of mine you took? I realize that it's all in good fun, but they really do mean a lot to me."

Margie looks thoroughly confused. "Frank, I didn't take anything out of your yard, well besides that surge protector, but I returned it days ago." She pauses and considers. "But if some of those people taking pictures in your yard took something, I'll replace it." She looks guilty. "I didn't mean to create a viral sensation by moving things around, nor did I anticipate that it would draw even more people to our street."

She's embarrassed and telling the truth, I realize. Aw hell. I sigh and rub my temples.

"No, no, don't worry about it," I say. Though internally, I'm dying a little. I'm missing the vintage candle cutouts that belonged to my late wife, and a piece of my heart is missing with them.

"What are you missing?" Margie insists.

"No one would even notice but me. It's not your fault. Just part of the risk of putting things outside where anyone can see and take them. Though why someone would want to steal Christmas decorations is beyond me."

"Okay, well. I'll be off then. See you at the Christmas Market set up on Wednesday?"

I nod. But anxiety roils through my stomach as I think of all the projects waiting for me inside my workshop that need to be finished in time for next week. And then there's the little girl who is still in my care for two more days. And, of course, my regular job that I go back to Monday. I should have extended my vacation. Maybe Jason was right. Maybe I've taken on too much.

Margie studies me but doesn't say anything. She turns to leave, and Julia rushes at her, throwing her arms around Margie's legs. "Have a good day, Miss Margie," she whispers. Margie pats her shoulder affectionately, and a small piece of my heart emerges from its ashes.

Chapter 23

MARGIE

DECEMBER 10, PRESENT DAY

I've entered my Bat Cave Era. I have shut out all distractions, closed my blinds, and confined myself to my kitchen. I've spent hours hunched over my stovetop. My lower back aches from being on my feet nonstop bent at an angle, and my heavy breasts make the whole process all the more painful and difficult. But I've committed myself to this Christmas Market, and I don't want to disappoint Amelia, myself, or my fans.

Because my fans have risen to the occasion. When I realized that a lot of Frank's recent popularity was stemming from his yard's viral social media trend, I devised a way to hijack it. I asked my followers and their friends to take a photo of themselves with a sign that says "Margie's Machinations are better than Santa's Balls" and use the same hashtags people have used in their selfies with Frank's front yard Santa. Three winners will be chosen to win a gift basket from me that includes a sampling of my delicious treats and a gift card for more items from my store. It didn't take long for the photos to begin intermixing with those of people in Frank's yard. Additionally, for every photo posted with the sign, one dollar will be donated toward my charity fund.

I was a little worried the Junior League and Garden Club would look down on my marketing techniques as distasteful, but it turns out that when you are doing a fundraiser that will directly benefit them, they are more than up to the challenge. A quick glance at Instagram shows high society women holding jars of jams and ornaments, dressed in their country club finest, and signs that legitimately say "Santa's Balls" on them. I'm not sure whether to laugh, cheer, or both.

I do feel a little bad about this campaign tactic, but #SantaBalls took off for both of us before our mutual truce. As did my plan to rally the Junior League and every Garden Club member in a hundred-mile radius to my cause. Guilt tugs at me just a little when I think of Frank's charity choice. But I justify my push to win by reminding myself how much it will help the local community.

With my radio blasting classic rock and my window shades pulled down, I enter into the zone so completely that I lose track of time. When my stomach lets out a ferocious growl, and I begin to feel light-headed, I glance at the clock. 5 p.m. I worked straight through lunch. My back spasms in realization. Wincing, I walk to my fridge and pull out turkey, cheese, and mustard, then grab a loaf of bread. Turkey sandwich for dinner will have to do tonight.

"News on the hour, every hour," the radio DJ says in my quiet kitchen. "An ice storm system is sweeping through the Deep South and expected to move through North Louisiana beginning tonight and continuing into tomorrow." I roll my eyes. I'm sure the panic button has already detonated on more than half the community, and all the milk and bread are now gone from the grocery store. These dire warnings happen at least once a year, and nothing ever comes of them but disappointed children hoping for a snow day. The DJ encourages us to wrap our pipes and make sure we have flashlights while I munch on my sandwich and let my mind wander to everything I still have left to do for the Market. Setup begins Wednesday, and it's already Sunday.

I still need to pull my signage out of storage, and I probably need to buy some Christmas decorations to add to my booth. I've stocked up on my best-selling jam and jelly flavors already, but I'm making a new jelly flavor for Christmas this year—apple pie a la mode. I start to stand, and my hamstrings scream in protest. Enough standing and cooking for one day. Not wanting to waste time, I decide that I can at least pack up everything I've canned and labeled so far.

I limp out to my she-shed, ignoring the line of cars in front of my house that have, by this point, become part of the scenery. I've been a lot less stressed since I decided to ignore the traffic and focus on what I need to get done for the Christmas Market. I pull out the boxes with the cardboard dividers in them and start loading the filled and labeled jars into them. Amelia's husband, Rhett, is coming over Tuesday to help me carry them into the convention center.

I move steadily, repacking all fifty jars back into the original mason jar boxes, but when I get to the end, I come up two short. Huh. I walk around my shed, looking beneath the coffee table and behind couches. Nothing. How did two jars just disappear? I must have brought them into my house, I decide. Or maybe left them there when I brought the others out here for labeling. Resolved to look for the two missing jars tomorrow, I head back over to my house. My legs are screaming at me to sit down. I swallow two ibuprofen, then pour a finger of bourbon over ice and slide onto my couch, propping my feet up in front of me on the coffee table.

As I sip my bourbon, I tell myself that if I ever agree to do something like this again, I'll make sure I have a couple of months to prep, not just a couple of weeks. As loath as I am to admit it, I'm getting too old for all-day cooking sprees like this. I take another sip of bourbon. The warmth of the liquor soaks into my body and relaxes my muscles.

The longer I lay there and let the bourbon swim through my system, the more freely I allow my thoughts to wander. It's not long before I fixate on Frank, a place my thoughts wander far too often these days. I picture how sweet he is with Julia, the way his wrist felt beneath my touch when I helped patch up his hands, how he looked kneeling before me in my shed.

I shudder, remembering the way his hand found my leg and stayed there. Warmth floods my stomach and moves lower. And I can admit to myself that it's more than just the bourbon causing that feeling to flood my system. My brain snaps to the moments I've seen Frank in flannel chopping wood in his backyard like he stepped right out of a Brawny paper towel commercial. There's just something about a man who isn't afraid to get dirty and work with his hands.

I take the last sip of bourbon and put the glass on the coffee table next to me. I lay back on the arm of my couch and close my eyes. With no one else around to watch me, I allow myself to indulge in a forbidden fantasy: Frank and me together. I imagine the way his calloused palms would feel moving up my arms, how his scruff would scrape my cheek, how he'd press his body firmly into mine. These thoughts feel intoxicating, naughty. And I haven't thought of any real-life man like this since, well, since David.

And with thoughts of Frank taking off his flannel shirt in front of a fireplace, I drift off to sleep.

MY HOUSE IS COMPLETELY DARK, and I can hear a child crying. I wander through the halls, looking into rooms that shouldn't be in this house. Rooms full of piles of Christmas lights and vintage Santa Clauses. I keep going, looking for the crying child. I open the door to another room and it's full of basset hounds who all begin to howl when they see me. I slam the door shut and keep going, keep searching.

I open another door, and Frank is there, sitting in a dark room on my childhood bed. I step into the room, and he stands to greet me. He pulls me into his arms and kisses me. At first it's soft, but it gets deeper, more intense. My whole body heats up as I rip at his flannel shirt, silently begging him to take it off.

I hear the crying again and rip my lips from his, turning to continue searching. I have to find the crying child. She needs me.

I step away from Frank, but when I do, he's not Frank; he's David. I stumble backward and run down the endless, dark hallway, looking desperately for the child who needs me. Finally, I reach the last door at the end of the hallway and fling it open. And there, on the bed, sits a little girl with dark hair hanging in front of her face. Julia, I realize. I run to the girl and kneel in front of her. I push her hair back and realize that this girl isn't Julia, she's a young Amelia. I fall back and hug her to my chest. We cry and cry and cry. And when she pulls back again, she's my sister Jo, still seven years old, but there are bruises all over her cheeks and tears streaming down her face.

Her cries grow louder and turn into screams. I try to calm her, but she's inconsolable. A loud crack sounds, and I look up to see my roof crashing down over us. I scream.

And then suddenly, I'm awake. My heart is pounding, and sweat coats my whole body. I try to take deep breaths.

It was just a dream, I tell myself. *It was just a nightmare.*

I thought I left the lights on when I fell asleep in my living room, but I guess I turned them off in my bourbon-induced rest. I reach for the lamp and click it on, but nothing happens. That's when I realize that the whole house is freezing. I grab my phone and turn on the flashlight, using it to light my path to the drawer where I keep flashlights and batteries. I switch over to the bigger flashlight and head to my garage to check my circuit breaker. Maybe Frank managed to finally overload the power for the whole block with all those lights.

A quick investigation shows that no breakers were thrown,

though. Huh. All my blinds are still pulled down, so I can't see if Frank has also lost power. I pull them up and see… my God. Is that snow? Real-life snow?! I can't remember the last time we got snow in Louisiana. And I can't help it; the sight of it right before Christmas like this makes me smile.

But that's when I realize that it's not only dark inside my house, all the lights in Frank's yard are also off. It must be a transformer. Not ideal on the one and only night in a decade we have snow, but I'll be fine. I have roughly thirty-seven blankets in my house and can build one hell of a blanket nest.

Chapter 24

FRANK

DECEMBER 11, PRESENT DAY

"Papa, I'm scared," Julia says as she sits on my couch with multiple blankets piled on top of her.

It's just after midnight, but she and I both woke up when the power went out. There's a very distinct silence that happens when the central heat and white noise machines cut out in the house. Even the outside critters are mute because it's snowing. I open the blinds on all the windows so Julia can see the snow reflecting the full moon. It paints a haunted landscape, one I haven't seen the like of in years. The quiet is only interrupted by the occasional howl of the wind that sends leaves tumbling and branches shaking.

"Don't worry, Juju Bug. I'll start a fire in the fireplace, and we can both sleep in the living room tonight. It will be like camping." She brightens at my suggestion. I hand her a flashlight while I take another one. "I'm going to go into the garage and grab our firewood.

Good thing we planned ahead just in case, right Julia?"

"We were so smart," she agrees.

I step outside, and the snowflakes kiss my face. It slowly begins to collect on the ground, and it's like someone took a brush to the landscape and painted it clean, washing away the dark decay of winter. The moon glows boldly, even brighter with the electricity shut down.

I glance over to Margie's house and see that it is also completely dark. Worry pulls at me. I hope she's okay. But it would be weird to go over there and knock on her door at midnight, and would probably scare her. I won't do that... but I want to. I want to protect her, to make her comfortable and safe.

I shake my head, trying to clear those thoughts, and continue walking to my garage. I set my flashlight down and load my small wagon with firewood. I pick it back up, lighting the dark path back to my house. Never have I been so grateful to have a large, wood-burning fireplace. I start stacking the wood in the grate. Julia insists on helping, and soon, we have a nice pile going. It takes a few attempts to get the fire lit, but fortunately, the wood is dry, and we kept it that way inside the garage.

When the wood catches and crackles, it transforms my dark, ominous living room into a cozy, warm den. Julia leans into my arm and buries her cold nose into my shirt. A surge of pride moves through me, knowing that I'm taking care of my granddaughter. Together, we stare into the fire, transfixed by its flickering movement, lulled by its warmth. It's not long before Julia's slight weight sinks fully into me, and I hear her tiny snores.

I think of Cheryl in that moment, of how things might have been if she were here. How she would have taken Julia in her arms, held her tightly while I started the fire. And then, inexplicably, my mind turns to Margie, how she held Julia that night in her shed; the way Julia trusted her just like she's trusting me now. How much our rivalry challenges me and makes me feel alive again. How I wish she were here with us.

I stand, lifting Julia and carrying her to the loveseat near the fireplace. I lay her down and tuck the blankets in around her. She looks so peaceful, so rosy, lit by the warm flames. I take the larger couch, setting it up with a pillow and blankets. I can see out the window from where I lay, and I drift off to sleep as the snowflakes continue to cascade from the sky outside.

"PAPA, IT'S A CHRISTMAS MIRACLE," Julia whispers.

I groan, wondering in my half-asleep state why my entire body feels like it's been hit by a truck. My eyes flutter open. Julia's face is so close to mine that I can see the intricate mossy patterns in her earthen irises.

I blink again, look around, and realize I'm in my living room. On the couch. Right. No power. Snow. Julia steps back as I slowly sit up. My back is killing me. Too much time spent bent over my table saw, chopping wood, and sleeping on a couch. I am definitely not the young man I used to be.

"Papa, look!" Julia squeals, pointing to the window ahead of me. For a moment, I thought the power was back on because my whole house is awash with light. But no, that's just snow on the ground. And it's so bright, so white, that it's reflecting the sun into my house and setting it aglow. I have to admit, it is quite magical.

My phone buzzes on the small end table next to me. I reach for it and see that Jason has texted me at least ten times. I swipe it open to see urgent messages, asking if we are okay. I reply that we are fine. No power, but fine. He responds immediately telling me that the ice storm hit Dallas hard yesterday, and the news is saying that Ruston is practically shut down. I eye my phone's battery percentage. Thirty percent. I'm pretty sure I have a car charger tucked in a drawer around here somewhere.

"Papa! I want to go play in the snow! Can I build a snowman and make snow angels?" Julia is practically buzzing with excitement.

"Just hang on there, Juju Bug. First, let's get you something to eat. I think I have some Pop-Tarts in the pantry. Not nutritious, but it gets the job done."

"I want one of Miss Margie's cookies!" she squeals.

I can't blame the kid for that.

"Come on then, let's go see what we can round up. And then let's get that fire going again. I'll check my phone and see when they think power might be restored."

While Julia digs into her cookie, I open up the local news app and scroll through. It doesn't look good. Power outages cover nearly the entire northern half of Louisiana. And much to Julia's discontent, all that white outside is mostly ice. There are no salt and plow trucks nearby. They simply don't exist this far south of the Mason-Dixon line. That means we're stuck and at the mercy of the local power company. Fortunately, the governor issued a statewide emergency, so help is coming. But it won't be today, and it likely won't be tomorrow.

I'm grateful that my fear for Julia spurred me to chop firewood. We will be safe and warm. I wonder again about Margie. We'll go check on her later today, I decide.

AS THE DAY WEARS ON, the snow turns to sleet and then ice. I've charged my phone in my truck to make sure I can stay on top of power and weather updates, as well as let my son and daughter-in-law know that Julia and I are okay.

The only way to save everything in my fridge and freezer is to move it outside. So Julia and I make a game of hauling food into my oversized ice chest and piling snow and ice on top of it. Throughout the day, the temperatures rise slightly, just enough to melt the top surface of the snowy accumulation. But it is supposed to plummet again tonight, turning all that newly formed water into sheets of dangerous ice. After dropping a package of hot dogs into the ice chest,

I glance at Margie's house again.

"Come on, Julia, let's go check on Miss Margie. We have to walk carefully, though. No slipping," I instruct.

"I will tiptoe across the yard," she replies solemnly.

"Will you hold my hand so I don't fall?" I ask her.

"Of course, Papa."

Together, we traverse the slush in between Margie's and my yards, careful to avoid all the Christmas decorations now frozen and lifeless on the ground. At the sound of a sad woof, I turn to see Biscuit tapping his paws on the slush and instantly retreating back inside when the ground temperature registers. I still haven't been able to convince him to do his business outside since all this happened, but soon, I'm going to have to clear a patch of ground and carry him out before he has an accident in my house.

We finally make it to Margie's front porch and I'm relieved to see that most of the patio in front of her door was protected and kept dry by the roof above it. I knock and wait. I hear some shuffling from inside, and when the door opens, I'm greeted by what can only be described as a blanket monster. Margie must be wearing ten layers of coats, blankets, and socks beneath a very large quilt. Her nose is red from cold or perhaps strong liquor.

"Miss Margie, we wanted to check on you and make sure you're okay," Julia says proudly.

"That is very sweet," Margie agrees. "I'm okay. Just cold. But I've pulled out all the blankets and sweatshirts in the house and made myself a little nest."

I smile at the thought of her all tucked in like a baby bird surrounded by its mother's feathers.

"Do you have firewood? A generator? Something to keep you warm? It's supposed to get even colder tonight."

"No, nothing like that. But I did alright with my blankets last night. I'm sure I'll be fine again tonight," she insists.

"What about food? Can we help you move the stuff from your fridge and freezer outside so it won't spoil? I have an extra ice chest."

"Already did that," she says proudly. She shuffles, and her blanket pile slides off her shoulders a bit to reveal an oversized Louisiana Tech Bulldogs hoodie beneath.

"And batteries?" I don't know why I keep asking her questions like this. I feel compelled to help and protect Margie, even though she clearly wants none of it.

"Yep, got them too. I'm fine, Frank. I promise."

"Just promise me that you'll call me if you need anything, okay? Here, give me your phone. I'll put my number in it for you."

Margie plunges her garden glove-covered hand into the front hoodie pocket and retrieves her phone. I take my gloves off and take it from her. I add my contact number and then send myself a text so I have her number too.

"Feel better about everything now, Daddy?" she asks, raising one eyebrow.

My cheeks heat at her words, but I won't let her get the best of me. I roll my eyes. "Yeah, yeah. Look, we called a truce, and I want a fair competition for the Market. It's hardly fair if I'm competing against an ice cube."

"The Christmas Market is supposed to start next week. Setup is the day after tomorrow. I don't know how we're still going to be able to do it at this rate. I called Lia, and she said the convention center doesn't have power either. The roads are completely iced over, and no one can go anywhere."

She sounds so disheartened, and I hate it. "Well, that's one way to try to get me to give up on our bet, but I'm not going to cave that easily," I say with confidence. She lifts an eyebrow at me. There's that spark I love. "Have faith. It's a mess right now, but you know this Louisiana sun. It will come out of nowhere, and we will go from twenty degrees to sixty degrees in an hour," I say with conviction.

"You certainly aren't lying about that," she agrees.

"Okay, well Julia and I are going to go roast some marshmallows in the fireplace. Feel free to come on over if you get bored or too cold. Biscuit will even sleep on your feet for you and keep you nice and toasty."

"That dog of yours does seem to have an odd fascination with feet," she agrees.

"And I'm serious, Margie. Call me for anything, okay? Promise me."

She stares at me, studying my expression. And I can't help but feel that she's weighing my sincerity, unsure if I really want to help her.

Finally, she nods. "I promise."

Chapter 25

MARGIE

DECEMBER 11 , PRESENT DAY

It's freezing. I never thought the day would come in Louisiana where I could see my breath inside my house, but here we are. I open the news app on my phone and search for the latest power outage updates. It's not looking good. They are beginning with restoring power to the grocery stores and areas where utility trucks were already stationed, like larger neighborhoods. It will be at least another day before they make it out to these country roads if we're lucky.

I swipe over to my weather app. Outside temperatures are hovering in the upper twenties right now, but may dip into the teens tonight. I shudder and flex my fingers, trying to keep them warm. If worse comes to worse, I can run a bath. That, at least, is connected to my gas water heater.

Frank: Everything ok over there?

The text pops up on my screen as I close out my weather app.

Margie: I'm still alive if that's what you're asking.

Frank: No doubt it would take more than an unprecedented winter storm to kill off Margie Murphy.

I quirk a smile. I never thought I'd enjoy this, but I love that he doesn't back down from me.

An alert flashes on my phone, indicating that I only have ten percent power left. Shit. I need to go sit in my truck for a bit and charge my phone. At least I can turn the heat on in there for a bit. I dig my hiking boots out of the closet and grab my car keys. I suppose I don't need all ten blankets while I sit in the truck, so I opt for just one in addition to my hoodie and jacket.

The sun sets early this time of year, and at 6 p.m., it's already dark outside. I grab my flashlight, too. I walk to the front door and open it. The wind rips through the doorway, and it's nearly impossible to pull shut behind me. Rude. I reshuffle, wrapping my blanket around my head and shoulders in a cape that Darth Vader would be proud of. I tuck my keys and phone in my front hoodie pocket and prepare to yank my front door closed.

I thrust my blanket cape around me, reach for the handle of the door, and yank it closed. The wind tries to shove it back open, but I press on, leaning with my full body weight. I finally get closed, only for the wind to crash into me like a charging bull, slamming me into the door behind me with a loud thwack. *Very rude.*

I focus on the fifteen feet or so between where I stand on my front porch and my truck, trying to decide the best way through the slush and wind to arrive safely at my destination. I take one cautious step. The concrete is steady beneath my boot, so I take another.

This isn't so bad.

Another gust of wind barrels across my yard, scooping up dead leaves and rustling them in great, whirling swathes into the side of my truck. It startles me, but I manage to keep my balance. I just have to go slowly. Step, pause. Step, pause. It's fully dark now, the nearly full moon the only thing shedding light on my surroundings outside the scope of my flashlight.

Another gust sweeps through my yard, howling through the trees like a banshee on the wind. This time, it slaps into me hard and seems to grow hands, grabbing my blanket cape and twisting it around my body until I'm locked up tight like a newly bound mummy. I totter, my body threatening to topple like a freshly chopped tree. But I manage to keep my balance. I say a silent prayer of gratitude that no one can see me in this state. I slowly begin to turn in a circle, trying to unravel out of my blanket cocoon.

I hear a crash. I turn and look around but I can't see anything. It's too dark, and the wind is making my eyes water. I'm beginning to regret my attempt to charge my phone. I should have just waited until the morning.

Another gust of wind, this one even stronger, slams into me. I have to lean into it to stay upright. The crash comes again, louder and rumbling, but I can't move my legs enough to gain ground. Like a bug trapped in a spider web, I thrash in an attempt to find the source of danger.

And that's when I see it: the giant red ornament from Frank's yard is rolling straight toward me, and I am right in line to be its bowling pin. Just as I consider that my best option might be to go to ground, it slams into me, spurred on by wind and likely a healthy dose of karma. And with my arms tightly bound within my blanket prison and my feet unable to gain traction on the ice, I have nothing to protect myself as I fall face first. I managed to twist my body, saving my face, but my ankle goes one direction while the rest of my body goes the other. I feel it pop, and the pain shoots through my leg like a dagger. I scream, but my agony is devoured by the howling wind.

"Fuck you, Santa balls!" I yell, making myself feel only moderately better.

At least now that I'm on the ground. I can roll out of my blanket straight jacket. I get to work on that first, slowly rolling my entire body across my icy front lawn until I'm both free and freezing. Next, I try to stand. But as soon as I place weight on my ankle, I buckle, pain gripping me in its vice and taking me back down.

I am so screwed. Maybe if I sit it in the snow for a bit until my ankle is numb I'll have better luck. But I know the temperature is dropping rapidly, and that option could quickly turn to hypothermia.

Should I crawl? I could barely walk more than five feet, but I suppose it's worth a try. I roll onto my hands and knees, and the wind whips into my face, stinging my eyes. I place one hand down in front of me in the icy snow, and it immediately soaks into my garden gloves, which were not meant to keep in heat. I slide my knee forward and cry out in agony as my ankle drags. Right. No crawling.

I could call an ambulance, but the road is a complete mess. I don't even think it could get through. I look up through the strands of hair whipping around my face and clinging to the sides of my mouth. My gaze immediately catches on the giant red ornament. Frank. He is very lucky we called a truce. I reach into my hoodie pocket, grateful to find that my phone still has five percent battery. I fumble through my contacts and call Frank. It rings. Once, twice, three times. No answer.

I try again. Tears threaten to spill as my body trembles violently from the freezing air and feral wind biting into me. I imagine myself as an intrepid explorer atop Mount Everest, staring down her last packet of food. I blink. This cold is really getting to my brain. I try calling Frank again. This time, someone answers, and I nearly weep with relief.

"Hi, Miss Margie! This is Julia. How are you?"

"Hey, Julia. Listen, I need you to go get your Papa."

"He's out in the garage chopping up some more firewood. He's going to have to call you back," she chirps.

"Julia, this is an emergency. I need you to–" The phone disconnects. I look down, and it's dead.

"Fuck," I whisper. Tragic fantasies begin to spin out in my head. I see myself lying frozen on the ground, slowly blacking out, my death imminent. No one would find me until the roads clear, and even then, only because of the smell. I try to crawl again. I get to my hands and knees, and I am simultaneously relieved and terrified when I realize I can't feel my hands anymore. Though that makes gripping my flashlight impossible, too. I stick it in my hoodie pocket and try to move forward.

I take one crawling step forward, drag my leg behind me, and collapse with pain. I scream in frustration. I think of that man who had to saw his own arm off with a rock to escape being trapped in a crevasse while hiking. If he can do that, I can make it back to my house just eight feet or so away. I get up again. I grit my teeth and begin to crawl. I collapse twice more. I push myself up and keep going.

I just want to close my eyes and give up. Logically, I know that's dramatic. It's not very far. But pain and extreme cold are affecting my ability to think clearly. Which is why when a beam of light hits me, I think I have passed out and wandered into a hallucination.

"Margie!" a male voice calls distantly. I crane my head, trying to make sure this is real. "Dammit, Margie. Hang on. I'm getting to you as fast as I can. This ground is slick as hell." I close my eyes and wait. I start counting, trying to block out the pain.

A strong hand grabs my upper arm and rolls me over. "Oh my God. Margie! Are you okay?"

Frank. He's here. But all my words are gone, swallowed up by pain and wind and frozen earth.

"Hang on, okay? Let's get you off the ground."

I feel his arms beneath my shoulders, pushing me up to a sitting position. "That's right. Good girl. You're sitting. Take a breath now let's get you to a stand. Ready? One, two, three."

He yanks me upright, and I shove off the ground on my good foot with all of my waning energy. But, inevitably, I place weight on my bad ankle, and a scream tears out of me. "My ankle," I manage to chatter out.

"Dammit. Okay. Here, wrap your arm around my shoulders. Just like that. Good girl."

Together, we trudge slowly back to my house. Frank manages to wrench the door open and gasps.

"Dammit, Margie, it's like a meat locker in here, barely any better than outside. You can't stay in this. But we have to get you out of those soaking clothes immediately."

"You aren't get-tt-ting in my pants," I chatter out.

Frank looks at me incredulously. "Well, darlin', I'm flattered that you can still manage to flirt with me when you are in very real danger of hypothermia. But let's save that until you're warmed up."

I can barely manage to process what he said before he asks me to point him in the direction of a bathroom. "Please tell me you have a gas water heater and that your pipes aren't frozen," he mumbles to himself.

He gets to work, turning on my bathtub. By some miracle, the pipes begrudgingly yield water to us. "Thank God," Frank whispers. "Okay, we can't put you immediately into hot water. We're going to start with warm, and gradually raise the temperature, okay?"

I nod.

"Go ahead and take your clothes off," he says.

"Are you s-s-s-serious?" I chatter.

He rolls his eyes. "Believe me, Margie. When I'm ready to make a move on you, it will be a lot more fun than this." The slightest hint of color tinges my cheeks. He must be trying to distract me.

"T-t-turn around," I say.

He does so immediately. "I'm going to be right here in case you need help. I promise not to look at you inappropriately."

I believe him. I pull my flashlight out of my pocket and click it on, aiming it at the ceiling so that it floods the bathroom in low light. I'm so cold that I can't get my fingers to function correctly. I manage to get my hoodie and shirt off while sitting on the closed toilet and keeping my weight off my ankle. And that's when I realize I have a big problem.

"Um, Frank," I say, embarrassed. "I need your help. First, can you h-h-hand me-e a t-t-towel?"

He reaches for the one hanging on the back of my bathroom door and hands it over without looking at me. I use it to cover my boobs. "I c-c-can't unhook my bra."

Every muscle of Frank's body locks up for a split second. "That's gonna be hard to do with my eyes closed."

"It's okay. I'm covered."

He turns and sees me with the towel over me. Slowly, he steps around me and begins to unhook the cold, frozen band. I can barely feel his fingers because I'm so cold, but I feel the tension release when he's done.

"And my jeans b-b-button," I mumble.

"Lean back," he says, then kneels in front of me. I can feel his warm breath on my stomach. And, despite the dire situation I'm presently in, I find that I'm embarrassed for Frank to see my stomach rolls.

"I think I've g-got it," I say as soon as he gets the button and zipper undone.

"Here, let me help. I promise to keep my hands to myself," he says with mock seriousness, then he pulls the soaked jeans off my legs. When he gets to my damaged ankle, he takes his time, trying not to bump the injury. "You can keep your underwear on, but let's get you in the bathtub. We need to warm you up."

He helps me stand. I clutch his bicep with one arm and my towel with the other. Together, we scoot toward the tub.

"Okay. I'm going to close my eyes. You drop the towel and hang onto me as much as you need to, okay?"

I nod.

He squeezes his eyes shut. I drop the towel and ease myself toward the waiting tub. It's slow going, but I eventually sit on the edge, then move my feet in one at a time. The warm water on my cold skin makes me yell in pain. It's like a thousand bees stinging every inch of me, waking my body back up.

"Just take your time," Frank says, his back now to me where he stands in the door.

And slowly, ever so slowly, I lower myself until I'm all the way in the tub. I reach for the shower curtain and pull it closed, giving myself some privacy.

"I'm in and covered."

"How are you feeling?" he asks gently.

"Horrible. Every part of my body hurts."

"Do you think you'll be okay to stay there for about twenty minutes while I go back to my house and check on Julia? She's sitting with Biscuit in front of the fire, and she's well-behaved, but she's still so young, and I–"

"Go. I'll be fine," I say. My voice catches on the last word as the shock and pain of the last thirty minutes begin to crash down around me.

"You can't honestly think I'm leaving you here alone tonight?" Frank says incredulously. "I'm just going to check on Julia and get something to help get you back over to my house for the night. I have a roaring fire, plenty of food, and a little girl who will be very happy to have a slumber party guest."

I can hear the smile in his voice as he talks about Julia, and it helps my body thaw just a little more.

"Frank, you don't have to–"

"But I want to," he says, cutting me off.

Tears sting my eyes. He wants to help me. He wants to be there for me. He wants to take care of me.

"Okay," I finally allow.

"Good. Now you stay there and add a little bit more warm water every few minutes. Do not attempt to get out of that bathtub without me in the house. If you fall, then you'll be frozen and naked when I show up to rescue you this time."

I can't help it; a laugh escapes me—a great, gasping laugh born of exhaustion and hysteria. His warm, gruff chuckle joins in. And soon the walls of this old house are echoing sounds of joy and contentment I once thought was lost to them forever.

Chapter 26

FRANK

DECEMBER 11, PRESENT DAY

As I slog back through the slush to my house, I finally let the emotion of the last hour wash over me. Finding Margie laid out on the ground shot panic through my entire body. For a brief moment, I thought she was dead, that I was looking at the corpse of the woman I was coming to care for.

And I know that now. I care about Margie. As a friend, yes, but as more than that, too, I think.

I want to be the one there for her so she's not alone when a random winter storm system descends on Ruston. I want to be able to help her when she's injured and cut firewood up so that she's safe and warm. I want to sit with her and drink coffee while she gives me hell and stare at the half-smile she flashes when she's genuinely amused. I want to hold her all the time. Hold her hand. Hold her as we watch a movie together. Hold her in bed. But I'm not sure if she wants any of that. If she can trust anybody enough to let them try.

And even if Margie only ever wants to be my friend, I'll accept it. Because I can admit to myself now that I'm just as lonely and stubborn as she is.

I finally make it to my house and open the door, the wind nearly knocking me over in the process.

"Hey, Juju Bug," I call out. "You okay?"

She comes to meet me, Biscuit at her heels.

"Is Miss Margie okay?" she asks immediately.

"She had a bit of an accident. Hurt her ankle really bad. You were a smart girl to come get me out of the garage," I tell her, pressing my hand to Julia's cheek.

"She said it was a 'mergency. And Mama always uses that word when we have to go to the hospital. Does Miss Margie have to go to the hospital?

"Maybe when the roads reopen. But she will be okay for now. Listen, Juju Bug. I have to go back over there and help Miss Margie come over to our house. While I do that, can you set up a place for her to sleep on the big couch?"

She nods her head vigorously. "Like a sleepover!" she declares.

"Sort of. More like a hospital. Do you think we can be good nurses to Miss Margie?"

"Oh yes, I know all about hospitals," Julia declares.

"Alright. I won't be gone too long. Just like last time. You stay inside with Biscuit. I'm going to get my ATV and see if I can get it to go over the snow and drive Miss Margie back over, okay?"

IT TURNS OUT THAT MY ATV works well driving over the slush—as long as I go slowly and stay away from icy concrete. I probably break ten Christmas light bulbs on the trek from my garage to Margie's front door. But, for the first time in a long time, I don't care about the Christmas lights. Not even a little.

When I arrive at Margie's front porch, I park it and go inside her house, making my way back to her bathroom. I call out to let her know I'm there.

"Still alive," she croaks.

The anxiety in my chest eases a fraction. I take a breath and aim for levity.

"So, you turn into a raisin yet?"

"Still just a plump grape," she quips back. And I'm so relieved to hear her voice steady and sharp again that I nearly melt into the floor.

"Well, that's an encouraging sign. Think you can get out and put on some dry clothes? Julia is anxious to play nurse."

"I can certainly try."

"I'm going to help you. And before you start throwing protests at me, remember what I said about being naked on the floor, alright?"

She lets out a dark chuckle. "Fine, but if you catch sight of something you don't want to see and have nightmares about it, that's on you."

"Believe me, they wouldn't be nightmares," I say, heat creeping into my voice. She doesn't say anything, but I hear the tub water slosh slightly. "Okay," I say, clearing my throat. "Let's do this." I walk over to the closed shower curtain and hold a towel up in front of me. "Can you stand?"

"I guess we're going to find out," Margie says.

I stare at the towel in front of me as Margie pushes the shower curtain back. I keep staring at the towel as I hear her move and let out whimpers of pain. My arms tremble with the desire to drop this damn towel and help her, but I keep holding it, determined to show her that she can trust me to keep my word.

"Well, this is embarrassing. I can't stand up on my own," she says. I can hear the defeat in her voice, and I hate it.

"I'm going to kneel down and stick my arms out for you. I'll keep my eyes closed. You just grab onto me, and I'll help lift you, okay?"

She mumbles to herself, then finally. "Fuck it. Fine."

I chuckle. I stare at the towel as I kneel down and then close my eyes when I place the towel on the floor. I feel a warm, wet hand grab my forearm, then another. The touch is grounding and firm. I latch my hands onto Margie's damp forearms, helping to steady her.

"On the count of three," I tell her. "One, two, three."

She yells out in pain and topples forward. I catch her, not even hesitating to wrap my arms around her torso, holding her up so she doesn't fall. I'm so intent on making sure she doesn't topple over that it takes us both a solid five seconds to realize that Margie, soaking wet and almost totally naked, is pressed up against my body.

My eyes fly open, and I see that she's looking at me, mouth agape, as words fail us both.

"It's okay," I rasp out. "I know this is awkward as hell right now, but I'm not going to drop you and let you hit the floor."

"Close your eyes!" she squeaks.

I slam them shut again immediately.

"God, what did I do in my life to deserve this level of debasement," Margie whispers to herself.

"If it makes you feel any better, one time when I was out working on the farm, I accidentally mooned a visiting group from the Senior Home. Poor old ladies just wanted to enjoy their field trip and pick a few pumpkins, and instead, they happened to all be present when my back pocket got caught on a nail and ripped off the whole back side off my pants.

"Probably made their year," Margie murmurs.

We both chuckle.

"I'm going to lean over and grab this towel. You just hang on to me."

"As if I had any other choice."

I slowly bend down, reaching toward the ground where I dropped the towel earlier. Margie hangs on to me for dear life. I work to counterbalance her body and not topple over. I am almost there. The towel is within my reach. I grasp it with the tips of my fingers.

And that's when my heel slips on a puddle of water. My heel shoots out from under me, and I fall back. I manage to keep one hand on Margie as we both go down. I catch myself on the heel of my hand and let out an "oof" as Margie slams into me.

"Oh my God!" she yells out. "Are you okay, Frank? I'm so sorry."

We lay there for a moment, looking at each other in the flashlight-lit room, breathing heavily. And even though I promised not to let my eyes wander, I can't help that I can still feel every single place where her soft body presses into mine. Even through my jeans and flannel shirt she feels delicious. I groan in pleasure despite the pain.

And suddenly, her weight is off of me.

"Margie? Are you okay?"

"Physically? Yes? Emotionally? Debatable."

"Are you decent?"

"Never. But I'm covered. Mostly."

I look over and see her lying next to me on the floor. She grabbed the towel and managed to cover herself up. I roll my head to look at her face, and she does the same.

Time beats between us.

"Frank," she whispers.

"Mmmhmm."

"This tile floor is fucking freezing."

We erupt into unhinged giggles. My laughter rises from deep within my soul, shaking my body. My shoulders rock against the frigid bathroom tiles. I gasp as tears roll down my cheeks. And I'm not sure if it's the absurdity of the moment, hysteria, or relief that Margie is okay, but it's cathartic, a needed purge of emotion.

I push up on one arm and stare down at Margie. Her features are cast in stark shadows from the flashlight. "Come on then, let's get you off this frozen floor."

"Before we find ourselves in another precarious position, would you mind grabbing some clothes out of my room? I'll sit up and cover myself, and then we can do the shuffle hop out of here."

"Good point," I admit.

"But do hurry; my ass is about to turn into a pair of ice cubes," she says.

"Don't make me start laughing again, or your whole body will be an ice cube by the time I finally bring you clothes."

"Just call me Han Solo."

Chuckling, I walk into the bedroom that's connected to her bathroom. She verbally directs me to her t-shirts, sweatshirts, and sweatpants. And, to her credit, Margie only hesitates a moment before directing me to her underwear drawer. Still, I blush a little as I pull out underwear, a bra, and some socks. I deliver the requested clothes and step away while Margie works to get her clothes on from where she sits on the bathroom floor.

"Alright, I need your help again, Mr. Do-gooder," Margie calls out. I walk back into the bathroom, ready to help lift her up. "I've just about got all my clothes on but need to stand to pull my pants up all the way.

I lean over. Margie slides her arms over mine and grips my shoulders. "This will be easier if we do this bear hug style. That way, I can lift with my knees, and we have a more concentrated center of gravity."

"I'm surprised you haven't had enough of me pressed up against you for one night," she quips.

"That's not possible," I murmur.

She hesitates, and for a moment, then she throws her arms around my neck. She smells like the fresh, clean scent of her bath soap mixed with hints of cinnamon and coffee. I inhale deeply.

"On the count of three. I'll lift, and you push up with your good leg." This time, we execute the stand without toppling over. She quickly pulls up her sweatpants the rest of the way. "Now, put your arm around my neck. You're going to have to hop, but we'll go slow. My ATV is waiting outside, and I'll load you up on the back and drive you over to my house."

"Makes me feel just like a dead deer," she says.

"Now give yourself some credit, Margie. You're definitely alive and more like a bear than a deer."

She swats me playfully and shakes her head. And then, together, we hop and scoot through Margie's dark, cold house. We have to pause every few steps to catch our breath and rest our muscles. But, eventually, we make it to the front door.

"Before we go, is there anything you need me to grab from your house?"

"Just my toothbrush," she instructs.

I help Margie get situated on the back of my ATV, and then I climb into the driver's seat. I crank it up, letting it warm up for a minute. I tap the gas pedal gently. It spins a little on the icy ground. I hit it again, and it lurches forward. Margie slams into my back.

"Well, shit, Frank. You're going to break my other ankle at this rate."

"Turn your body, put your legs around me, and hang on. There's no need to get wet all over again."

We both catch that big bucket of innuendo at the same time. "Well that was awkward," Margie says, claiming the elephant in the room like it's her job.

"I don't think there's been a single moment tonight that hasn't been awkward. No point in changing things now."

She shifts behind me, sliding her legs around me slowly, careful to protect her injured ankle. She scoots in close until her front is pressed into my back. Her arms slide around me, locking across my chest. The position brings us close, most of our bodies touching. I tap the gas and she jostles into me even more. And I don't hate it. Not one bit.

Finally I get the ATV moving at a slow, steady pace. I have to pause a couple of times when it starts to slide or spin. Every time it lurches forward, Margie grips me more tightly. It's a heady feeling. When we finally make it to my house, I pull up as close to the door as I can, then hop off. Julia throws the door open, and Biscuit woofs in greeting.

"I'm sorry we don't have a wheelchair, Miss Margie. Our hospital is missing a few things. But we have a bed ready for you," Julia says solemnly.

"Well, now, I appreciate the lack of wait time, doctor," Margie says.

"I'm your nurse. So is Biscuit. Papa is your doctor."

"Well, thank you kindly, Nurse Julia."

I help Margie off the ATV, and together, we shuffle hop into my house.

Chapter 27

MARGIE

DECEMBER 11, PRESENT DAY

When we make it into Frank's living room, I moan at the sight of the roaring fire. It's so warm and cozy in here that I'm tempted to crawl over to the fireplace rug, curl up like a cat, and fall asleep. And the smell of the crackling wood brings me back to the bonfires of my youth.

"Your bed, Miss Margie," Julia says, pointing to the large couch in the room.

Frank helps me hop over. I sink into the deep cushions and sigh. It's only a moment before my adrenaline comes crashing down around me. And as my body acclimates to the warmer temperature, I begin to feel my throbbing ankle. The pain seems to increase steadily until it feels like someone is throwing rocks at my ankle on repeat.

"We need to elevate your foot," Frank says. "And I know you don't want to hear this, but we need to put ice on it."

"I'll get some!" Julia says, then darts off. She returns a moment later with a bag of frozen corn they stuck outside.

"Perfect, Nurse Julia. Thank you," I tell her.

Julia and Frank fuss over me, making sure I'm comfortable. They cover me with blankets, cushion me with pillows, and stoke the fire. It almost makes me uncomfortable having people fuss over me like this. I'm not used to anyone taking care of me—ever. And while I know Amelia and Rhett would be the first people to show up if I asked, I hate asking for help. It makes me feel weird like I'm putting other people out.

But Frank and Julia seem to enjoy doting on me like this. And seeing them happy warms a long-dead piece of my soul, waking it up like a phoenix emerging from the ashes.

Once I'm settled, Frank retrieves hot dogs from his ice chest outside, and together, he and Julia roast them over the indoor fireplace. I watch from my spot on the couch as they cook together. I study the way Frank shows Julia how to thread the hotdog on the skewer properly. With infinite patience, he instructs her on how to hold the skewer in the fire so it doesn't burn the hot dog to a crisp. He lets her try to get it off the stick and into a bun herself. She misses the first time, and the hot dog tumbles to the ground. In a bout of speed I didn't think was possible, Biscuit appears from the shadows, snatches the dropped hot dog up, and scarfs it down. Julia looks like she's about to cry at the mistake, but Frank intervenes, telling her it's okay and that Biscuit wants to participate, too.

Occasionally, Frank glances over his shoulder to check on me. His eyes twinkle in the dancing firelight. The warm glow makes his cheeks rosy. His smile as he interacts with his granddaughter is infectious, and I can't keep my own smile off my face as I watch them.

It's not long before Julia shouts, "I did it!" And soon, we all sit on the couch enjoying our fireplace-cooked hot dogs and a can of baked beans Frank warmed over the fire. It's not gourmet, but this is the best meal I've had in ages.

As we eat, Frank and I listen to Julia share stories of exploring her Papa's yard and about her school friends. And when she mentions her last stay at the hospital, Frank glances at me uncomfortably. He doesn't know that Julia told me about her autoimmune disease, I realize.

"It's okay," I murmur. "Julia told me all about her illness when she came to visit me that night in my shed."

"Oh," Frank says.

"And Miss Margie told me that being sick sucks," Julia announces proudly.

"Did she now?" Frank asks, his warm chuckle rumbling through my bones.

After dinner, Julia yawns loudly. Frank glances down at his watch and startles. "It's nearly ten o'clock. Come on, Juju Bug. Let's go brush your teeth and get you settled into your couch bed for the night."

Every part of me is aching to help Frank get Julia ready for bed, but I know it's not my place, and besides, not much I can do with a bum ankle. Instead I content myself with petting Biscuit's snout that he places on the couch cushion beside me. The beam of a flashlight alerts me that Frank and Julia are returning to the living room, followed by her soft giggles.

Julia, now dressed in a princess nightgown, leggings, and socks, scrambles onto the loveseat where her bed is already waiting for her. Frank kneels beside her, and together, they say bedtime prayers. Frank kisses Julia's forehead and tucks her blanket in tight around her. It's almost like watching the movie of a life I could have had. I blink back the fantasy and chastise myself. Amelia and I did just fine on our own. We never needed anyone else, especially not a man.

Though right now, I kind of want one.

Frank steps away from Julia and sits down next to me on the couch. He leans back, closes his eyes, and lets out a long sigh. I study the flecks of gray in his beard and hair, admiring the way they enhance his masculine beauty. Age, I've found, tends to sharpen someone's features, not dull them. He snaps his head up and looks straight at me, immediately catching me staring. His mouth quirks. He loves that he caught me.

"Quite a night, huh?" he whispers. The fire crackles around us, and already I can hear Julia's faint snores from the couch perpendicular to ours.

"I'll say. It's been a while since a man got me naked, and that's not exactly how I imagined it would go down if it ever happened again."

Frank blinks, surprised. He tries to stifle a laugh but only manages to shove it inward, making his whole body tremble.

"I admit that I've never quite experienced a woman throwing herself at me like you did tonight," he says, mischief lighting his tone.

"More like toppling onto you. If I were throwing myself, you'd know it. I'd at least try for something in the realm of sexy. That was more baby horse emerging from the womb, not a woman trying to seduce the man she's attracted to."

"Are you?" Frank asks, his voice suddenly a husky whisper.

"What? A horse?"

He chuckles quietly. "No. Attracted to me?" His icy blue eyes tunnel into me, seeming to cut off my airway. His gaze darkens as he studies me. He's serious, I realize.

I look away. "I don't know," I reply honestly.

"Well, that will humble a man pretty damn quickly," he replies. And even though he says it jokingly, I know I've hurt his feelings.

"It's just that, well, Frank," I turn my torso to face him. "It's been a really, really long time since I was attracted to anyone. And I'm not your typical beauty queen. I'm a hard worker; I have to be. I can't rely on anyone but myself, and Amelia depended on me almost her entire life." I cut myself off and look away, mad at myself for saying too much.

I feel his calloused palm slide over the back of my hand.

"Hey Margie, it's okay. You don't have to tell me anything you don't want to." His voice rumbles and mixes with the crackling fire. "But, I think I'm attracted to you," he sighs.

"You think?" I ask wryly.

"Well, it's been a while for me too. And, shit. This is awkward. But you should probably know one way or another. I have only ever been with one woman. My wife, Cheryl, and we got married when we were twenty. Only ever had eyes for each other," he smiles sadly and seems to stare down a tunnel into the past.

"Did you finally irritate the snot out of her too?" I ask, trying to get a smile out of him.

But his smile collapses, folding in on itself into a frown. "No. Or maybe. She always tolerated my bullshit. No, Margie, Cheryl passed away three years ago. Cancer. And she took all the light out of my life with her. Well, almost all of it," he says and glances at Julia for a moment. "And honestly, I never thought I'd want to find something like that again. Didn't want to. I didn't think anyone could ever live up to her."

He glances at me, and I wilt. I am certainly not perfect Cheryl.

"But the thing is," he says, leaning closer to me, fingers intertwining with mine. "I had it all wrong. It's not that someone should or could replace Cheryl, because my wife was her own person with her own unique path in the world. I loved her in a way that only she could be loved. But I still have love in my heart to share with someone else."

He pauses, running his hand through his hair. "I am not very good at this," he sighs. "What I'm trying to say is that I like you, Margie. In a more-than-friends way. And I don't want you to be Cheryl. I like you, just as you are."

"But I'm kind of mean," I admit, biting my lip.

He huffs a laugh. "Yeah, but I kind of like it."

I study his expression, admiring the way his crows' feet deepen when he smiles. "You are something else, Frank Campbell," I say and squeeze his hand back. It's the only place we touch, but it feels weighty and important.

"Well, Frank, it may have been a few years since you took a roll in the hay with your wife, but a man hasn't laid hands on me since I was young and beautiful. And then he abandoned me as soon as life got too hard."

"You're still beautiful," he says quietly, squeezing my hand. "And I know about life's hard knocks." He glances at Julia. "And I have a pretty good track record of sticking around regardless."

God, this man, and his perfect words.

"I just, I don't know. I'm not used to this kind of attention," I shuffle uncomfortably.

"I get that. And there is no pressure from me, okay? I'm here and I enjoy spending time with you—even when we are trying to throw each other to the wolves. And I'm happy to have your friendship if that's all you're willing to give. But maybe we could start by talking more? Sharing parts of our lives that don't involve undermining the other?"

"Or rescuing each other from the frozen tundra?"

"Hey, I'll come to your rescue any time, Margie."

"That's not something I'm used to. No one has ever done that for me," my joy fades as I slip into memories.

"Well, let me try, okay? Let me show you that I'm a man of my word."

I consider him, mulling over his request. He's not asking to date me. He's not trying to jump into my bed. He's asking me to consider him as a person beyond just our ongoing feud. A friend. Maybe more eventually.

"Okay," I agree.

He dips his head, and I catch a glimpse of his smile as he does so.

"Can I put my arm around your shoulders?" he asks cautiously.

"Considering you've already had my naked body plastered against you tonight, I don't think that will hurt anything."

He slides in, his arm going around my shoulders and pulling me in. I cautiously lay my head on his shoulder and close my eyes. I inhale, taking in the smell of woodsmoke from the fire, the pine of his tiny Christmas tree, and the smell of sawdust still clinging to his shirt. It's intoxicating, and I briefly consider burying my nose in his flannel shirt and just living there for a while.

My eyes feel heavy, and just as I start to doze off, I snap my head up. "Frank?"

"Hmmm," he grumbles, letting me know that he, too, had fallen asleep.

"Where are you going to sleep?" I look around and take in Julia asleep on the other couch in the living room. The rest of the house is far too cold to sleep in without the roaring fire.

"Sleeping bag," he mumbles.

"Oh my God, I took your bed," I hiss.

"Oh, speaking of, let's get that set up for you. I'm gonna need you to stand so I can unfold the futon."

He rubs his eyes, then pushes off the couch, wincing. He's got to be sore after lifting my ass all evening. Nevertheless, he reaches for me to help me stand and hobble out of the way. Then he unfolds the sleeper sofa. He's so weary, and the fold-out bed can clearly hold two people.

"Frank, let's share it. There's plenty of room," I insist.

"Trying to get me into bed already, Margie? I thought we were going to take this slow."

"Ha ha, very funny. You really think I would do that with a child in the room? What kind of monster do you think I am?"

"The kind who unplugs her neighbor's Christmas lights."

"Oh, whatever."

"Listen, it's fine. I can grab a sleeping bag and sleep on the floor. Biscuit will love it."

The dog in question lazily wags his tail in response.

"I appreciate you trying to be noble. But you and I aren't exactly young anymore, and we have both pushed our bodies in ways I don't much like to think about tonight. I'm going to use your restroom, and when I get back in here, we are both going to share this bed like mature adults."

All the fight seems to have left him because Frank nods and then helps me make my way to the restroom. By the time I re-emerge, he's waiting for me outside the door. While I was occupied, he changed into flannel pajama pants and a long-sleeved t-shirt. He also set up the futon with two pillows and two blankets.

"Only if you're sure?" he asks wearily, inclining his head to the bed.

I nod and practically flop onto the sleeper sofa. Even with the fire, it's still chilly, so Frank doesn't need to worry about me shedding my hoodie or sweatpants. He climbs in beside me. Each of us tucks in under our own covers. And any concerns I might have had over sharing this sleeper couch disappear immediately as I crash headlong into sleep. And just as I'm drifting off, I swear I feel the faintest brush of lips against my temple.

Chapter 28

MARGIE

DECEMBER 22, 1998

Despite my best efforts, the most I've been able to get Josephine to do is eat a sandwich I brought to her room. Which is why I'm shocked when she emerges from her makeshift cave in jeans and a t-shirt this morning and sits at the breakfast table without my prompting. Amelia brightens immediately at the sight of her mother, and my heart thrums with tentative hope.

"Hey, Mommy," she says, throwing her arms around her. Jo winces slightly, then reaches for her daughter and hugs her in return. My shoulders relax as I dare to hope that Jo is beginning to return to herself.

When we were kids, Jo was so much like Amelia. Sweet, loyal, introspective. I was the lava to her ocean, the briny pickle to her delicate mousse. And while we differed in almost every respect, we were inseparable. If I was out in the garage trying to build a table with Dad's saw, Jo was quietly trailing behind me with a glass of lemonade and a book in hand to observe. When I insisted on building a bonfire, Jo gathered twigs to help me light it. When other kids picked on my sister, I was quick to slam a fist into the faces of her bullies; consequences be damned.

I study the dark circles under her young eyes and her sallow cheeks and consider driving to her house and facing down her husband myself. But that man is dangerous, beyond just the usual bully sort. His default is violence first, and David isn't wrong in urging me to use caution around that man.

Amelia snaps me out of my reverie when she leaps up to turn on the Christmas station. "Rocking Around the Christmas Tree" crackles to life and infuses my cozy kitchen with comfort and joy. Even Jo cracks a small smile that she tucks away behind her coffee mug.

I'm just sliding the second batch of pancakes onto the table when I hear the gravel crunch in my driveway. David. My gut twists with the conversation we still need to have, but not now. Not when we're finally having a comfortable moment with my sister and niece. I grab an extra plate and sit it on the table just as the car door slams. Jo winces, but Amelia lights up, ready to see David. Already, I'm trying to figure out how to tell her that he won't be around here much longer.

"JOSEPHINE!" a male voice laced with fire and whisky calls from outside my front door.

My stomach plummets. Jo loses all color and begins trembling. Her eyes flare as she slowly scoots back the chair. She's ready to bolt or commit murder. I'm not sure which. Amelia whines like a puppy with an injured paw.

"Come here, baby," I whisper to my niece.

"Josephine! I know you're in there. You open this damn door right this minute before I blow the handle off with my rifle!" Dale screams.

Shit. He has a gun. My body shifts from frightened to militant. This man will not harm these two. I won't let him. Quickly and quietly, I move Amelia to my pantry closet.

"Hide here, baby. Don't make a sound," I whisper.

"But Mama," she says, tears sliding down her rounded cheeks. Sticky syrup still clings to the edges of her mouth.

"Your mama is going to be okay. Your Aunt Margie is going to handle this, okay, baby? But whatever you do, do not come out of here. Promise me." Amelia nods and clings to the stuffed bear she pulled out of my childhood things and has taken to carrying around with her.

A warning shot fires from outside, and Jo screams. My heart hammers in my chest as I rapidly form a plan. I yell out. "Just wait a minute, Dale! I'm getting out of the shower!" I'm hoping to buy a moment of time.

"Open the damn door, Margaret. She can't stay in there forever. She's gotta come home where she belongs!"

"One second!" I call out.

I grab the phone and call 911. When the operator answers, I quickly outline the situation and give them my address. Another gunshot, and the door rattles. "Hurry. Please," I whisper into the phone as I hang up.

I round the corner to the front door and find it already open, the doorknob demolished, and a jagged, splintered hole where it once was. Dale looks wild, unhinged, like a bear with his foot caught in a trap. He's staring at Jo like he's either going to kill her or throw her in the back of his truck and disappear into the woods. Jo is trembling and quietly pleading for him to stop.

"Dale put the gun down, and let's talk," I say with a confident, steady bravado I don't feel.

"How dare you keep my wife locked up in your house away from me?" he slurs.

I don't fully process what he's saying and don't put much stock in it. He's obviously drunk, angry, and armed. I have to diffuse this situation before things escalate to the point of no return. I try again.

"Just put the gun down, Dale. You don't want to do something you'll regret now, do you? Something that will keep you from your wife forever?"

I see the moment of doubt cross his face as he wavers. His hand, holding the gun, drifts down to his side.

Josephine whimpers again, and I watch as Dale's foggy brain tries to process his situation. He reaches out and grabs Jo by the arm, and yanks her to him. I want to run and pull her back, to punch him and kick him in the balls. But he has a gun, and I know any sudden move from me could end in death.

"Now you're coming back with me. Where's our girl?" he growls.

Jo only whimpers. I straighten my posture, a cobra ready to strike if he comes close to the little girl hiding in my pantry.

He shakes Jo and yells, "She is our daughter. Both of ours. She belongs to us. You will go get her from wherever you stowed her away, or so help me, Josephine." He lets go of her arm and shoves her, causing Jo to stumble and crash into the hard linoleum floor.

"Now!" he rages.

Panic begins to build inside me. Will Josephine go get Amelia from her hiding place? Can I somehow tackle the gun from his hand while she goes?

I step forward, unsure of what I'm about to do when the door creaks open behind Dale. He starts to turn, but it's too late. A cop slams into him from behind, taking him down to the floor. Another officer enters the house and kicks the gun away. In a matter of moments, Dale has been cuffed as he lies pressed to the floor, screaming obscenities while his arms are wrestled into handcuffs.

I feel like I'm having an out-of-body experience. Distantly, I hear Jo's quiet sobs from where she still lays where she was knocked to the floor. The flashing lights from the cop cars outside my front door cast an eerie red and blue sheen to everything. Police haul Dale up and outside. And all the while, Christmas carols continue to play a haunting soundtrack alongside the violent scene before me. I'm locked in place, every joint frozen, every breath shallow.

"Margie! Oh my God, Margie!" a voice calls. I blink, the world passing by me in slow motion. Arms wrap around me, and I inhale David's familiar scent. "What happened? Are you okay?"

"Ma'am," an officer says quietly. "Ma'am, we need to get a statement."

I blink again, and the world snaps back into real-time. "Amelia," I say, and run to the pantry. When I open the door, I see her huddled on the floor, arms wrapped around her knees and the ragged teddy bear. She's rocking back and forth and sobbing.

"Oh baby, come here," I say as I fall to the floor and pull her into my lap. "It's okay, baby. Everything is okay now. I've got you. Your mama is okay."

The officer leans against the door frame, his black hair falling into his eyes as he studies us, considering the situation. Finally he squats and sits on the floor next to me.

"Ma'am, I know that this is the last thing that you want to do right now. But this is the only way we can find out what happened and protect everyone involved," he says gently.

I nod, and then, while I rock my niece in my lap, I cover her ears gently with my hands and tell him everything. David watches from where he stands just outside the pantry door, sadness etching his features. But I can't think about him, not right now.

"He's being taken into the station," the officer finally says.

"We will be pressing charges," I assure him as he stands. He nods and retreats, leaving behind a void of pain and crashing adrenaline. My head pounds, and the wave of all the emotions hits my body like a tranquilizer gun. I feel the crash but know that I can't stop it. I can't stand still. My sister and my niece need me.

David helps me up while I still hold Amelia in my arms. I carry her to my room and tuck her under the covers. I pick the cheeriest Christmas movie I can find on TV. I go back to the entryway for Jo and guide her into the bed beside Amelia. I crawl in next, pulling them into me. It's a tight fit in my double bed, but we all need each other right now.

David murmurs something about making sure the door will close and disappears. I wanted him to fight for me, to fight for the girls I love. But I know now that will never be the case with him. And, as I hear the door to my house close and the shuffle to cover the spot in the door Dale blew apart, I know this is the death knell in our relationship.

I thought it would hurt more. Logically, I know it should, but I can't manage to think past my family next to me.

Chapter 29

FRANK

DECEMBER 12, PRESENT DAY

I sleep fitfully, my muscles aching as I spend my dreams riding my ATV through the snow, unable to see anything around me. I'm freezing, searching for something… no, someone. But I don't know who it is. I push my foot down on the pedal, urging my ATV to crawl through the snow, frigid air swirling around me and ripping the breath from my lungs. The vehicle's wheels catch and spin, over and over, until I've lost track of where I am. My body is freezing, and I'm disoriented in the ghostly pale woods. It's as if I'm stuck indefinitely, with no clue how to move forward or retreat. Panic begins to seize me, making my heart churn. And I'm not scared for myself—but because someone needs me and I can't get to them. I hit the gas and the wheels spin in place again.

A light flares to life in the distance. It's warm and inviting, full of warmth, welcome, and hope. Determination filters into me. I focus and ease into the gas pedal. Slowly, my ATV moves forward, the snow melting as I get closer to the light source. I'm no longer spinning out in the ice but propelling forward, chasing that delicious heat.

"Papa," a voice echoes around me, like a voice in a canyon. I look, searching for its source. When I don't find it, I keep going.

"Papa, are you okay?" My whole body rocks.

My eyes fly open, my heart thundering inside my chest.

"Papa?"

I look up to see Julia leaning down over me, her face framed by messy, dark hair.

"Everything okay, Juju Bug?" I grumble out.

"Yes. But I'm hungry, and you weren't waking up. I would get myself some cereal, but you told me not to go outside for any reason, even to get milk."

"That's a smart girl," I reply.

"Do you think Miss Margie would mind if you helped me?" she asks.

"Why would she mind?"

"Because you are keeping her warm," Julia replies in a tone that suggests that I'm an idiot.

That's when I realize that I've got my arms wrapped not around my pillow but tucked firmly around Margie, holding her against my chest. She smells good, like cinnamon, coffee, and apples. I guess we both got cold in the night.

"Right, well, it did get chilly last night," I say casually.

Margie stirs in my arms, body moving against my own. And all I want to do is pull her in closer, to hold her against me, and breathe in her cozy scent. She stretches, then freezes. I watch as her hand slides up and over mine, where it's wrapped around her waist.

"Sorry," I whisper. "The spooning was an accident."

"Sure it was," she murmurs, but she doesn't pull away.

"Yay, Miss Margie is awake too!" Julia cheers. "Now we can all have breakfast together."

"Yes, well, don't forget Miss Margie is still injured," I say, reluctantly pulling away from the woman in my arms.

"And I am going to be the best nurse and bring her breakfast," Julia says delightedly. "I'll go change and get the tray," she says, darting off.

As soon as she's gone, I murmur, "Sorry about that."

"It's fine. Really. We must have been cold in our sleep," Margie says. I'm surprised by the lack of bite in her tone. And although I enjoy it when we battle, I like this even more.

"I just want to make sure we're okay?" I ask. I rest my hand gently on her shoulder, and she rolls over to look at me. Her autumnal hair falls around her like a starfish.

"Okay," she agrees. She moves and winces. "Except my ankle feels even worse."

"Don't worry. Nurse Julia and Doctor Campbell will take care of you."

I STREAM THE LOCAL NEWS reporting on the weather and road updates over my recently charged phone. The precipitation has moved out of the area, but the cold temperatures linger, keeping ice coating all of the roads. Electric company personnel work through the night to restore power to our area, but the outages are vast and encompass far more than just Ruston.

I'm grateful to have Margie here with us. Julia is wonderful company, but this perfectly encapsulated moment in time allows us to pretend to be a family together. We spend time playing "Go Fish" and pulling out dusty board games. Turns out Julia is an ace at the "Game of Life," and Margie cleans up at "Guess Who?"

It doesn't take long for Margie to fit seamlessly into our space. Throughout the day, I check on her injured ankle. The color has deepened to a mottled bluish-black and looks terrible. When I attempt to rotate it to get a better look, Margie cries out in pain. Julia makes it her personal mission to place snow and ice in grocery bags and place them on Margie's swollen ankle. Fortunately, I am well stocked with Tylenol and ibuprofen, though I don't know that they do much good. Margie will need to get to a hospital once the roads are cleared, but we still don't know when that will be.

We stay in touch with Jason and Emma, who are still stranded in Dallas. Although most of the highways have been cleared, they couldn't get to their house in Ruston right now, even if they wanted to. When we FaceTime, I try to encourage them to enjoy their alone time together and tell them that Julia is in good hands, especially since my neighbor is staying with us. Jason lifts an eyebrow at this revelation but says nothing.

I charge up Margie's phone using my truck. When she turns it back on, she's immediately flooded with texts and voice messages from Amelia, sick with worry. Margie calls her, and even though her phone isn't on speaker, I can still hear Amelia lay into her about scaring her half to death. Margie finally manages to explain what happened, and I pretend not to notice that her hands tremble at the re-telling.

When she hangs up, Margie turns to look at me. "Well, the Christmas Market has been moved back a week. Poor Lia still wants to save it. She's put so much work into it. But I don't know if anyone will even be able to come to it at this point. We need the sun to emerge and the frigid temperatures to move back up north where they belong."

"Guess that gives me more time to make inventory, especially since I can't get to work right now anyway."

"Once again you have the advantage," Margie says, nodding at her battered foot. "Good thing I managed to make a bunch of items before this happened. I just hope they aren't frozen solid."

"No need to be a sore loser."

"Who said anything about losing?" she demands. Her cheeks flush, ready for battle.

The sight of her so alive and ready to challenge me, despite everything that has happened over the past twenty-four hours, charges my desire for her even more. I lean toward her as if hooked and reeled in by something supernatural. I can't help my forward momentum, but I force myself to stop, aware that I told her we would take things between us slowly. And friendship doesn't mean kissing. Margie stares at me, eyes darting across my face, my lips, my eyes. But she doesn't pull away. Slowly, so slowly, she leans toward me.

My lips hover over hers, and we pause mere centimeters apart. I can feel her warm, minty, toothpaste-scented breath coast over my lips. It's intoxicating, igniting a flame inside my belly. I lean forward again until our lips are a hair's breadth apart. I tilt my head, allowing my bottom lip to brush against hers just the slightest bit. It sends shockwaves of desire rolling through my body. I'm shaking, I realize. Actually trembling with desire. I cup her jaw, my thumb brushing along her cheekbone.

"Papa!" Julia calls, running into the room.

Margie and I pull apart like we were struck by lightning, both of us breathing like we hiked up a hill. It takes a second for me to pull myself out of my desire-addled state and focus on my granddaughter. I rub my hand over my face and down my beard, which has grown out over the past couple of days without an electric trimmer to keep it close-cropped.

"Papa, I just saw a reindeer!" Julia shouts. "Do you think it was one of Santa's?"

"We still have a couple of weeks until Christmas, but maybe it was here early checking things out," I say. My voice is raspy, still clogged with desire after the almost-kiss that just passed between Margie and me.

"That is so neat! I can't wait for Santa to come. Do you think he'll bring me an American Girl Doll? Oh, or maybe a kitten? I really want a kitten," Julia continues. And I'm both flustered by her interrupting the moment and relieved she didn't pick up on anything different between Margie and me.

"I'm not sure if now is the best time for a kitten, Juju Bug. I think Santa has to get permission from your parents before placing an animal under the tree."

She visibly wilts, but only for a moment. "Maybe Santa will bring Miss Margie a kitten. You live alone. I bet you and a kitten would be good friends," she says. "And then I could come over and visit it all the time. I'd help take care of it."

Julia seems so hopeful, and I hate having to take any form of joy away from her.

"Well, now, Julia," I start.

"What Santa brings is always a surprise," Margie says at the same time. "So there's no telling. But what do you think we should try to cook over the fire for dinner tonight?"

Margie is so skilled at redirecting Julia that she doesn't even notice. I should take notes.

THE REST OF THE DAY PASSES in quiet moments. We cook canned ravioli in a pot over the fire. Not the healthiest dinner, but it gets the job done. Julia takes her role as nurse seriously, even pretending to take Margie's blood pressure. Margie, to her credit, plays along, though she shies away when either of us tries to inspect her still-swollen ankle.

All too soon, it's dark outside again. I charged my phone in the truck again today, and when Julia begs me to play Christmas music, I can't deny her. I stream instrumental versions of classic Christmas songs. And in between the roaring, crackling fire lighting the darkened room, the woodsmoke, and the small Christmas tree, this moment feels like something snatched straight from the pages of a storybook. By eight p.m., the soft, instrumental music has lulled Julia to sleep, and Margie and I are the only two awake.

"It's still so cold," she says, rubbing her hands together. "I wish I would have thought to grab my liquor."

"Fortunately, I keep it in stock. As long as Jack Daniels is okay?"

She smiles fondly. "Hell, I'll take anything at this point. Yes, please."

"On the rocks? I'm sure I can get some snow or…"

"Hell no, I'm freezing. Room temp whiskey is chillier than normal anyway."

I pour us each a glass and settle onto the couch next to her. We sip in silence, enjoying the violin strings singing out "I'm Dreaming of a White Christmas."

"I don't think this is quite what the composer had in mind," I say, looking at the icy ground outside my window.

"I don't know, it's kind of cozy," Margie says. "And it made me stop trying so hard to do everything and actually take time to enjoy the season."

"Without all the annoying Christmas lights," I smirk.

"You said it, not me."

"Why don't you like Christmas?" I ask, turning the mood solemn.

"What makes you think that?"

"Just the way you get so, I don't know, irritated about all of it. The lights, the music, the trees."

She sighs. "Well, to be fair, I think any neighbor would get upset about those lights of yours."

"Maybe. But it's something else," I insist. "You mentioned something about it when we went to the Christmas Tree Farm together."

She hesitates and takes another sip of whiskey. I let the silence hang between us, allowing her to decide what to do with it.

"Once upon a time, there was a young woman," Margie begins, her voice raspy. "She was a lot, as some people might say. She talked often and without a filter. Most men were scared of her, and most women thought she was a bitch. But she didn't mind. Not really. She thrived on pursuing the things she loved and watching over her little sister. But then, one day, the young woman met a man. This man thought her stubbornness was funny. He admired the way she figured things out and pursued what she wanted without apology. And slowly, the young woman began to see what this whole romance thing was really about. She found value in companionship and began to share her life with the man." Margie pauses and takes another sip of whiskey.

"But as much as the young woman wanted companionship and romance, she was, at her very core, a protector. And when her sister and her niece were abused by a terrible man, she would stop at nothing to protect them. She'd sacrifice anything, even herself, if it meant keeping them safe. And it turns out her man only wanted a strong, persistent woman if she was those things for him and him alone. In the end, the young woman chose those who needed her, not the man who thought he wanted her."

She tosses back the last of the whiskey and sinks into the couch.

"Well, that man sounds like a dickhead," I say, taking the last swig of my Jack Daniels.

She chuffs. "Or a perceptive genius who knew when to escape a bad situation," she says, looking down into her now-empty glass.

"Margie," I hesitate. "You chose Amelia and… her mom? Over him?"

She nods.

"I think that makes you brave."

"Don't coddle me," she says, sounding defeated.

"I'm not. I mean it. I would do the same as you did for my sons. For Julia. I get it."

She looks up from her glass at me, tears hovering on the edges of her lower lashes. She glances at where Julia sleeps, then back at me.

"I suppose you do," she says simply.

The desire that formed between us earlier snaps to life again. But I'm cautious with it this time, intent on keeping it burning. I don't want to let either of us snuff it out before it has a chance to kindle this time. We stare at each other intently.

"I think we should go to sleep," Margie says, breaking the silence and sitting her glass on the side table.

"Okay," I allow.

We slide under our individual blankets, then roll to our sides to stare at each other.

"I'm scared," she finally says.

"Of what?"

"That when this is all over, when I go back to my house, and we stop playing at family here, that this thing between us will disappear. That maybe I'm imagining it all."

"Margie, I promise. I'm not going anywhere." I hesitate. Consider. "Can I kiss you?"

Her cheeks flame. An eternity seems to pass. Finally, she whispers, "Yes."

I lean in slowly, giving her time to back out if she wants to. But this time, when I get within an inch of her lips, she surges forward, pressing her mouth to mine. Our teeth clash, and noses knock. Nothing about the kiss is smooth or enjoyable. Margie immediately pulls away.

"Well, that was awkward," she whispers, and we both laugh.

"Let's try again," I say. I lean in slowly and press my lips to hers. I move my mouth gently, allowing us to get used to the sensation. I raise my hand and cup her face, and she reaches out and slides a hand around the back of my head, her fingers tangling in my hair. We find a rhythm, lips moving against lips. Heat rushes down my chest and into my core, simmering and growing. And when I feel her tongue trace the seam of my lips, I let out a quiet gasp and open for her. It's strange kissing someone new. Strange, but wonderful and delicious. We're tentative and exploratory, both of us becoming reacquainted with something we haven't explored in years. I ache to keep going, to learn her body, but I know we're not ready for that, not yet.

Especially not with a child in the same room. We seem to have that thought at the same time and pull back to look at the sleeping child in question.

"That was… nice," Margie whispers.

"Just nice?" I ask.

"It was very nice?" she asks and chuckles.

"I'll take it," I agree. "Good night, Margie."

"Good night, Frank."

I move back to my side of the sleeper sofa and find my pillow. I settle in, but before I go to sleep, Margie's hand finds mine beneath the blankets. And, together, we fall asleep.

Chapter 30

MARGIE

DECEMBER 13 , PRESENT DAY

Light surges to life behind my sleeping eyelids, waking me. I blink and squint, trying to figure out where I am and what's happening. I notice the familiar sleeper sofa, but everything looks different. And I realize that's because the room is illuminated by overhead fluorescent lighting and not just the warm flicker of a firelight. The power is back on.

I hear a groan beside me and turn to see Frank burying his face in his pillow. His granddaughter mimics him, doing the same.

"What time is it?" Frank mumbles.

I reach for my phone. "It's five a.m.," I say.

"Too early."

Frank climbs out of bed and turns all the lights back off, then gets back in. Without hesitation, he reaches for my hand and clasps it. He doesn't want this to end, either. But with the power restored, it's only a matter of time before we have to stop pretending.

"I SHOULD GO BACK TO MY HOUSE," I insist, looking down at my still-swollen ankle and internally wincing at the suggestion.

"No, you should go to the hospital and get that looked at," Frank insists. "I heard from a friend who lives down the road a mile or so that the crews are clearing the streets over by him now. We've got about another hour before we can get out. I'll take you to the hospital then. But, in the meantime, I'm going to make a real breakfast with the help of electricity."

"Papa, are you making eggs and bacon?" Julia asks.

"And toast and hashbrowns," he agrees.

Soon, the kitchen is filled with the smells of salt and fat, and all the fried goodness that makes breakfast the best meal of the day. He even has his coffeemaker up and brewing, and that first sip is the best thing I've tasted in a week.

"Your mom and dad are coming home today, Juju Bug," Frank says to his granddaughter. We both expect her usual cheeriness, but instead, she visibly wilts. "What is it, Julia? Are you going to miss playing with Biscuit?"

"I don't want to move to Dallas," she says. "I don't want to be brave." Then she starts to cry.

"Come here, Julia," I say, opening my arms to the little girl. She comes to me readily, curling up in my lap. "It's going to be okay. Remember what you told me? This is just for a short time. And then when you get back, we should have a party at my house."

She peeks up at me. "Really? A party? Can it be in your she-shed?"

I chuckle. "Of course. You can bring Biscuit, too."

"And Papa," she insists.

I glance at Frank, whose heart is fully in his eyes. "And your Papa," I agree.

THE CRUNCHING AND GRINDING alert us to something going on outside. I can't jump up, but Julia readily investigates, reporting that big trucks are driving on the road with giant shovels attached to the front and salt shakers on the backs.

"I guess that means it's time to go to the hospital," Frank says. "Julia, I know you don't like going–"

"I will go to help Miss Margie at the hospital," Julia says confidently. "Because I know more than the doctors and nurses do."

We both smile at her. Frank encourages her to get dressed.

It takes a little bit of shuffling, but soon, I'm sitting in the passenger seat of Frank's truck, blinking at the snow and ice reflecting the bright sunlight back at me. Everywhere I look, things are melting and dripping: branches, the house, Frank's yard decorations. It's as if the world is mourning that things have to go back to the way they were.

Our drive to the hospital is quiet, both of us lost in our own worlds. Even Julia seems to sense that we all need a moment to process everything and sits quietly in the rear seat of Frank's extended cab, staring out the window.

The hospital is quiet when we arrive. It turns out that most people stayed inside their homes and out of trouble during the ice storm. When I go back to a room, I tell Frank that I've got this.

As if to reinforce my claim, Amelia bursts through the hospital doors. She runs to me, wraps me up in her arms, and starts sobbing. She murmurs about how scared she has been and how upset she is that she couldn't get to me. I glance up to see Amelia's husband, Rhett, shaking hands with Frank and murmuring words of gratitude. And, despite being surrounded by white walls, a thick cloud of antiseptic, beeping monitors, and ringing phones, I suddenly don't feel so alone.

That is until Frank takes one last wistful look at me, eyes crinkling, and turns to walk out of the hospital's automatic doors with Julia's hand tucked inside his own. When he leaves, I feel his absence like a physical thing. My memories of David leaving start to overlap with the present, and panic rises in my chest. I have to stop this right now. I close my eyes and inhale Amelia's familiar scent, focusing on the way her arms wrap tightly around me. I exhale.

"Come on back, Ms. Murphy," a nurse says.

Amelia follows me back to the room and sits in a chair beside the hospital bed. When the doctor comes in and inspects my ankle, I see Amelia wince. I do, too. After more than two days, my entire foot and ankle look like they've been chewed on by a beaver and spit back out again.

"Let's get some x-rays and go from there," Dr. Patterson says.

IT'S NOT LONG BEFORE the doctor returns and pulls the x-ray up on his computer screen.

"You see this right here," he asks, using a stylus to indicate a small line. "That is a hairline fracture. The good news is that I don't think this will require surgery. The bad news is that you aren't going to be able to resume normal activity for at least eight weeks. Let's get you in a walking boot and see how that goes."

Although I'm relieved to be able to walk out of the hospital on my own two feet, I'm disoriented. I still feel like the past forty-eight hours were a fever dream I've been forcefully awoken from.

Amelia helps me get settled at home, fretting over me the whole time. She and Rhett make sure all my groceries are back in my house and even run to the store to help me restock. They stay for a while, catching me up on the chaos that erupted over the past two days. Amelia and Rhett lost power at their house, but their road was one of the first ones cleared. Their power was restored less than twenty-four hours later. And when they couldn't reach me, they tried to drive to me but couldn't get through. Amelia said they were on the verge of asking their neighbor if they could borrow their ATV and a jon boat to haul me out of my house like an inner tube behind a ski boat when I finally called her.

"Lord, that's all I need. For this community to see me ride in a jon boat behind Amelia on an ATV."

"Maybe you could hold up a sign advertising your business," Rhett deadpans, and we all laugh.

"I'm so glad Frank came to your rescue. I feel sick just thinking about what would have happened if he wasn't there. Your old neighbor certainly couldn't have done that," Amelia says.

"I'm grateful too," I say quietly, still feeling strange about acknowledging our time together in Frank's house to someone else. That time feels sacred, like a secret held just between Frank, Julia, and myself.

I clear my throat and change the subject. "So, what about the Christmas Market?"

"Ugh. It's been a mess, but it's still on, just postponed by a week. The roads are being cleared as we speak, and I think everyone is ready for a little Christmas cheer. But, Aunt Margie, do you think you'll still be able to participate with your foot in a boot?"

"I can cook a little more if I need to, but I just about have everything ready to go. Though, oddly, a few things are missing from my inventory. I'm short two jars of peach jam, one of my 'Kiss the Queen' aprons, and even some of my labeling supplies are missing. It's weird. I never misplace my inventory."

"Probably just lost in the shuffle somewhere," Amelia says. "Besides, your YouTube and Instagram campaigns to get people to donate to your charity has taken off like wildfire." Amelia chuckles. "That was so very you, Aunt Margie. I can't wait to see the final sales and donation counts."

THE NEXT DAY IS QUIET, and I find myself mourning the loss of company more so than ever. I have always enjoyed being alone, but after a saturation of time with Frank and Julia, everything feels lifeless. The longer the quiet goes on, the more I question whether any of it really happened at all. The only thing grounding me in reality is my booted foot and the continued surges of pain it causes.

I pick up my phone and consider texting Frank, but it feels desperate somehow. Like I'm chasing someone who has better things to do. My pride just won't let me do it. I can't stand the thought of being scorned and looking like a desperate fool in the attempt to establish something that was never truly there to begin with.

The walking boot is manageable, if still painful on my swollen ankle. It at least allows me to shift my weight to the heel of my foot and get around better. I'm heel-to-toe walking slowly through my house to my coffeemaker when a knock sounds at my front door. My heart beats with hope that I desperately try to squash.

"Just a minute," I call out, then make my way to the front door.

I'm mentally preparing myself to have to tell the young men at the door that I am not interested in becoming Mormon, thank-you-very-much, but when I open it, a familiar face greets me and sends a surge of relief through my body that is so potent that I actually go weak in the knees and have to catch myself on the door frame.

Frank swoops in to catch me, his arm sliding around my waist. "Sit down, Margie. I've got you." His deep voice rumbles through me and only serves to weaken my knees further. I should be embarrassed by my visceral reaction to his presence, but all I want to do is crawl into his arms and stay there.

"Stay here for one second; let me just set this down," he murmurs. He's gone for a brief moment, and then he's back, his arm finding my waist.

"I'm okay, really," I insist, clutching for my dignity. "Just a little bout of weakness." But I don't let go of him. I want to reassure myself that he's really here. As if he knows what I'm thinking, Frank breaks out into a wide smile, the kind that shows his laugh lines in all their handsome glory. All I can do is stare, mesmerized by how even more attractive they make him.

"Come on," he whispers and presses a kiss to my forehead.

He helps me to the kitchen table and then retrieves his mysterious package.

"Roads are back open. This calls for a celebration," Frank says, sitting down a brown bag dotted with grease spots and a drink carrier with two lattes. "I went by Lattes and Lagniappe for some goodies."

"Where is Julia?" I ask, slightly embarrassed that I just now realized she's missing.

"Her parents arrived in town yesterday and came straight to my house. They missed their little girl. It's why it took me longer than I wanted to come check on you. I had to reassure them that Julia was well and ready to return to them."

The warmth that's been steadily growing in my belly since Frank arrived spreads to encompass my heart.

"Oh, I didn't expect you to come check on me," I say, looking down at the table, unfamiliar shyness creeping in.

I feel Frank's hand slide over mine where it rests on the table. It's warm, calloused presence is comforting. I look back up at him.

"I told you I'm not going anywhere," Frank says seriously. "Besides, what kind of man would I be if I just abandoned you after my daring search and rescue?" His eyes crinkle. "Now, where are your plates? Let's eat."

It turns out that Frank, unsure of what I wanted, picked up both savory and sweet items. There are a couple of breakfast sandwiches and Amelia's favorite chocolate croissants. And my coffee? Milk and cinnamon. He remembered. That detail, more than anything else, sends my heart fluttering. I'd never admit it to anyone, but one of my greatest desires was to be with someone who saw those little details about me and memorized them without prompting. I realize that I know how Frank likes his coffee, too.

"Let me guess," I say conspiratorially. "That's a honey latte."

"With cinnamon on top," he finishes for me.

"I thought we weren't doing morning coffee together unless you won the charity bet?" I challenge.

"The bet was coffee at my house on Saturdays. This is neither my house nor is it Saturday," he responds easily.

"And your work?"

He sighs and settles back in the chair, slowly spinning his coffee cup and looking at the cardboard insulated holder. "The farm is a mess, and they still don't have power. I'm going over tomorrow to help them clean up and figure out how to manage the crop that more than likely received irreparable damage in the storm." He sighs and rubs his face. "It's going to be a mess. I mostly work on crop planning and harvest schedules these days, but they need all the help they can get cleaning up broken branches and damaged land. They are giving the team one more day since many of them still can't leave their own houses. But once we go back tomorrow, I'm going to have to halt working on my pieces for the Christmas Market. I think I'll be okay. Let's face it, I'm a new business. I'll be lucky to make a handful of sales."

"Ah, but you're also handsome Santa Claus with the Yard of the Year," I encourage. "Don't count yourself out of the race just yet."

"Handsome, huh? Do you like me in the Santa suit, Margie?"

I flush instantly, from the bottoms of my feet to the tips of my ears.

"You do!" he crows, laughing. "Oh, this is too good. Margie, for someone who dislikes Christmas, I find it surprising that you have a Santa fetish, but I love it. Perhaps you and I were meant to be, after all."

His words throw an instant serious cloud over the moment. Frank reaches for where my hands cup my coffee cup and cradles them. His thumbs trace lightly along my knuckles. It's strangely erotic. His light touch sends waves of desire coursing through my body. And when I look up from our hands, I see that he's staring intently at me, his own desire touching every one of his features.

"Margie, I– Um. I would like to take you out on a date."

"Okay."

"Really? I expected you to fight me on it."

"Do you like it when I fight with you? Because I can turn this into an argument if you want me to."

He swallows. "Maybe a little. Sometimes."

"Fine. Frank, I don't know if that's a good idea. Perhaps we still need to sort through the yard insanity you've got going on first."

"Consider it sorted. I don't have to turn them on anymore."

I balk. "Seriously? You can't do that."

He raises an eyebrow. "I thought you hated the lights."

"I mean, I do," I allow. "But they are so very you, and the people around here love them."

"But you hate them. And Julia got overwhelmed by them. I don't know. Maybe they are a piece of my past I need to let go of."

"What do you mean?" I ask cautiously.

"The Christmas lights. They were my late wife's favorite thing. I do them as a memorial to her, as odd as that seems. That and because Julia loves them. But apparently, even she thinks they are too much now."

I watch as his mood turns dour, his thoughts getting caught up in the past. He pulls his hands back in retreat. *His late wife. Oh.*

"I think I'm the asshole here," I grudgingly admit. "I never knew. I mean, how could I have, I guess? But still. The lights bring you joy and a lot of other people happiness. I never stopped to consider anyone beyond myself."

I swallow and continue. "Do you want to talk about her? Your late wife?"

Frank's whole expression drops into sadness. "Do you want to hear this? Really? You and I are starting to, I don't know, build something between us. It seems like past loves are not the best topic of conversation."

"Frank," I say, reaching to grab his hands this time. "She is part of you. A big part of you. And I want to know everything about you. So yes, tell me about her. Will I be jealous? Probably. But that's only because she got so much time with you. She had your heart for what I imagine was a very long time. But she also helped you become the man you are now and raise the amazing kids you have. So yes, I want to know about her, know about you."

He blinks, surprised, but a bit of his smile returns.

Chapter 31

FRANK

DECEMBER 14, PRESENT DAY

I didn't think I could fall in love again after Cheryl. But right now, with Margie's words, her request, her thoughtfulness. It might be possible. And she's right. The only way I can move forward with Margie is to share every part of me, even the parts that still hurt to think about.

I squeeze Margie's hands.

"Cheryl was my high school sweetheart," I sigh. "And I always thought that I was the luckiest man alive to meet the great love of my life in the very first woman I ever dated. I didn't have to wade through ugly dating and break-ups. I was drawn to her instantly, and she to me. We just clicked. W-e dated all through high school, and once we graduated, I went to technical school to learn the ins and outs of farming, and Cheryl became a nurse. We had a simple life, really. Just like how we found each other, everything always felt like it was meant to be.

"We weren't perfect, of course. We argued on occasion, usually over stupid stuff. Cheryl loved the holidays, especially Christmas. I thought buying lights and decorations was a waste of money, but she was having none of it. She brought some lights from her childhood home the first year we were married. And then, every year after, she bought something else in the post-Christmas clearance sales. Within a few years, we had a modestly decorated yard. And my calloused heart slowly changed as I saw how much joy those decorations brought her every year.

"And then our first child was born. Jason is the mirror image of his mother. He has her dark hair and eyes, just like Julia, actually. And he loved those lights as much as she did. It's amazing what having a child does to your brain chemistry. I went from doing a fair impression of the Grinch every year, to shopping with Jason and Cheryl for new things to add to our yard. And then our second son, Drew, came along, and, no surprise, he also loved the lights. It just became our thing."

I pause and look at Margie to see how she's handling all this. But she hasn't faltered and continues to watch me steadily, intently.

"Our lives were not remarkable. We were a simple family, but we did our best to provide for our children. Once the babies came along, Cheryl wanted to be home with them, so she switched to working one weekend shift every other week, which meant I got that as one-on-one time with my boys. I loved it, being a dad, being a husband."

I see Margie's shoulders sink slightly, but she doesn't say anything. When she notices I'm staring, she clears her throat. "Please continue, if you're comfortable doing so."

"You seem upset. I don't want to hurt you, Margie," I hesitate.

"I have some painful things in my past, and some of your words are landing on tender places in my soul. But it's okay. I mean it. I want to hear your story," she encourages.

"You're sure?" When she nods, I continue. "All this to say that we had a good life. We struggled financially some, but love managed to fill in the cracks. When our boys grew up and moved out, we mourned their departure, but it also drew us closer to each other."

I have to stop, remembering the look on Cheryl's face when Drew left for college, the way she held in her tears until we drove off from his dorm. The way we clutched each other and cried with deep, heaping sobs. The feeling of loss as we passed by Drew's bedroom. The overwhelming silence that permeated every room of our home. But it also forced us to reconnect as husband and wife. And slowly the tears were replaced with shared laughter and wrinkles. With cups of coffee on the front porch.

"But the boys always came back for Christmas to help decorate. And when Jason and Emma married, and then again when Julia was born, Cheryl and I thought we had won the lottery. A little girl in the family brought new life to us. And you see how she is. Julia is a ray of light, a happy child with a big imagination. And then, everything changed again. It seemed like all the good things we had in life for so long were an early advance on the bad things we'd have to pay back later. First Julia got sick, and then Cheryl got sick."

My voice catches on the last word and Margie moves her chair closer to mine. She slides her arm around my shoulders and squeezes me. She's quiet, allowing me to decide how to proceed. I take a deep breath.

"Julia had a lot of weird things happen. Swollen joints, she couldn't walk. Jason and Emma were worried messes and were constantly taking her to hospitals in Dallas and New Orleans. And Cheryl was not herself. At first, I thought she was depressed over Julia's health, but then she had so much pain that even sitting up in the morning hurt her. By the time we finally took her to the doctor, we learned she had late-stage myeloma. It goes without saying that it didn't end well."

I take a moment and rub my hand over my eyes, steadying myself. "We only had a short time with her after that. Cheryl didn't want to do aggressive treatment. She told me she was too tired and in too much pain. I was furious at her for giving up, but ultimately, it was her choice. We lost her just six months later. That was just over three years ago."

"I was devastated and became a shell of myself. I lost hope, lost my joy. I pulled it together for Julia. She became the only person who could make me smile. And Biscuit became my constant companion. It's like he knew I needed something to ground me in this world instead of constantly pining for the world to come. He would follow me around the house and sit on my feet."

"He's good at that," Margie concedes.

"And when, six months after Cheryl's death, three-year-old Julia asked for 'lights' at Christmas, I found something I could throw myself into. Still do. It's probably not healthy, but it's cathartic. It's like I'm aggressively telling the world that I haven't forgotten my late wife, and they can't either."

We sit in silence for several minutes. I feel drained like my soul has been rung out and left to dry.

"You are a strong man, Frank Campbell. And I hate that life dealt you such a raw hand all at once," Margie finally says, emotion clogging her voice. She pulls me into a hug, and I allow my head to fall to her shoulder, soaking in her warmth and comfort. It feels good, all of it. The emotional purge, the tight embrace. Margie.

I lean back and look up at her. Clearing my throat, I say, "And I didn't think I could ever find happiness, at least not like that, ever again. I found it in Julia, in my sons. But I thought my heart would forever be buried in the cemetery with Cheryl. I was content with that. And then," I swallow. I reach up and brush a lock of hair out of Margie's eyes, marveling at the glints of copper and gray. "And then I met you."

"Frank, I don't know what to say," she confesses.

"You don't have to say anything. You don't owe me anything. I just wanted you to know that, in your own stubborn, caring, chaotic way, you helped bring me back to life."

She brushes her thumb across my cheek, swiping a tear away. Then she leans in and kisses my forehead in benediction. My heart soars as if the chains have been tossed away, and it feels light, free, and reinvigorated.

I lean into her, slowly pressing my lips to Margie's. They are soft and full. She kisses me back, pouring her own emotions into the kiss. Our mouths are slow, exploratory. Our kisses are full of emotion and care. It's the comfort I didn't know I needed. I open my mouth and she does the same. Our tongues slide together tentatively, just like that night in my house. There is no way I'm letting this go, letting it melt away permanently with the ice storm. She tugs me into her, her full breasts pressing into my chest. I groan, surprising us both. She leans away slightly, her expression asking if this is okay.

I reach up and cup her face, pulling her back to me. She comes willingly. I slide my hand over her thigh, loving the curves I find there. I greedily reach for her hip and tug. It's a bit clumsy with her boot, but I manage to get her to straddle my lap. Her weight grounds me, and heat licks down my spine.

She pulls back. "Frank, I'm too heavy to sit on you like this. I'm going to break you in half." She laughs a little, but I can tell she's self-conscious.

"I'm not that delicate, baby." And I pull her into my waist more tightly to prove my point. She gasps when she feels how aroused I am. "Is this okay?" I whisper. "I know we said we were going to take things slow."

"This is perfect," she whispers. "But I'm afraid I don't have much experience in this department. So you better let me know if I mess something up."

I laugh. "I don't think that's possible," I say.

"Want to bet?" she asks with mischief. "What if I bit you?"

"Then I'd spank you," I say, and I thrust into her. She gasps.

"I do believe I like this new form of fighting, Mr. Campbell," she says huskily.

"It only gets better from here," I say, then I plunge back into the kiss.

I feel Margie's fingers play with the hair at the back of my neck. I slide my hands along her back, tracing the length of her spine. I devour the small sounds of passion that she makes, moving my mouth to her neck to draw out more.

It's been a long time since I've done anything like this. Even before Cheryl's death, she was sick, and before that, we were dealing with the emotional storm of Julia's illness. Sex became a rare luxury with my late wife, and when we did, on the rare occasion, make love, it was the sex of longtime partners who took from each other in comfort. This passion is something I had forgotten about. Something I didn't realize I still possessed. I love it. I crave it. I need more of it.

I give myself over to making out with the woman in my lap. I go with my instincts, my hands roaming over her body. She's more tentative, her hands locked in place behind my neck.

"It's okay," I whisper into her ear. "You can touch me wherever you want to. You have my enthusiastic consent."

She laughs but takes me up on my suggestion. Slowly, cautiously, Margie's hands move to my shoulders, then down to my chest. Her hands twist into my shirt, pulling, gripping, holding on for dear life. I let my hands slide down to her ass and pull her into me. It's intoxicating.

We grind together there in her kitchen, our coffees gone cold. I lean in and whisper, "Maybe we should take this somewhere more comfortable."

She hesitates. Then, "Okay."

Just as we start to stand, a knock sounds at the front door. I freeze, disoriented. The knock comes again.

"Shit," she mutters. "Amelia. I forgot," she murmurs in irritation. She tries to scramble out of my lap and nearly topples over when her boot slams into the chair leg.

"Hang on, I'll help you." I help her balance and stand, then rise in front of her. Margie stands about four inches shorter than me, and I reach down to pat her tousled hair down into something slightly more contained.

"Tell me the truth, do I look as chaotic as I feel?" she asks.

"Um," I start.

"Don't you lie to me, Frank Campbell."

I laugh, loving her directness. "I mean, your lips are swollen, and you have some beard burn here," I say, pointing to her neck.

"Dammit," she mutters. The knock comes again.

"Margie? Are you okay? Hold on, I'll get my key," Amelia calls through the door.

"I'm coming!" she calls out, then looks at me. We both laugh at the innuendo, fueled by the desire still coursing through both our bodies.

I lean in and whisper, "Maybe not today, but soon you will be." And then I peck her cheek and retreat to the bathroom to get my raging hard-on under control.

I listen as the front door opens and Amelia and Rhett embrace Margie. I run the cold water and cup it in my hands, thrusting my face into it. It's the closest thing I've got to a cold shower at the moment.

When I step out of the bathroom, I see Amelia fussing over her aunt. "Are you sure you're okay? You're flushed. Do you have a fever?"

"I said I'm fine," Margie says, pushing her away.

"Oh, hi Frank," Rhett says softly. The room freezes and everyone turns to look at me. I rub my hand along the back of my neck.

"Um, hi," I say.

"Oh, I didn't know you had company, Aunt Margie. Where are my manners? How are you Frank?" Amelia walks up to me and gives me a hug, like we've known each other for years. "I can't thank you enough for all you did to help my aunt during the ice storm."

"It's nothing," I try to brush off the praise.

"It's everything," she says firmly. And, in that moment, I can see Margie's influence shining through the eyes of her niece.

"Frank here stopped by to check on me," Margie says.

"Well, isn't that kind?" Amelia says. "Are you coming with us over to the convention center?" When it becomes clear that I'm not sure what's going on, Amelia furrows her brows in confusion. "Didn't Margie tell you we were coming over to help her move all of her booth supplies in for the Christmas Market since she's down with a bad foot?"

"Oh, that's right," I allow. "Sorry. I was just caught up in thinking about all the work I still need to do." The lie slides off my tongue easily. I don't want Amelia to know anything is happening between her aunt and me until Margie is ready for her to know. "Y'all go on ahead. I was just about to head back to my house and finish up a few of my own pieces. I'll bring them over to the convention center later this week."

I start walking toward the door to leave but pause as I go to pass Margie. I want to kiss her goodbye, but I know this isn't the time and place. So I settle with, "It was good to see you. I'll check on you again later." She stares at me. The weight of emotions passing between us is tangible.

Amelia clears her throat, and we both dart our glances away. I hurry to the door.

"Frank," Amelia calls out. I pause and turn to look at her. "I'm so glad to see the two of you are getting along now. I think this means that, despite all the recent hurdles, this Christmas Market is destined for success."

I smile weakly, grateful to step outside into the cool air and clear my head. But as I walk back to my house, I can't hide the grin that seems to have found a permanent place on my face.

Chapter 32

MARGIE

DECEMBER 14, PRESENT DAY

The entire time Rhett and Amelia help load up my Christmas Market supplies, I'm a distracted mess. I try to pay attention to their conversation, but I'm still lost in that earth-shattering kiss. No, not just a kiss. That was a full-on make-out session. I didn't know I had that in me. I thought that part of me had shriveled up like a dried date. And yet, when Frank's lips touched my neck, I had an out-of-body experience. The rough brush of his beard, paired with the gentle caress of his full lips, will be a source of my fantasies for the rest of my life.

"Margie?" Rhett's gentle rasp breaks into my thoughts. I stare at him, confused. "I asked if you want those boxes in the shed closet loaded up too?"

"Oh, um, yes. Sorry. Those need to go, too."

He nods and goes to grab them. I have got to pull myself together.

It's not long before we're loaded up and driving to the convention center. Unfortunately, it is illegal to drive if your right foot is broken, so I'm at the mercy of whoever wants to shuffle me around Ruston at the moment.

Once we arrive, Amelia and Rhett start hauling in my supplies. I can at least tuck my table banner in under my arm, and slowly haul it to one of the two main tables by the convention center stage. Frank's booth will be right next to mine, so we can keep an eye on the status of the competition. I find myself smiling at the thought of him in a Santa suit, encouraging people to buy his wood carvings and signs. And I'm disappointed that I didn't once think to ask Frank if I could see his work while I stayed at his house. Though, I suppose I had other things on my mind over those two days.

I'm still feeling the injuries from my icy debacle and have to pause often while we set up. Fortunately, it doesn't take long to get things squared away.

"So, who is going to be your assistant for the Market?" Amelia asks.

"Well, aren't you?" I ask indignantly.

"Aunt Margie, I have to run this whole event. There is no way I can do that and help you run your booth."

I glance at Rhett to inquire if he'll help me, and he immediately bursts out laughing. I raise an eyebrow, but he just keeps laughing and shakes his head no. My fists find my hips. "Now you listen here, Rhett Hebert, you are my nephew-in-law, and when I need help–"

"Aunt Margie, he's going to be helping me, his wife. You have to find your own assistant," Amelia says.

"But nobody likes me!"

"Well, maybe you should try being nice," she encourages. I fold my arms and harumph. She continues, "Besides, that's not true. Lots of people like you. They're just scared of you."

"That's not helpful," I say, dryly.

"Sure it is; just consider the list of people who aren't scared of you and ask one of them," Amelia says as if that's as easy as pie.

"Well, it's a short list, and you and Rhett are occupied. Katie and

Jacob are in Dallas. Frank is my competition, and Annie Mae is in assisted living."

"I think you're forgetting the one person who has never been afraid of you, not even when you threatened her livelihood," Amelia says, trying to stifle a laugh.

"You don't mean Greta?" I say incredulously. "That woman exudes storm clouds and 'stay away from me' vibes like it's her job. That is not exactly good for business."

"Maybe she can scare people into buying your stuff," Amelia shrugs.

"I'm not sure whether to scold you or applaud you for your boldness."

Amelia laughs. "I learned it all from you, Aunt Margie."

"Can't argue with you there," I sigh. "Fine, I'll call Greta. Just remember that when your shoppers run out of here crying, this was your idea."

IT TURNS OUT THAT GRETA is delighted to assist me with the Market. I was shocked when she readily agreed, but then she confided that her real desire was to get to learn more about Frank, or as she is now calling him, "Sexy Claus." I have probably made a terrible mistake in allowing this to proceed, but I don't have any other options at the moment.

I'm mollified by the fact that Frank has stopped by my house every day since he brought over chocolate croissants and coffee. Well, mostly mollified. Except for the fact that Frank has decided that he is going to both court me like some kind of old-timey gentleman, and convince me to like Christmas.

It started small. He showed up one day with two packs of instant hot chocolate and marshmallows. He insisted I make myself comfortable while he heated them in the microwave and then served them up. We sat there for a solid ten minutes before he realized I hadn't taken a single sip of my hot chocolate.

"What's wrong?" he asked, melted marshmallow fluff clinging to his mustache.

I sighed and considered my words. But finally decided that if Frank really wanted to date me, the real me, then I needed to be myself. So I told him flat out that I didn't like hot chocolate. The way his jaw dropped made me laugh.

"Who the hell doesn't like hot chocolate?" he asked, offended.

"It just has a lot of bad memories attached to it. Besides, Lia always liked hot apple cider year-round, and drinking that at Christmas makes me far happier than the hot chocolate."

The next day, he showed up with apple cider packets.

When the knock comes at my door today, I'm already smiling as I hobble to the door. When I swing it open, Frank is leaning against the door frame, smirking like my own personal catnip. "Can I come in?"

"By all means," I say, swinging the door wider. "What's on your Kris Kringle agenda today? Baking cookies? Hanging stockings by the chimney with care?"

"I thought we might try watching a Christmas movie after I get off work tonight," he says, pulling me into a hug. His sawdust and pine scent wraps around me in a heady cloud.

"Tonight, huh? Like a date?"

"Something like that," he agrees easily.

We haven't so much as kissed since that day he came by my house to check on me. I know we agreed to take it slow, but I can't help but think that I imagined the whole thing. I want to kiss him again, but I'm scared he'll reject me and shatter my slowly building self-confidence into shambles. Especially since he hasn't initiated more than a hug since that time.

"Your house or mine?" I ask.

"Yours. My house has plenty of Christmas spirit already. Yours is the one that needs to be de-Scrooged."

I push him playfully, but he just laughs.

"And what about your items for the Christmas Market tomorrow? All done?"

He sighs. "Almost. But I'm tired, and I want to relax when I get home from work. I think I'm just going to sell what I've made so far. Besides, the Junior League will be very happy when you win the charity competition."

"You can't give up on me now," I say. "Just because we're this," I say, gesturing between us, "Doesn't mean you have to hand the competition win to me."

"Good Lord, woman, I'm not handing you the win. I'm just not going to break my back anymore because I'm tired, need my energy for the Christmas Market tomorrow, and I'd rather watch a movie with you tonight. Is that so terrible?"

"I s'pose not," I allow.

"Alright, I've got to get to work," he sighs and pulls back. I miss his warmth immediately. Frank presses a chaste kiss to my forehead, then turns and heads out to go to work for the day.

I love it. I hate it. I want more. And I hate myself for wanting more. This is exactly the position I never wanted to be in again—waiting on a man to care for me back.

Chapter 33

MARGIE

DECEMBER 22, 1998

When I wake up, the TV is blasting music from the DVD home screen of Miracle on 34th Street. Amelia is tucked into my side, my old teddy bear clasped under her arm, snoring softly. I turn to find Jo, but she's left my bed. I take my time scooting out from beneath Amelia, laying her down on the bed to continue sleeping off the day's trauma. I tuck her in and turn off the TV.

My neck is sore from falling asleep sitting up, and my shoulders ache with the coiled tension of fight or flight that flooded my body just a few hours ago when Dale made his violent appearance. The house is silent, lit only by the small Christmas tree in my living room. I wander to the front door and see that David temporarily patched the rifle-blasted hole for us. Tonight, at least, Dale is in jail. I flip the front porch lights on, then head to my guest room to check on Jo.

I ease my head into the door and peer inside. I expect to find Jo's sleeping form in the bed, but instead the bed is neatly made. Dread creeps up my spine and taps me on the shoulder. Something isn't right.

I step into the room and quietly call for my sister. When I don't get a response, I begin to spin out theories of Dale showing back up and grabbing her. I start to leave the room and call the police when I notice the envelope on her pillow. My heartbeat thrums in my ears and my stomach plummets as I reach for it, dreading what I'll find inside.

I turn on the bedside lamp and open the envelope. I unearth a piece of paper torn from a spiral notebook; side edges as jagged as the pain now ripping through my heart. I study the craggy, smeared handwriting, noticing how many of the words are scratched through or smeared as if my sister's writing was keeping time with her erratic thoughts.

Margie,

I have to go. Dale needs wants will come after me. ME. Not Amelia.

You must think I'm terrible. I am. I know it.

I'm leaving my daughter. But I'm not good for her, Margie. Not a good mom. I've only ever brought her pain. I can't take care of her. I can barely keep myself alive. I thought, for a moment this morning, that I could do it. I talked myself into it. I walked into the kitchen, determined to be the mother Amelia needs.

But as soon as I made the decision, Dale appeared. It was an omen, Margie, a sign that I can't be around Amelia anymore if she's going to live safely.

I don't want to keep moving forward. But I will. I will keep going because I don't want Dale going after our daughter. This is the best thing I can do for her, for you.

I'm sorry. I know you must hate me. Both of you. But that's something I will bear to keep her safe.

I am grateful for you. Amelia has always loved you most. She's in the best possible hands. It gives me peace to know that.

Thank you for taking us in. You've always been the better sister.

Please don't try to find me. I'm going somewhere far away. I am going to leave a note at my house for Dale, so he'll know that I'm not in town anymore when he gets out of jail.

I love you. I'm sorry. Jo

"Dammit," I snarl to the empty room and crumple the paper in my hands.

I sink my face into my hands and finally let myself feel everything that's happened over the past twenty-four hours. I never cry. It's not in my DNA. I power through and punch the problem in the face or cower it into submission. But, for the first time in a long time, I feel utterly helpless. There is nothing I can do to fix this.

And so, I let myself feel it all, and then the sobs start. Great, gasping sobs rack my body as I cry for my sister and think of all the ways her piece of shit husband destroyed the wonderful young woman she once was. I cry for Amelia and the parents she will never have, for the mother who has abandoned her. I cry for David because I know, without a doubt, that the path forward has been inexplicably chosen for me. He will go his own way, we will break our engagement, and his life will move on without me. I cry for his dashed dreams for both of us.

And then, finally, I cry for myself. I cry for the future I might have had in Charleston, for the family I pictured when I saw David kneeling in the yard with Amelia. I cry for the loss of my sister, my best friend for most of my life. I cry for the role of mother that's been thrust upon me, one I considered for the future but was not prepared for. And I cry for the person I will have to become in order to survive this and give Amelia the life she deserves. I will have to sacrifice many of the things I've craved: a future husband and my career.

My face is swollen and mottled by the time the tears finally stop.

I stand and look at myself in the mirror before me. I look like a ghost as if I've aged ten years in a single day–and perhaps I have. I study the woman before me, and the longer I look at her, the more I see past her shortcomings to her strength. I have always taken care of shit myself, always relied on myself to make sure that everything is as it should be. I allowed myself this moment. I felt sorry for myself. But, in reality, this time in my life is no different from all the others. I only have myself to rely on. But Amelia has more than just herself–she has me. And I'll be damned if I let anyone hurt my little girl.

Chapter 34

MARGIE

DECEMBER 18, PRESENT DAY

I've been a nervous wreck all day. I can't wait for Frank to come over and watch a movie tonight, but I'm terrified that he either won't show or that he will and tell me he's decided we are better off as friends. Or worse, he won't do or say anything at all and just keep me in this weird limbo we've found together.

But when the knock taps at my door right at seven p.m., I exhale and open the door. Frank stands in the door frame, lit by my front porch lights against the night sky and wearing red and green flannel, the perfect nod to Christmas. It's like he just entered the set for his cover shoot. I swoon, just a little. I open the door all the way and he steps in to hug me, just like he always does.

Biscuit follows behind him, and Frank looks at me sheepishly. "Hope it's okay to bring my dog? I should have asked earlier, but I've been working so much this week that Biscuit has been lonely and moping around the house."

I nod, "It's fine as long as he's on flea meds."

"I'd never let bugs infest my buddy here," he says, looking down. He glances back to me, and for just a second, I think he's going to kiss me. Then the moment slides past us like it never existed. My heart sinks.

"So, what movie did you have in mind for tonight?" I try to play it off like I'm not worried.

"I thought *It's a Wonderful Life* might be a good one," he says.

"Too long. Too sad. How about *Die Hard*?" I ask.

"That is not a Christmas movie," he says immediately.

"Is so," I insist.

"*Miracle on 34th Street*?" he tries again.

"I am trying not to cry, remember? Let's watch a movie with some Christmas joy."

He sighs and considers. "I know just the one. Come on, let's fix some apple cider."

"Spiked apple cider," I insist.

"As my lady commands," he says. And I swear there is a damn twinkle in his eye at his words.

I fix the apple ciders while Frank sits on my couch with Biscuit at his feet and navigates through my streaming services until he lands on the movie he wants. I settle in next to him, careful to preserve a slice of space between us, refusing to seem desperate.

"Seriously?" I ask when he selects the movie.

"What? It's a classic! Everyone loves Tim Allen. And it's not sad," Frank insists.

"It is a little sad; I mean, the way Scott Calvin starts packing on the pounds in record time makes me feel a little depressed," I say.

Frank nudges me with his elbow and we laugh, then settle in to watch *The Santa Clause*. Watching a movie together should be comfortable, but instead, the whole time, I'm hyper-aware of where Frank's body is in proximity to mine. We're not touching, but I can feel heat radiating off of him. He grabs the remote and pauses the movie. Biscuit stirs at our feet, getting up to turn in a circle and lay back down again.

"Margie, is everything okay?"

"Fine. Why?"

"You're just fidgeting a lot."

I fidget again, take a moment to try to steady myself, then give up. "Look, Frank, this is weird."

"Okay, I admit turning into Santa is weird but.."

"Not the movie. This," I say, pointing between us. "I don't know how to read you. Last week, we were making out in my kitchen like teenagers and talking about dating. And now you barely touch me. Did I do something wrong? Do you want to just be friends? Because if you do, then please have the decency to tell me because this not-knowing thing is driving me insane."

He stares at me for a moment, starts to talk, pauses, and starts again. "Margie, I thought you wanted to take things slow."

"I mean, I'm not ready to jump into marriage or anything, but you seemed to enjoy the kissing, and I definitely did. And then *nothing*. Was I bad at it? I mean, I know it's been a really long time, but going from you sticking your tongue down my throat to forehead kisses is a pretty drastic shift."

"No, it's not that. I thought you wanted me to slow down. Amelia showed up that day, and you seemed freaked out. And I don't want to scare you away. I thought I was laying it on too thick. I wanted to show you that I'm not going anywhere, no matter if things are physical between us or not."

"What are you saying? Did you like the kiss?" I need him to be clear.

"Hell yes, I liked the kiss. I can't stop thinking about it, to the point of distraction. I can't work on my woodworking projects when all I want to do is come over to your house, throw open your front door, push you up against a wall, and kiss you until I can't breathe."

"Oh."

"Yeah," he says, rubbing the back of his head.

"Well, why didn't you just say so?"

And then I reach for him. My lips meet his in a clash of lips and teeth, and he responds in turn. We're desperate for the touch we've both been yearning for for days.

Frank leans back slightly. "Margie, I don't want you to feel like you have to–"

"Frank. For goodness sake, shut up and kiss me."

And he does. His lips slide over mine, and his tongue licks into my mouth. I reach behind him and allow my hands to trail down his back, exploring him in a way I wasn't brave enough to do the last time we kissed. He groans, and his mouth finds my neck again, reigniting memories of his touch. I gasp with pleasure.

My hands find his chest, and I slide them over his pecs. I love feeling the muscle beneath his shirt. "Frank," I murmur between kisses. "Will you take your shirt off?"

He freezes, and embarrassment washes over me. I must have gone too far and asked for too much.

"Sorry, no, you don't have to. That was weird." I start rambling.

He reaches for the top button of his flannel shirt and unbuttons it. Then moves down to the next, releasing it slowly, so painfully slowly. I watch each button as he slides it free and reveals another tantalizing inch of skin. I could orgasm from this sight alone, this slow, deliberate unveiling. I can't look away. And when he finally unfastens the last button, he eases the shirt off his body. I allow myself to stare. He's fit, his body honed by a lifetime of hard labor. He's not etched and defined like a bodybuilder but lean and corded. Dark brown and gray hair dusts over his chest and down his stomach. I reach for him slowly and allow one finger to touch his chest. I trace the outlines of his muscles. It's oddly sensual, and he shivers with desire.

"God, why is that so sexy?" he grumbles, watching my finger's progression across his torso.

He reaches for my hand that's exploring his body and gently pulls it to his lips. Slowly, he guides my wandering finger into his mouth, licking it and sucking it. The sensation shoots heat straight to my core, and I groan. He looks at me, mischief in his eyes. "Now, your turn. Will you take off your shirt?"

I swallow and hesitate. But fair is fair, I suppose. I reach for the top button and try to seductively unbutton mine like he did, but I feel like an idiot. My cheeks heat as I fumble with the buttons.

"Let me help," Frank says gently, then reaches for my shirt buttons. With each one he unfastens, his knuckles brush my skin. It's heady. I want to lean into the touch, but I hold steady, letting him take his time as he unveils me.

When he reaches the final button, he pushes it open and stares his fill. I try not to squirm, but I'm curvy and not used to anyone looking at my body. I know I have stretch marks and cellulite, and I certainly don't toil away on a farm.

"Beautiful," he sighs. "May I touch you?"

I blink, surprised at his easy assessment. "Please," I whisper.

His hands trace the lines of my bra, exploring. When his fingers brush my nipples through the material, I groan.

"I really, *really* want to put my mouth on these," he rasps.

"Let me help you," I say, his desire making me more confident.

I reach behind me and undo my bra clasps, letting it slide to the floor. I want to cover myself. I'm fifty-two, and my large breasts aren't exactly perky and cute. But Frank reaches for them immediately, massaging them, his callouses feeling delicious against my skin. He looks up and meets my stare, his eyes glazed with desire. He leans in and kisses me, his tongue delving deep. He rubs my breasts and then eases me back onto the couch and crawls over me. His weight on top of me, his skin touching mine, sets me on fire. Our jeans rub together, and I can feel his length pressing into my core.

Slowly, he moves from my mouth down to one of my breasts. And when his mouth finds my nipple, I swear I see stars. He takes his time, licking, exploring. And then he moves to the other one, giving it the same deliberate attention.

"Beautiful," he whispers over and over. I've never been worshiped like this. Hell, I've only ever had sex with David, and that was decades ago, but he never made me feel like *this*.

"Margie," Frank whispers. "You have to tell me when you want me to stop, okay? I don't want you to feel like you have to do anything."

"Please don't stop." I didn't want to beg, not to a man, not ever. But I can't stop the plea that falls from my lips.

"Do you have a condom?" he asks.

I burst out laughing. "Frank, I haven't had sex since I was twenty-five."

"Well, I haven't used a condom since I was eighteen," he says, laughing at himself.

"Look, we're both clean, obviously. And the pregnancy ship sailed away with menopause when I was forty-seven. I think we're okay," I say wryly. "Though I may be terrible at sex. There's no way of knowing."

"Well, there is one way of knowing," Frank says with mischief, and then he kisses me again slowly, languidly.

After a few more minutes, I reach for the button of his jeans. He allows me to unfasten them, and we work them off together until he's down to a pair of...

"Are those Christmas boxer briefs?" He looks at me and blushes a deep shade of crimson.

"Yeah, well, I didn't think you'd be seeing these tonight. Cut me some slack."

I cackle and then he reaches for the button of my jeans. My laughter dies immediately. He leans back and helps me get them off, stopping to pull that damn boot off my foot along the way. Once that barrier is gone, I start to feel nervous. I'm practically a born-again virgin, and Frank was married, sexing it up for years.

"Hey, it's okay," Frank says, brushing my hair back from my face. I hate feeling weak, but I have to be honest with him if this is going to work.

"I'm just nervous. I can't really remember what I'm supposed to do," I confess.

"Just trust your instincts. And remember, we can stop anytime. I promise."

I nod, believing him. I'm so grateful that this moment right now, one I thought forever lost to me, is with him. He reaches for my underwear and slowly pulls them down my body and over my thighs. Then, he does the same with his own. I stare at the space between us, where we are bare before each other. My stomach swirls like a thousand dandelion seeds have taken flight inside of it. I glance up at his face and study the vulnerability there. And I remember that he has only ever had sex with one other person, too. And it's been years.

I reach up and cup his face, pulling him to me. He comes willingly. "It's okay to be scared," I whisper in his ear. He shudders. "We've got each other."

He reaches under my good leg and hikes it up over his hip. Then, slowly, he moves himself against my center, testing the water, getting the both of us used to the sensation. We let out simultaneous groans. He does that a few more times, and it's making me want to crawl out of my skin. I need him.

Finally, he eases into me. He goes slowly, mindful that it's been a very long time for me. And though I'm impatient, I'm glad that he takes his time. He stretches me, and the feeling is delicious, tight, and a little painful. I breathe deeply, forcing myself to relax and take him. When Frank slides all the way home, he gasps in pleasure.

"You feel so damn good," he rasps. He continues to move gently at first, but soon, my hands slide to his hips, and I'm urging him to move faster and deeper. The slight pain at his intrusion has given way to full-throttled pleasure as we lose ourselves in each other. I delight in every kiss, every thrust, as my body blossoms back to life under his touch. And, sooner than I hoped, we're both tumbling over the edge, calling out our pleasure as we come together.

Chapter 35

FRANK

DECEMBER 18, PRESENT DAY

I stare at the woman beneath me in awe. She's beautiful like this, her guard down and her heart open to me. It's a privilege not many get to witness, and her trust overwhelms me.

"You okay?" I ask her, brushing her hair back from her face.

"Fantastic," she says. "You?"

"Yeah, fantastic," I agree.

"Frank, do you want to spend the night? I mean, I know we have the Christmas Market tomorrow and all, but it's late and—"

"I'd love to," I say immediately. Probably too quickly.

She smiles. And it's so warm and genuine that it takes me aback. "My God, you are so beautiful," I tell her, the words escaping my mouth before I can stop them.

She rolls her eyes, but I can tell she likes the praise.

"Come on then. Let's take a shower and get to bed. We both have to be up bright and early tomorrow," she says.

I push myself off of her, then lean over and pull her to stand up next to me. I can tell, now that the sex is over, that she's feeling awkward. And I won't have that. Not at all. So I lean in and kiss her lips gently, pulling her naked body into mine and holding her close. Our hearts seem to find the same rhythm as our skin touches in every place possible. When I pull back, I can see that her anxiety has ebbed. I reach for her hand and together, we walk to her bedroom. Well I walk and she holds onto me, limping slightly.

After our showers, we crawl into Margie's bed. It's a double, so there's not much room for two adults, but I don't mind. I am in my Christmas boxer briefs and she dons a t-shirt and underwear. And as I pull her into me, relishing being the big spoon, I can't help but inhale the scent of her hair and sigh. Cinnamon, coffee, cider.

I hear Biscuit settle in on the floor beside us, and for the first time in a long time, I drift off to sleep in peace.

LOW WOOFS WAKE ME. Biscuit needs to be let out. Half asleep, I start my rote motion of rolling out of bed and into my slippers to let him out. But when I try to move, I realize there is someone next to me. I lean into Cheryl, pulling her close and pressing a kiss to her neck. But then her scent hits me. *No, not Cheryl.*

I blink and try to focus my sleep-blurred vision. Rusty hair and curves for days.

Memories of last night slam into me in a rush. My cheeks heat with pleasure, and my stomach heaves at the sudden and intense feeling of guilt. I thought of Cheryl as soon as I woke up this morning. *Is this a betrayal to my late wife? Are these thoughts about Cheryl a betrayal to Margie?*

I roll out of bed, and Margie murmurs, "Where are you going?"

"Letting Biscuit out, I'll be right back."

But the whole time I'm walking him outside, my thoughts are a tangled mess. I was so sure about last night. I promised Margie

I'd never abandon her, and I won't. But I've got to get my head on straight. I didn't expect this weird rush of confusion brought on by the muscle memory of having my wife in bed next to me for three decades would cause this morning.

I can't believe I woke up thinking about Cheryl. Not to mention the fact that after thirty committed years to one woman, I moved on to someone else. Does that make me a bad person? Did I just throw away a decades-long promise to my late wife?

I pace and mull it over as I watch as Biscuit trots across Margie's yard to mine, sniffing around. That's when I realize I forgot to turn on my Christmas lights last night. And with Margie in my arms, I even managed to forget my annual tribute to Cheryl.

I slide my hands up and yank at my hair, feeling conflicted and antsy, like a swarm of bees is threatening to escape from beneath my skin. I need to get my head on straight. I made Margie a promise not to abandon her, and I won't. But she deserves better than this conflicted version of me.

As I walk across my yard, I study every Christmas decoration, remembering when I got it. The wooden cut-outs of Peanuts characters were purchased when Jason was eight and obsessed with *A Charlie Brown Christmas*. I keep going. The candy canes that line the walkway were Cheryl's contribution from her parents' house. Next to them sits a wooden cut-out of a fox wearing a Santa hat. I smile sadly, remembering that this was the very first wooden cutout I ever made on my own as a gift to my late wife. Each item is a memory, a connection to my life over the past thirty years.

What would Cheryl think of me now, wandering like a forgotten ghost through the Christmas wasteland of my own front yard?

Movement catches my eye and I glance over to see a red fox dart across my front yard. The color of its fur reminds me of Margie's hair. I halt my walk, fixating on its sly movements as it prances gracefully across the dead grass. Even Biscuit stands still.

Goosebumps run up and down my arms. Is this some sort of cosmic coincidence that I was just staring at and remembering the fox I made for Cheryl? Should I abandon my pursuit of Margie?

But then it trots over to one of Cheryl's candy canes, pausing to sniff at it. The fox turns its head and looks directly at me. Chills shudder through my body as the feeling of the supernatural washes over me. We stare at each other, this wild creature and I, and we seem to have a silent conversation. Then it drops its gaze, seeming to bow to me, as if acknowledging and accepting my guilt and pain. When it looks up again, I swear my burden feels lighter.

And then, quick as a wink, it darts off into the forest behind my house, startling a cardinal along the way.

What just happened? Was that some sort of cosmic message from my late wife? Is she… okay with me moving on? I need to sit with it some more. Regardless, I can't quite shake the feeling that the fox granted me permission to step out of my grief and back into life.

BY THE TIME I GET BACK INSIDE her house, Margie is in her robe and starting a pot of coffee. The sight of her wild, fox-colored hair seems to reinforce that it's okay to pursue this. She's so casual and vulnerable, and the knowledge that she's comfortable around me like this helps ease the lingering vestiges of my guilt.

I walk up behind her and pull her to me, granting myself permission to relish how she fits against me. She hums with contentment.

"We need to head to the convention center in about an hour," she says, turning in my arms. She leans up and presses a gentle kiss to my lips. She pauses and studies my face. "What is it Frank, are you okay?"

I shrug. "I'll be fine. Just letting my thoughts linger in the past for too long this morning."

Her brows furrow in concern. "Want to talk about it?"

I look down. "I'm not sure. I just want to be good to you, Margie. To give you all of me. And that means working through grief and guilt when it rears its ugly head from time to time."

She pulls me into her arms and holds me tight. "Whatever you need, Frank. I'm here."

My arms come up around her and I squeeze her back. This feels... right.

After a moment I whisper, "What about that breakfast, hm?"

She leans back and studies me, then a smile creeps across her face. "I thought we could both use a hearty breakfast to help us power through today."

"What do you have in mind?" I murmur, lips pressed to her forehead.

"Eggs, bacon, the usuals," she says.

"Okay, I can handle fixing that," I say easily.

"No sir, I'm cooking for you," she insists.

And I love that our natural banter centers me, draws up my joy. She makes me feel playful and a bit wicked. I lean into it.

"While I kind of like it when you call me 'Sir,' I must insist on cooking. You are going to be on your injured foot all day, and this is the least I can do to make things easier. Now, go sit."

She lifts an eyebrow at me, and for a moment, I think I'm in for another battle of wills. I crave it, desperately wanting to lean into the desire and challenge she stirs up within me.

Finally, she cocks her head and, voice laced with sultriness, says, "Yes, Sir."

The sentiment shoots electric desire down my spine. I pull her in tightly and kiss her deeply. *This is right. I know this is right.* She kisses me back with equal enthusiasm. Breathing heavily, I lean back. "Now go be a *good girl* and sit down," I grumble.

She takes a step past me, swats my ass, then keeps going, settling in at the kitchen table. "Frank, do be a dear and fix me a coffee."

"Yes, ma'am," I say good-naturedly and fix her cinnamon coffee just the way she likes it.

WE HAD TO PART WAYS before heading to the convention center for the Christmas Market. I had to take Biscuit home, and Margie's assistant for the day, Greta, is driving to her house to give her a ride. I offered to drive her, but Margie insisted that she already had plans, and the last thing we needed was for the entire city to be gossiping about the rivalry-turned-chemistry happening between us. I told her I thought that would only drive up our sales, but she rolled her eyes and patted my shoulder as if to say, "Oh, you poor, sweet fool."

I recruited Jason to help me today, and he's meeting me at the convention center.. Fortunately, I had already spent most of my week loading up my trailer with all the wares I planned to sell over the next three days. I only have a few more things to grab, including my Santa suit, and then I'm on my way.

I call Jason when I arrive at the convention center, and he meets me out in the back parking lot with a dolly. Together, we haul everything in. Once inside, I see that Margie has already set up her space, complete with a plaid tablecloth and a hand-drawn sign that says "Margie's Machinations." I hear her infectious laugh before I see her. My body seems to move in her direction of its own accord, seeking her like she's my true North. I make myself stop, aware that no one knows we have moved our tentative friendship into something far more intimate.

But when she looks up and we lock eyes, I can't seem to catch my breath. Then Margie winks devilishly and turns back to setting up her booth.

"She's out for blood," my son mumbles. "Best get everything set up, Dad."

I force myself to turn my back to Margie and do my best to set up my booth. I made a special sign for my new business: Julia's Jems. I thought my granddaughter's name added a certain amount of charm to my business. When Jason sees the sign, he has to blink back emotion and pulls me into a hug. After that, it becomes easier to focus on my purpose: selling my woodworking to support Julia's hospital bills and winning money for Ronald McDonald House so other kids have a place to stay while they receive treatment.

I set the carved bears up along the side of my booth, and the wooden signs go up on the makeshift stand behind me. "Welcome" and "Hey, Y'all" invite people to stop by and consider new front door decor. On my table, there are smaller wooden carvings: coasters and cutting boards, small jewelry boxes, and table-sized desk signs. And my booth wouldn't be complete without an abundance of Christmas decor.

I reach into a box I brought with me and pull out one of my many strands of lights, running it along my booth table's edge. I set up a small, pre-lit Christmas tree behind the bears and even grabbed a wireless speaker to pump Christmas music into my space. Now, all I'm missing is my Santa suit, but I'll wait to put that on about fifteen minutes before the Christmas Market opens.

"You have got to be kidding me," Margie says. I turn to look at her and she has her hands on her hips, one eyebrow lifted. "I can't escape my obnoxious neighbor's Christmas lights and music, even here."

I lift an eyebrow and place my hands on my hips, mirroring her stance. "I always come to win, neighbor."

Amelia appears between us, twisting her hands anxiously. "Now, you two, play nice."

We both turn to stare at her, and I can practically see the sweat forming on her brow. We let her sweat it out for a few seconds before Margie cackles.

"Relax, Lia. We've got this," Margie says, patting her niece on the shoulder.

"Besides, I'm here to keep her in line," Greta says, looping her arm through Margie's. Then Greta turns to look at me, eying me from boots to hair and back down again. She lets out a low whistle, then looks at Margie. "Just friends, indeed."

Margie's cheeks heat immediately, and I feel a surge of desire hit me like a tidal wave. But Margie just rolls her eyes and follows her friend back to her booth.

Today should be fun.

"Alright, I've got the donation and sales meters set up on the stage behind you," Amelia says. "May the best seller win. We open in thirty minutes."

I grab the cash box and hand it over to Jason. "I'll be right back."

TEN MINUTES LATER, I emerge in my full Santa costume. I should probably be embarrassed, but I'll do anything to win this competition, even lay my dignity on the line. I didn't bother with the fake beard. I've been letting my own grow out since the power outage, and I rather like the longer look. It is more gray than brown these days, anyway, making me look like a slightly more youthful Santa. I didn't bother with stuffing my belly, either. It's going to get hot today, and the last thing I need is extra layers.

"Well, hot damn. I want to sit on his lap." I turn to see Greta giving me the once-over. I duck my head in embarrassment. When I look back up, I catch Margie staring at me unapologetically. When she catches my eye, the heat between us snaps to life. And suddenly, my Santa suit is just a little too hot.

Who would have thought this outfit would be the thing to get her attention? If that's the case, maybe I'll keep it out year-round.

All the vendors are set up and ready for the Christmas Market. And then a bubble of conversation fills the convention center. I turn to look at Margie one last time before I have to focus on work.

"It's showtime," I tell her in my best Beetlejuice impression.

THROUGHOUT THE DAY, shoppers crowd in. It turns out most of the locals know all about my yard and Santa costume, and many show me their own photos they took sitting on my literal lawn ornaments. Santa's balls were the hit of the season. *Thanks, Margie.* I smirk to myself at the knowledge that my fierce neighbor, who was on a personal vendetta to go Grinch on my lawn, inadvertently helped make it Yard of the Year.

But when I glance over at Margie's table, I see people are also showing her phone photos and erupting into laughter. And every time someone does this, a member of the Junior League—who set up a table right next to Margie—adds a donation to her jar and knocks my lead back another notch. *What is happening over there?* Judging by the amount of people giggling devilishly and loading up on Margie's jellies and jams, nothing good.

Jason stands, breaking my stare at my competition-turned-lover, and tells me he's taking a quick break to run to the restroom and get snacks.

I turn my attention back to the people approaching my booth. A little boy, about three years old, looks up at me wide-eyed. "Are you the real Santa?" he asks in awe. I glance up to see his mom—or maybe his babysitter?—who is dressed like she's on the way to the club, eye-screwing me. I shuffle uncomfortably. *What is it about this Santa suit?*

I turn my focus back to the little boy and answer his question. "I'm one of his brothers. The real Santa has a big white beard and a bigger belly. But I can tell him what you want for Christmas."

"Do you want to sit on his lap?" the woman asks. The little boy looks from her to me and back again, nervous.

"You can just tell me what you want for Christmas," I say gently.

"I'll sit with you," the woman says, looking at me suggestively. And I realize this is how women must feel all the time when men won't accept no for an answer. I'm going to have to be more direct.

"No, thank you," I say, still conscious of not spoiling the magic of Santa for the toddler looking between us.

"Oh, come on, Santa," she purrs, stepping closer and leaning in. "I'd love to take a photo with you. I've been a good girl."

I fumble my words, embarrassed and surprised that she didn't accept my polite no.

"I believe he said no," a firm voice says from my right. I look over and see Margie, hands on hips and auburn hair wild, ready to grab this woman by her hair and drag her out of here. God, I love it.

"And what are you going to do about it?" The woman asks, daring to stand up to Margie. But she has chosen the wrong woman to mess with. I want to de-escalate the situation and search for a way to do so.

"Now, now," I try. "It's okay. She was just moving along."

But the woman in question steps in closer to me and slides her arm through mine, staking a claim. "Oh, I don't think so," she says.

I try to pull my arm out of hers, but she holds on tight. What does she think she's going to accomplish with this? She can't overpower me, and we're in public. Margie moves in closer until she's right in the woman's face.

"He said 'No.' And I highly recommend that you respect his consent before I show you what it's like to have someone place hands on you when you don't want them to." Margie's nostrils flare and her hair seems to stand up like it's charged with electricity.

I make my move, not stopping to think. I pull out of the stranger's grasp and move to stand next to Margie. "Now, we don't want to upset Mrs. Claus," I say through clenched teeth and a false smile. I pull Margie into my side, and when she turns to look up at me in surprise, I plant a light, chaste kiss on her lips.

When I pull back and look around, everyone looks shocked. Well, everyone except the toddler, who has moved on to my bowl of candy canes and is helping himself to as many as he can grab.

"Well, hot damn," Greta says. "I knew it."

"Well, there's no accounting for taste," the woman snarls.

She grabs the little boy by the hand and makes a hasty retreat. But she doesn't make it far before she is stopped by security and Amelia, who looks like she just ran the length of a football field to get help.

Fortunately, the woman exits with security without much fuss, but I'm left feeling like a layer of grime clings to my skin. Margie squeezes my hand.

"Are you okay?" she whispers.

I let out a long exhale. "I'm okay. That was just weird. But," I hesitate. "I did like you coming to my rescue."

She smiles softly. "I don't like to get violent, but when push comes to shove, I'll protect those I care about."

A throat clears. We both turn to look at Greta. "Well, this has been a lovely show. And while I would love to gloat and tell Margie, 'I told you so' for the next two hours, we have a customer base to tend to."

We both turn to see the crowd staring at us, some holding up phones and recording the whole thing. Right.

Jason finally arrives back at my booth from his restroom break and looks around with confusion. "What did I miss?"

JESSICA BOOTH

Chapter 36

MARGIE

DECEMBER 19, PRESENT DAY

My blood is still boiling when I return to my booth, and it's only made worse by Greta's low, knowing chuckle. "I never thought I'd see the day," she says, shaking her head and laughing to herself.

I choose to ignore her and focus on my customers. A lot of people here know me from my YouTube channel and ask to take photos with me. And so, I have to fake it 'til I make it. Fortunately, my hostile #SantaBalls takeover, or I guess I should say "reclamation," seems to have been successful. Throughout the day, people stop by to show me their photos, and the Junior League makes promised donations and keeps track of everything. They are just as invested in me winning this competition and helping beautify the city as I am.

Part of me thrills in the competition. I love knowing that I've pulled ahead of Frank in both sales and donations. But I can't help but think of Julia and children like her. Every time I make a sale, it's like another stone dropped onto the guilt in my heart until it's so heavy I can barely breathe.

I glance at Frank periodically. He seems to have shaken off the earlier incident and is embracing the attention his costume brings. He wore that damn Santa suit expecting to be asked for photos, and he rose to the occasion. Still, every time a woman flirts with him, I am tempted to go over there and start tossing tables.

I console myself with the memories of us together last night. The thought warms me immediately, and I'm already trying to figure out when I can sneak over to him and invite him back over to my place tonight. Take that, you little flirts.

THE FIRST DAY OF THE CHRISTMAS MARKET closes at 6 p.m., and I feel like I've run a marathon. Every inch of my body hurts, and my broken ankle throbs in time with my heartbeat.

"I can go pull the car around so you don't have to walk too far," Greta says kindly. I know I must look like roadkill if even *she* is being nice to me. I nod.

Then a warm voice rumbles, "It's okay. I'll take her home."

I look up and see Frank back in his usual plaid shirt and jeans. He looks just as exhausted as I feel.

"I bet you will," Greta snarks. We both turn to glare at her. "What? The jig is up. You two kissed in front of half of Ruston."

"It was a chaste kiss," I insist.

"Margie, it may have been a small smooch, but there was so much heat between you two that it nearly set my underwear on fire, and I'm more than a decade older than you."

"Greta!" I say, laughing. God, I love this woman who always matches my energy.

"Um, Dad?" Jason approaches us, eyeing where Frank and I stand a little too close.

I start to step away, but Frank slides his arm around my shoulders and pulls me in tightly to his side. This isn't how I wanted to tell his son that we are…what? Sleeping together? Dating? I shudder. The air feels thick with tension like maple syrup is clogging the space between us.

Frank looks at his son, and Jason looks between us. Finally, he exhales. "Dad, I'm happy for you, okay? Just surprised, is all. It's a little weird for me, but I love you and hate how sad you've been these past three years. You deserve to be happy." My whole body relaxes at his words, and I sink more deeply into Frank's embrace. He continues, "So I'll see you back here at the same time tomorrow?"

"Thank you, son," Frank rumbles, then releases me to pull him into a long embrace.

Jason clears his throat. "Julia is going to stop by the Market for a bit tomorrow. I hope you're ready for the chaos. She thinks she's going to help run her Papa's booth."

"Oh, no doubt," Frank chuckles.

OUR DRIVE BACK HOME IS QUIET. Frank turns on the radio to the Christmas station and eyes me to see how I respond to "Silver Bells." But I'm so exhausted that not even my long-held Christmas trauma has the energy to rear its ugly head. He holds my hand across the truck's console, and this feeling of his hand tucked into mine, holding it protectively, is almost as good as having him in my bed. *Almost.*

By the time we park in my driveway, I'm half asleep, lulled by the gentle sway of the truck, the soft Christmas music, and the slow swirls of Frank's thumb over the back of my hand.

"Come on, let's get you inside," Frank says. He hops out of the truck and runs around to the passenger door, opening it before I can consider doing it myself. He helps me out of the truck and into my house.

"I can walk just fine in this boot, you know," I insist.

"Oh, believe me, I know. I just want to feel important, so let me," he insists.

"You're ridiculous, you know it?"

"Only for you," he says and kisses my cheek. His beard scratches softly against my cheek, and even in my exhaustion, my body wakes up, ready for more of him.

"Don't you need to check on Biscuit?" I ask.

"Emma and Julia went over about an hour ago to let him out. He'll be alright for a while still."

Once we get inside, I collapse on the couch. "I can't believe we have to do this again tomorrow. I love my niece, but I'm not sure I have it in me to do this again next year."

"You just need some food and a back massage," Frank says.

"I won't argue with you there. I think I have some leftover gumbo in my fridge. I made it a couple of days ago, and it only gets better the longer it steeps. There's enough for two. Just give me a second, and I'll go heat it up."

"You're going to stay right there," Frank says. And, I'd never admit it to anyone, but I love it when he gets bossy with me. No one else has ever had the courage to do so, and that's usually how I prefer things. But with Frank, letting go of my constant need for control and trusting that he'll catch me if I fall does something to me.

He stands and walks out of the room, returning a moment later with a glass of water, two ibuprofen, and a bottle of Four Roses bourbon tucked under one arm.

"My prayers have been answered," I sigh. I take the proffered pills and water, then watch him pour up two small glasses.

"I'm going to put the gumbo on the stove to start warming up, and I'll be right back."

I can already smell the heady scent of peppers and sausage filling my house when Frank slides in next to me on the couch and picks up his bourbon glass. The heat of the drink filters through my body, loosening up my tight muscles. It's delicious.

"What a day," Frank sighs, moving his hand over mine where it rests on my jean-clad knee.

"Yeah," I agree. "At least we confirmed that whenever there is danger and my 'fight or flight' kicks in, my response will always be fight."

"Was that ever actually in question?" Frank says, smirking as he sips his bourbon.

"I s'pose not," I allow.

"Thank you for coming to my rescue. Not sure what I would have done without you."

"You were handling it. I just let my emotions take the wheel. Good thing you were more level-headed."

"Not sure that I was, though," he says. "After all, I staked my claim on you in front of half the city, including my son, without a second thought."

I tense. "You didn't have to–"

"I wanted to," he cuts me off. "But I should have asked you first."

"I didn't mind." I turn my hand over beneath his so our palms are touching.

"Let me go get that gumbo," he says, leaning in to kiss my temple. "Then the massage."

We eat like starved wolves, devouring our meals and restoring the calories we blazed through over the course of the day. The warm gumbo and bourbon turn on my internal heater until my whole body feels ablaze. Or maybe that's just a hot flash. Either way, I'm burning and start fanning my face with my hand.

"Just take your shirt off, Margie. I don't mind. Plus," Frank says, his voice dropping in register. "I'm ready to give you a massage now."

I shudder but reach down and pull my shirt over my head like it's on fire.

"That's a good girl," Frank rumbles, gaze heating. Maybe the sentiment should make me roll my eyes, but it only heats me up further.

"You're making me sweat, and that is *not* sexy," I say dryly.

"I disagree," he says. "Let's go to your room. You can lay down, and I'll work you over." I swallow. Hard. "Your shoulders look tense." I raise an eyebrow in response but don't say a word. I push myself to a stand and hobble into my bedroom, Frank trailing behind me.

"Take your bra off," he instructs.

I don't hesitate, holding his gaze as I reach behind me to undo the clasps. My bra drops to the ground between us, and Frank follows its path downward, his gaze catching on my full breasts. His tongue darts across his lower lip as he stares. I love that he looks at me like I'm a slice of warm apple pie.

"Sit," he purrs.

I do so, and he kneels down to help get the confounded boot off my foot. When my leg is free, the ache of my injury hits immediately, and I wince. Frank glances up from where he kneels before me and studies my expression. "Lean back. I'm going to make you feel better."

When I do, he reaches up and pulls my pants and underwear off, leaving me bare. "Beautiful," he whispers, then presses a gentle kiss to the inside of my calf. It's like a firework igniting at the point of contact, exploding up through my leg and directly into my center.

"I do like it when you kiss it better," I say huskily.

"Later," he insists. "Lay down and roll over. I'm going to rub your shoulders."

I pout but do as he says. He straddles my hips and traces the lines of my shoulders. "So tense," he says, then his hands begin to do as he promised, and he works me over. His knuckles find the knots in my shoulder blades, digging in to press them out. It hurts so good. His calloused fingers create delicious friction along my skin as he works every spot, lingering to make sure he's done his job thoroughly.

When he reaches my lower back, he uses his fists to work the muscles on either side of my spine, and I groan with pain and pleasure. He skips my ass and goes straight to my thighs and calves. He pauses for a moment, and I hear a rustling. Then he's back, and I feel his bare elbows digging into my hamstrings in lazy, addictive circles. I'm lost in a haze of touch and sensation, hyper-aware of every single place his body touches mine. And when he finally reaches my ass, he rubs it and then gives me a little slap.

"Hey," I protest. But he just chuckles.

"Roll over," he says.

Slowly, I push my exhausted body over. The room is dim, but a low lamp on my nightstand is enough to reveal his bare chest and tight jeans.

"Feel better?" he asks.

"Yes. Much. Thank you, Frank. I'll return the favor tomorrow. Right now, I can barely move."

"We're not done yet," Frank says, then he grabs my hips, pulls me to the edge of the bed, and lowers himself to the floor in front of me. I push up on my elbows and look down to where he kneels. I might die from the sight.

He pushes my thighs open and I try to close them back. "Relax, baby," he insists. Slowly pushing me back open. "I promise, this will feel good."

I swallow. "I've never done this before," I admit. His hungry gaze softens. "I promise, if you don't like it, we'll stop. But Margie, don't get too in your head about it. I promise I love it. Try to relax," he says, then places a gentle kiss on the inside of my thigh. I melt back into the bed.

"Okay," I agree. I'm nervous, but I try to give myself over to the moment, helped along by the knowledge that he said he enjoys this.

I feel his warm breath on me first, the sensation delicious against my sensitive skin. Then there's the slightest press of his lips on me. I tense. "Relax," he whispers again. "I've got you."

The first brush of his tongue sends sparks searing through my body. The second licks up my spine. He goes slowly at first, allowing me to adjust to the overwhelming sensation of his mouth on me. After a few minutes of gentle teasing, he settles in and devours me with enthusiasm. And he didn't lie; Frank is utterly, completely enjoying this. His beard creates friction against my skin in sharp contrast to the gentle movements of his tongue. And as he sucks and licks, my body begins to quiver.

"That's right," he mumbles between licks. "It feels good, doesn't it?"

His words are like lighter fluid on my desire. I give myself over to the sensation, rocking my hips in time with his mouth. And then he slides a finger into me, and I can't breathe. Another. "Oh my God," I whimper. "Feels. So. Good."

All my embarrassment has been chased away by pleasure. I open myself fully to him, getting drunk on the sounds we're making and the sensations chasing through my body. I feel my core tighten, coiling, winding. Frank keeps up with my rhythm, pressing more deeply inside of me. And when he curls his fingers slightly, I ignite. Crackles of lightning sizzle through my veins and into my breasts. I call out, unable to fight back against the tidal wave of pleasure as it washes over me in wave after wave. I'm lost to the current, so intense it almost hurts. Almost.

As I crash back down to earth, I feel Frank kiss the inside of my thighs again, gently, slowly. And then he stands and looks like he belongs to the world of fantasy. He's sweating, his length pressing against his jeans. And when I look up to his hooded gaze, he smirks.

Then, without hesitation, he unbuckles his belt and pulls off his pants and boxer briefs. He crawls on top of me, where I lay limp and exhausted, and presses a kiss behind my ear. "How was that?"

My only response is a whimpered, "Wonderful."

"I told you so," he chuckles darkly. He keeps kissing me, pressing gentle lips against my neck, down my chest, and across my breasts. It doesn't take long before my body is heating back up again. I didn't even think that was possible. I move up the bed and he follows me. He kisses me deeply, running his hand across my body.

I reach for him, stroking cautiously, still not totally confident in my sexual prowess. But Frank responds enthusiastically, and I guess I'm doing something right. Because, after just a few strokes, he pushes me back and settles himself between my thighs.

"I've been looking forward to this since last night," he whispers, then thrusts into me.

Despite our raging desire, Frank takes his time, moving slowly, allowing us both to enjoy the sensations. We're tired, but desire heats our blood and keeps us moving. His languid thrusts and gentle caresses are intoxicating. And as he reaches the place deep inside of me that sends bolts of pleasure through my body, I gasp, and he follows me. Together, we find our releases in a tornado of gasps and whispered "yeses."

When it's over, he collapses beside me, throwing an arm across my body. We lay there in the low light, and, in a matter of moments, I hear his gentle snores. I smile in contentment, grateful for this second chance at life and, maybe, a second chance at love.

Chapter 37

MARGIE

DECEMBER 20 , PRESENT DAY

The second day of the Christmas Market is filled with even more people. Greta and I barely have time to breathe, let alone eat. My body aches from all of yesterday's activities–both practical and carnal. But I push through it, letting autopilot take over as I meet and greet fans. Lust and attraction go a long way in helping me power through the day.

And when I hear a familiar, "Hey, Miss Margie," my heart thrills in recognition.

"Julia!" I exclaim, opening my arms to her embrace.

The little girl doesn't hesitate, running into me and wrapping her whole body around my torso. When she pulls back, she's all smiles and delighted to show me her costume. "I'm Papa's elf helper today," she preens, spinning in a circle to show off every jingle bell and holiday touch.

"Are you sure you don't want to be my elf?" I ask, teasing.

She glances at Frank, who is trying to hide his bemused grin, then back to me. Julia leans in and whispers, "I think that might hurt his feelings."

I nod seriously. "You're right, of course." Then she gives me one more hug and dances back over to her Papa's booth.

Throughout the day, Julia takes her elf duties very seriously. And her enthusiasm means the donations start piling in. Soon, Frank's sales and donations have caught back up to mine, and the Junior Leaguers and Garden Club members begin to fret. I'm secretly glad about it though. Frank's is the better charity, and if he wins fair and square, then the society ladies have no one to be mad at but the local shoppers.

Still, I don't want to just hand Frank the win. That's not in my nature. And so, I settle in, greeting shoppers, offering up samples, and cheering anytime someone makes a donation. In the last hours of the Market, there is a mad dash to both our booths as the whole community pitches in donations and buys wooden signs and peachy jams. They have become just as invested in our competition as we have.

And when Amelia's voice rings out over the PA system to let everyone know there are only fifteen minutes left until we close the competition, she has to get her friend and coworker, Beth, to help collect the money and make sure donations go to the right places. By the time it's over, Frank and I are so close in sales and donation collections that Amelia declares she and Beth will need time to calculate sales and donations before announcing a winner.

I plop down in my folding chair, bones aching from the constant standing and sitting of today and lovemaking last night. I've downed at least six bottles of water over the course of the day and only had to take a bathroom break once.

And even though the competition has officially ended, shoppers still line up to buy out the rest of my stock. We're down to just a few jars when I notice Greta searching frantically behind me. "I could have sworn there was another box back here," she mumbles. "I set it

aside just in case we needed to refill anything last minute."

But her search is in vain, and soon my table is completely empty and my cash box is full. A rather good problem to have.

The PA system squeals to life, and everyone covers their ears. "I have an announcement to make," Amelia says. "We have a winner for our charity competition."

The entire room collectively holds its breath as they turn to look at where she stands on the stage. "The competition was fierce, and the donations were generous. We had to recount everything twice to make sure. But, at the end of two days, we have a winner—by just seventy-five dollars!"

"Congratulations go to …. Margie Murphy!"

The entire room erupts in applause, and I'm surrounded by the Junior League and Garden Club like a group of cheerleaders around a winning Super Bowl player. My heart surges with the thrill of the win and the celebration happening around me. But then I spy Julia in her elf costume hugging Frank, and my excitement wanes.

I push through the crowd and limp to the stage, standing beneath it. I reach for the microphone and Amelia hands it down to me.

"Thank you everyone, for your support of this Christmas Market and of both Frank Campbell and myself. You have made this event a true success and supported both your local economy and small businesses alike."

I catch Frank's eye, expecting to see disappointment, but I only see pride radiating from his face.

"But I'm afraid that you missed a donation, Lia, and thus the results aren't quite right."

She looks down at me in confusion. I reach into my pocket and pull out the money I stashed there right before I walked to the stage. "This donation is for Frank's charity on behalf of his little elf, Julia. And it's seventy-six dollars, so I'm afraid we have to turn over the crown to Santa and his elf."

The room is silent; the only sound is a shriek from the oldest member of the Garden Society. And if I hadn't already been a town albatross, I certainly am now.

I clear my throat. "Congratulations, Frank."

"We did it!" Julia cries out and bursts into a fit of giggles. And, just like that, the rest of the room cheers with her.

Frank walks toward me, shaking his head, the ball of his Santa hat flopping back and forth. When he gets to me, he leans down and whispers in my ear. "Why?"

I hand the microphone back up to Amelia and then look back at him. "Because your charity was more important, and I don't need any of the other local ladies snooping around in your yard. You already have me for that."

And then I throw my arms around Frank, pull him down to me, and kiss him in front of everyone. The cheers turn deafening. Frank pulls me in tighter, and for the first time in a long time, I feel like I did something worthwhile.

Chapter 38

MARGIE

CHRISTMAS EVE 1998

I can't bring myself to tell Amelia that her mother is gone. Not yet. I'm going to let her enjoy this last Christmas before her entire world comes crashing down. Instead, I offer her a generic truth.

"Your mama needed a break and went to stay somewhere else for a while."

"Will she be back for Christmas?" Amelia inquires.

"I don't think so, baby, but you and I will still have a great Christmas. Want to help me make the cranberry sauce for lunch tomorrow?"

"You can make cranberry sauce?" she asks in wonder. "I thought you bought it in a can from the grocery store."

"Oh baby, that stuff isn't the real deal. Come on. I'll show you. You want it tart, a little sweet, and smooth. Just enough to cut through the saltiness of the turkey and dressing," I instruct.

I've decided that the only way to survive this Christmas is to stay as busy as possible. Though any time "Rockin' Around the Christmas Tree" comes on the radio, it revives memories of Dale shooting his way into my house, and I have to turn the radio off before I heave my guts into the nearest trash can.

Amelia and I stir and cook our cranberry sauce, adding a bit of orange rind in the final steps. She loves it so much that when she begs to do it again, I can't say no. I tell her we can make extra, can it, and give it to friends for Christmas. She's delighted and starts listing all the people she wants to make them for. "And we'll save one for Mama, too." I wince but say nothing.

I've tried calling Jo multiple times, but every time, it goes straight to voicemail. I'm at war with myself. Do I keep trying to track her down? Do I call the police to report her as missing? But she's not missing. She's an adult and made an adult decision to leave for her own safety. The guilt and fear make it difficult to focus on much of anything, so I commit myself to Amelia's needs the best I can.

Once we're done with the cranberry sauce, we move on to preparing dressing and baking a pecan pie for Christmas lunch. And just as Amelia is convincing me that we need to make cookies for Santa, I hear a knock at the front door.

My emotions war between panic and hope, unsure of who will greet me on the other side. I peer around the corner and see David through the window. I sigh, heart heavy, and swing the door open. We've had one brief phone call since everything went down yesterday. He checked in with me to make sure we were both okay. I expected him to be with his parents for dinner tonight, and I'm both happy and sad to see him here this evening.

"Come on in," I say, greeting him with a hug.

"Hey Margie," he says, pressing a kiss to my temple. "I won't keep you long. I just wanted to stop by and make sure you're okay."

I nod. Part of me wants to run, but I hold firm. "Yeah, we're hanging in there," I say.

"And I need to talk to you about Charleston," he says, casting all of the happy emotions I managed to conjure today into a mud puddle.

"I know," I say on an exhale.

"Mr. David!" Amelia cheers and runs to hug him. He bends down and hugs her back.

"Amelia, baby, why don't you go into my room and turn on a Christmas movie? Mr. David and I need to have a grown-up talk for a bit," I tell her.

Her expression immediately turns frightened as her eyes shift back and forth between the two of us. "He's not going to hurt you, is he?" she whispers. And the crack in my heart widens another fraction.

I kneel to her level. "No, baby. Nothing like that. I'll come watch the movie with you in just a minute. Time to start getting ready for Santa to come. Now go brush your teeth."

Amelia scurries out of the room, and I turn to look at David again. He's a good man. Kind, gentle, caring. But I already know he won't stick around in Ruston when his future is calling him somewhere bigger, not even for me. And he has no plans to become a dad in this way. I can't even blame him for it. Who's to say I wouldn't go running in the opposite direction if our situations were reversed?

These thoughts spin around in my head when he finally says, "Margie. I am sorry to have to have this conversation now, in the midst of the family trouble you are facing. I feel awful about it," he says, placing his hand over mine. The flicker of love once sparked to life between us burns in the small space between our hands. "I still want you to come with me."

His words surprise me. I thought this would be a breakup speech; that's what I had fortified myself for. Another weight hangs on my sinking heart because I know the life he wants for us is not possible now. My life is dedicated to the little girl in my bedroom who is waiting for Santa to arrive, the little girl who desperately needs a mother figure.

"David," I sigh, placing my hand over his. "I know you have to go. I'm proud of you. This is the opportunity of a lifetime." He brightens at my words, hope daring to glint in his brown eyes. I hurry, refusing to let it take root. "But my place is here, with Amelia. And it will be for the foreseeable future."

He wilts, considers, and then hesitantly continues. "What if you brought her with us?"

I close my eyes and grit my teeth against the emotion threatening to spill out of me. "David," I turn to face him, forcing myself to choose courage. "My place is here with Amelia. I can't take her out of state while this custody thing is just getting underway. And her whole world just got turned upside down. I need to keep things as consistent for her as long as possible while she mourns the loss of her parents. I haven't even told her what happened with her mom yet." I choke on emotion for just a moment, then pull it back in.

David's hand slides along my back, and he slowly rubs my shoulder in comfort. "We could wait it out," he tries. "See what happens with Amelia."

I nod. "We could, but David. You deserve to live your life. You shouldn't be waiting around for me when I am going to have to shift all of my focus to Amelia. We would start out great, making phone calls and seeing each other on weekend visits. But what happens when I can't come see you because I have obligations to my niece? Or when you try to visit but have a work event? How long before this thing between us festers into resentment? That is not a solid foundation for a marriage."

"Margie," he whispers, then pulls me into his arms.

We hold each other, and I blink back tears. For Amelia, I will do this. She deserves more than the cards life dealt her. So when I pull back from David, my tears are gone, and in their place is steady resolve.

"Okay," he says, looking down at our hands. "Okay."

I reach for the engagement ring on my left hand and pull it off, placing it in David's palm and folding his fingers over it.

"This is it then? After everything?" he asks.

I shrug and nod. I wish David loved me enough to fight for me, to want to stay here and support me. But I won't say it. My pride won't let me.

Instead we both stand, and I walk him to the door. "Merry Christmas, Margie. Amelia is lucky to have your love."

And with that, he steps outside, climbs into his car, and backs down the driveway and out of my life.

BY THE TIME I MAKE IT BACK to my room to check on Amelia, she's already asleep. I try to process everything that's happened, checking in with myself. It's time to put the past and that life path with David to bed. Amelia is my future now.

I carefully close the bedroom door and then head to my shed to pull out the carefully wrapped presents and bring them into my living room. I place them around the small, bent tree. I stare at the three stockings I hung with hope. I walk over and remove one, needing to rid myself of the visual reminder of Jo's absence. I focus on filling Amelia's stocking with Hershey's Kisses and Lip Smackers, throwing in some packets of apple cider for good measure. It's not much, but I'm grateful to be able to give her this small joy for Christmas.

Chapter 39

MARGIE

DECEMBER 23, PRESENT DAY

The few days between the Christmas Market and the days leading up to Christmas fly by in a whirlwind. Julia is over at Frank's constantly while her parents finalize details for their temporary move, which will happen after New Year's.

Between being trapped in my driveway by traffic and getting ready for the Christmas Market, I haven't done any Christmas shopping. I don't have a huge list of people to buy for, but Amelia, Rhett, Katie, Jacob, and Greta are on my list. And Frank now, too, I suppose. And Julia. Because buying gifts for a child at Christmas makes everything a little more magical. I've shut down my online store until after New Year's as well, knowing I need the time to heal and recover from both my injury and the Christmas Market.

I spend my days shopping and getting the ingredients for Christmas lunch while Frank goes to work. His yard lights still shine too brightly every single night, but I've noticed that the ones that shine directly into my windows have disappeared. I guess even Frank doesn't like the bright lights when we spend our nights together.

It's two days before Christmas, and I'm in my she-shed. I've got my wrapping paper out and have even conceded to playing Christmas music, allowing recent memories with Frank and Julia to filter over the bad memories of my past. The weather has leveled out to our usual Christmas temperatures in the mid-fifties. I don't have the heat on in the shed, though, and I'm getting chilly. I stand from my wrapping station on the floor and go in search of a blanket. But when I reach inside the small storage cabinet, it's not there. That's odd. I know I keep it here. It's nothing fancy, but it's soft and adorned with peaches–a gift from Amelia. I must have moved it and forgotten.

My phone buzzes. I open it and smile.

Frank: Just confirming our Christmas Eve date. My house. 6 p.m.

Margie: I'll be there. Want me to bring anything?

Frank: You're the only thing I need. We'll make this Christmas Eve one you can look back on and smile about.

I still haven't told Frank all the details of that Christmas Eve that changed everything. But he knows that Amelia became my ward almost twenty-five years ago after something traumatic happened at Christmastime. Thinking about that night lodges an icicle in my heart. I'm just glad that Amelia was too young to remember most of it.

Even now, this thing with Frank feels too good to be true. Part of me half expects him to up and move away, bidding me farewell to live my little life alone. I have to constantly remind myself that not every man is like that. And David wasn't a bad guy, but I couldn't commit to the life he wanted for us, and he couldn't commit to me.

But Dale destroyed my sister's life. And then Matt, Amelia's longtime boyfriend before Rhett, nearly did the same to her. I still hate myself for not forcing her out of that relationship sooner.

Trying to shake the bad memories off, I reach for my phone and text Frank.

Margie: Still coming over for dinner tonight?

Frank: I wouldn't miss it.

Even though we spend most of our daylight hours apart, the nights are just for us, like a secret tucked away in a treasure chest and buried beneath starlight.

Sighing, I leave my wrapping supplies out and walk back to the house. Red beans and rice for dinner. Simple, but I already know Frank and Julia like it, and that Biscuit will linger beneath my kitchen table, hoping for scraps. The thought reanimates another part of my soul I thought was gone with Amelia when she moved out. I love hosting, and getting to do so again lately has made me more happy and more pleasant to be around—even Amelia has commented on it.

WHEN A KNOCK SOUNDS at my door, and I hear the low woof of a basset hound, I slide the plates onto the kitchen table. I open the door and Julia flies in, making herself at home. Biscuit trots in behind her, leaving Frank holding a bouquet of red roses and white lilies with greenery tucked in around them. The sight is straight out of a movie. And it only gets better when he pulls a plastic container full of cookies out from behind his back.

"Snickerdoodles," Frank shrugs, eyes crinkling. "Julia insisted because you like cinnamon coffee."

I walk up to him and take his offerings. He kisses me on the forehead. But this time, I know it's because there are tiny eyes watching us, and if he places his lips on mine, neither of us will be able to stop ourselves from abandoning dinner for the bedroom.

"I love red beans and rice!" Julia sing-songs from the kitchen. "And Miss Margie, your Christmas tree looks beautiful!"

Frank lifts an eyebrow at me. I shrug. "I figure the place could use a little Christmas cheer."

"I knew I'd wear you down eventually."

"Don't let it go to your head," I say, poking him in the chest.

"Too late," he says, sneaking a quick kiss onto my lips. "Now you're just missing the mistletoe."

Dinner passes in comfortable conversation as Julia details everything she asked Santa for for Christmas. She is so very like a young Amelia that I can't help but smile as I remember the small, joyful memories of our past .

After dinner we sit on the couch and turn on *Rudolph*, the old claymation one Amelia loved. Julia curls up on my side and lays her head in my lap, and another piece of my heart thaws and melts. Frank reaches for my hand, and together, we watch an elf dentist, Yukon Cornelius, and Rudolph race to leave and then save Christmas. All these years later, I see myself in the outcasts and in the strange camaraderie formed on the Island of Misfit Toys. When the movie ends, Julia snores softly in my lap. I brush her hair back from her face, loving the warmth she brings into every space she enters.

"Amelia and I used to sit just like this, watching this same movie," I say.

Frank squeezes my hand. "Seems like a good Christmas memory," he says cautiously.

I sigh. "It was. One of the best ones. But most of my Christmas memories are tainted by the one where Amelia's father threatened me and her mother, my sister Jo, with a gun. My sister bailed on us after that, saying it was the best for everyone. Maybe she was right in some ways. Amelia and I were good for each other. But Jo could have stuck around and been part of our family, too."

"What happened to her?" Frank asks softly.

I hesitate. "She disappeared. Took on a new identity. Never contacted us. I spent many years after that tracking her down. I finally found her with the help of a private investigator. She fled to Ohio, of all places. Started a new life in a small city called Wapakoneta. She never married again, though that's not surprising."

"And you didn't reach out to her?"

"I tried at first," I say heavily. " But she never responded. I loved my sister. Still do. Enough to respect that she needed to start over and leave no crumbs for Dale to follow." My throat clogs. "And I realize now that it was a supreme act of bravery to leave her own daughter behind."

"It may not always feel like it," Frank says. "But Amelia got very lucky with you as her aunt and mother."

I wipe a tear away. "Oh, I don't know about that. Jo wasn't the only one to abandon me that Christmas. There was a man, David. We were… engaged. I thought we were in love, but looking back, I don't know if that was the case. But it was something promising. A future. He left me, too. Don't get me wrong, I *told* him to. I didn't want to lock him into Ruston, Louisiana, with a kid who wasn't his responsibility and a woman who couldn't make him her top priority."

"He didn't deserve you," Frank says solemnly.

I shrug. "Maybe not. But it still hurts, thinking back at the many people I cared about who left my life that Christmas. Like it wasn't worth it for any of them to stick around. Not for Amelia, and not for me."

The words lance the old wound that's been festering in my infected heart, making the pain and bile spill out. It hurts. A tear slips from my eye before I can stop it. Frank's finger catches it and brushes it away. I look up at him. "That's why I'm not good with people. I don't trust any of them—well, except for Amelia, of course. Why invest the time if they're just going to leave?"

Frank slides in closer to me, and his arm wraps tightly around my shoulders. "You are worth more than any of them, Margie. You are the strongest woman I've ever met. And that doesn't scare me, not one bit. It makes me want to be the man who can stand by your side and hold you up when the world comes at you and tries to bring you down. It makes me want to protect you, fight with you, and make love to you. You have no idea how incredible you are."

"You don't mean that—"

"I do," he says immediately.

"And I'm grateful that you're giving me a chance. I promise not to disappoint you," he says, kissing my temple.

"Don't make promises you might not be able to keep," I tell him, my cynicism resurfacing.

"I'm not going anywhere, Margie," Frank says. Then he slides his hand to cup my cheek and turns my face to him. He kisses me gently. And I know that kiss for what it is: a promise.

Chapter 40

FRANK

CHRISTMAS EVE, PRESENT DAY

I'm determined to make tonight perfect, to show Margie that not every man who enters her life is destined to ruin it. Julia is staying with me this morning while her parents Christmas shop, but they will be by to pick her up around 5:30, giving me about thirty minutes to freshen up before Margie arrives. My granddaughter jumps in to help me set my dining room table like it belongs in a Dickens novel. We pull out special candlesticks and Christmas-themed placemats. I even break into the fine china I've been meaning to get rid of.

Julia insists on personally decorating the table. Her six-year-old styling sensibilities are surprisingly discerning. She disappears into my yard for a few minutes and returns with a basket full of pine cones. When she asks me for a large glass vase, I dig through a box and find one. She places the pinecones inside and asks me to help her tie a bow around it. Next, she insists we hang up Christmas lights around the room to make the space feel magical.

"Santa would like this," she insists. And I do believe she's right.

I forgo the traditional Christmas meal of turkey and dressing, knowing Margie is cooking those for her own family tomorrow. Instead, I decided on salmon, salad, rolls, and cookies. The latter because Julia insisted she still needs to make some for Santa tonight. I admit I'm not the best chef. The salad came from a bag, the rolls were frozen, and the cookies were slice and bake, but I did spend some time with a YouTube video learning how to make salmon, and feel fairly confident in my ability. I'll wait to do everything but the cookies once Margie arrives, so dinner will be fresh.

The last thing I need to do is get Margie's Christmas present ready. I wasn't sure what to buy her. She doesn't go for flashy things like jewelry or purses. I asked Julia for her opinion, which I am beginning to realize is highly valuable. Her answer is simple, and she says it like it's obvious: "You should make her something, Papa. That's what I'm doing."

I still have some imposter syndrome surrounding my woodworking, but the Christmas Market showed me that people want what I'm making. I just hope Margie does, too. The whole time I worked on her gift this week, I kept thinking about what she did for me at the Christmas Market, about what her donation meant for kids like Julia. I poured every ounce of what that meant to me into her gift, sanding corners and taking my time with measurements. And I hope all of that comes through when she opens it.

I ask Julia to help me put away some of my largest yard decorations. Yes, it's still Christmas Eve, and we will have cars in front of my house tonight, but I've been slowly taking things down since Margie and I agreed to date. She didn't ask me to, and she probably hasn't even noticed. But I want to show her–and Julia–that their feelings matter to me. Still, I can't bring myself to put away the now infamous Santa Balls. The cars are already beginning to line my street to see the decorations. Today and tomorrow the traffic will be heavy, and then it should begin to ebb. It will be nice to find out what being neighbors with Margie can be like without all the extra viewers stopping by my house every night.

As the sun begins to set, Julia runs back inside to get a snack while I put the last few Christmas decorations in my shed. I check my watch. Five-fifteen. My son and daughter-in-law will be here in fifteen minutes. That will give me time for a quick shower and then, hopefully, the best Christmas Eve Margie has ever had.

I walk inside my house and notice that the kitchen light is off. That's strange. I thought Julia was in here getting a snack. She must have wandered into the living room. But when I go in there, it's just as silent.

"Julia?" I call out. Nothing. The bathroom, then.

I make my way through my house, calling for my granddaughter, but there's no sign of her anywhere. Biscuit sits at my feet and looks at me, and I wish he had some sort of Lassie instinct so he could tell me if Julia has fallen into the metaphorical well. Panic begins to creep into my chest, gripping me in a vice. I hear the gravel crunch in my driveway and know Jason and Emma have arrived. Hopefully, Julia is already outside greeting them. Maybe she never went back inside.

I hustle outside, but there's no sign of Julia. Jason spies my panic as soon as he turns off their car.

"What is it, Dad?"

"I can't find Juila. She was just here a few minutes ago, and now she's gone." I look between the line of cars on the street and the darkening woods behind my house. My pulse ratchets up to an unhealthy beat. "She wouldn't," I whisper. "I've told her a million times not to go in the woods alone."

I glance at the line of cars, and even more frightening thoughts involving kidnapping or being hit by a vehicle seize me. Jason and Emma begin to call for their daughter, and I can hear the sharp, unhinged pitch that colors their voices. I run to my workshop and grab flashlights and a jacket. I tell Jason and Emma to start questioning the people in the cars lining the street and to call the police. Then, together, Biscuit and I enter the woods.

Chapter 41

MARGIE

CHRISTMAS EVE, PRESENT DAY

My nerves flutter like a bunch of drunk flies in my stomach. I shouldn't be anxious. Frank and I have spent nearly every night together for the past week, but Christmas Eve still holds uncomfortable memories that I try not to look too closely at.

I take my time getting ready, at least more than I usually do. I'm not much of a makeup or dress person, but I brush mascara onto my top lashes and pick out something that's, well, not a t-shirt. It's a golden-colored blouse that Amelia helped me pick out for a wedding last year. I even grab my nice jeans–the ones I don't garden in. Taming my hair is another matter altogether. After a few attempts to get it to lay flat, I decide that Frank has seen it like this a million times and, without special hair products and appliances, making it lay flat simply is not going to happen.

I glance at the clock. It's 5:50. The drunk flies pick up speed inside my gut, and I feel vaguely sick. I grab the bottle of Buffalo Trace Bourbon I keep for special occasions and the small Christmas gift I wrapped for Frank. 5:55. Time to go. I methodically go through my house and turn off the lights–everything except the Christmas tree. I smile at the sight, acknowledging that I've allowed a little bit of Christmas joy to filter into my life this year.

I open my front door, shaking my head at all the cars still lining the street. I've gotten sort of used to their presence now, and it will be weird once they're gone again. Though not having to fight traffic to leave my house will be a welcome relief.

I glance down the road and see a couple going car to car and raise an eyebrow. Who knows what people are selling these days? I square my shoulders, ignore the cars in the road, and go to the side door of Frank's house. Steadying myself, I knock on the door three times and wait. We usually hang out at my house, but I'm glad we're at Frank's tonight. It's kind of nice not to have to worry about the dinner details.

I wait thirty seconds, and Frank doesn't appear. I wonder if he's in the shower? I knock again. Wait. Nothing. Panic flickers at the edges of my psyche. But no, Frank told me he'd never leave me. I reach for my phone and open up the texts.

Margie: Hey! I'm here at your side door. Probably hard to hear my knock over the loud Christmas music.

I stare at the screen, waiting for the read receipt to pop up, but it doesn't appear. I shift from foot to foot, trying to decide what to do. I could try to walk in, but this isn't my house, and I'm not sure that we are at that level of our relationship yet. I decide to call Frank. The phone rings and rings, and every unanswered moment causes my anxiety to spiral into a tornado of fear and rejection.

Frank is not David. I mentally repeat to myself. I glance at the driveway and see Frank's truck and another vehicle parked there. My panic grows. Is someone else over here? A woman? I reach for the doorknob, and it opens easily under my palm. I stand frozen, unsure if it's okay to cross this threshold without invitation.

I inhale and step inside. "Hey Frank, I'm here!" Nothing. The house is dark. I think I'm going to throw up. I double check my texts to make sure that we planned our date at his house tonight at 6:00. Then check today's date to confirm that it is, in fact, Christmas Eve.

Where is he?

I walk to his makeshift wood shop in the garage, but the lights are out here, too. Worry begins to take the place of abandonment fears. What if he accidentally chopped his hand off and is bleeding out inside his shop? I jiggle the handle, but it's locked. I peer inside and can't make out anything. I hear sirens in the distance, but they will have a hard time getting through the traffic when there's no shoulder to drive on or for cars to pull off on. *Is it for Frank?*

I dart through every room of his house, certain that Frank has collapsed somewhere and I just missed him. I leave the bottle of bourbon on the table and yell his name, taking the time to look in every room, check bathtubs, and even yell into the attic. He's not here. I check my phone again. He didn't call or text.

Dread takes the place of fear. Was all of this with me too much? But then, why is his truck here? The sirens grow louder, bringing me back to the night Dale shot his way through my front door. Trauma takes control of my brain, and I bolt, running back to my house. When I pass through my front door, I slam it shut behind me, then crawl into my bed and under the covers. I need to block it all out.

My whole body is wracked with shudders. I dry heave as my skin turns hot and then freezing cold in rapid succession. I feel like I'm dying, like I can't breathe. I cry out, then bury my face in my pillow and scream.

Frank isn't here. The police are coming. He left me. He. Left. Me. My brain gets stuck on that track, skipping back to it over and over again. As the sirens get closer, their sound yanks my past into my present. I pull my knees tight to my chest.

I try to make myself as small as possible. *Maybe if I can do that, all of this pain will go away.*

Chapter 42

FRANK

CHRISTMAS EVE, PRESENT DAY

I charge through the woods behind my house. But it's already completely dark outside, and my flashlight doesn't do much to illuminate the shadows tucked under thick stumps and tall pines. My imagination runs wild. I have visions of Julia being devoured by coyotes or her arm broken while she's trapped beneath a fallen tree. I'm panicking, and a distant part of my brain yells at me to calm down or I'll never be able to locate her.

I hear the sirens in the distance and have to fight the urge to puke. "Please," I plead to whoever is listening. "Please, I'll do anything. Just let me find my Juju Bug."

"Frank!" I hear Emma's muffled call through the trees. "Frank, come back. The police are here."

I hesitate. I desperately want to find Julia and every instinct is screaming at me to keep going, keep looking. But I need help.

"I'm coming!" I call back.

Biscuit and I make our way back out of the woods to my yard, where four police officers stand ready to greet me.

"Mr. Campbell," I'm Officer Jenkins, a policewoman in her late forties says to me. "I need you to tell me about the last time you saw Julia."

The last time. Those words sink into my gut. "I, uh, um. She was going inside to get a snack. It was about 5:00, and I was picking up some lights in my yard." I swallow, staring at the blades of grass illuminated by the flashlight beneath my feet. "I went back inside a few minutes later, and she was just gone. I searched my whole house, called for her, nothing. And then my son and daughter-in-law got here, and we started looking."

"No one in any of the cars saw her, at least no one we talked to," Jason says. Emma's face is pressed into his shoulder, and she's sobbing. *This is all my fault.*

"Okay, now let's talk this through," Officer Jenkins says. "Is there anyone who would have wanted to harm her or take her?"

"No," we all three reply immediately. "Everyone loves her," Jason insists.

"Okay, what about a place where she might have accidentally fallen into or gotten locked in somewhere? Think beyond just your house, Mr. Campbell. Is there any place nearby where she might have gone?"

I look to the woods again, but no. Julia promised me she wouldn't go in there without me. I don't think that's where she is. I run through possibilities and discard them just as quickly. I slowly turn in a circle until I spot Margie's house. And then I remember the last time Julia disappeared on me and where she went.

"Margie's shed," I say. And then I take off running. The police officers follow my pace, and Jason and Emma trail behind. When I get to the shed, it's dark and locked. My heart sinks.

"She's wandered off and into here before," I tell them. "My friend lives here."

"I'm going to see if the homeowner can open the shed up for us. What's her name?" Officer Jenkins asked.

"Margie Murphy," I whisper.

And then another wave of dread hits me. *Margie. Our date.* I wasn't there. I'm ready to collapse as everything around me spins around me like a tornado and shreds apart.

I hear the officer knock on her front door. "Miss Murphy? Ruston Police," Officer Jenkins calls out.

She doesn't come to the door and all the lights in her house are off. *Did she… leave?* I glance and see her truck is there.

"I can call her," I say, jumping into action. When I pick up my phone I see the missed calls from her and the unread texts. Dammit. I call her, but her phone rings through to voicemail.

I reach for the front door knob. It's unlocked. "Sir, you can't enter this house," the officer tries to stop me. "It's okay. She's my girlfriend." The words sound weird on my tongue, but I can't stop to think about that right now. There's too much on the line.

I go inside and turn on the lights. And, for the second time tonight, I'm calling out for a girl I love. "Margie! Margie! God, I'm so sorry. Margie!"

I hear a cry from her bedroom and bolt to the now-familiar space. The room is dark, with only a small sliver of light filtering in through her cracked bathroom door. I notice a lump under the covers.

"Margie? Oh God, baby. Are you okay?"

"Go to hell!" she shouts.

"Margie, I didn't mean to screw this up, and if you want me to leave, I will. But right now, can you please open your shed? Julia is missing."

She throws the covers off of her, unveiling wild hair and mascara-streaked cheeks.

"Julia's missing?" she rasps.

"Yes. That's where I've been. I should have called. I know. But I panicked. I'm still panicking. We can't find her and I thought maybe she went back to your shed. The police are here."

She rubs her face roughly with her hands. "One second, let me grab the keys."

Margie rolls out of bed and slides her unbooted foot into her well-worn tennis shoe, then power walks to her kitchen. She reaches for a hook where her keys hang and grabs one. Then she charges through her front door, not giving me a second look. She goes straight to the shed, fumbles with her keys, then slides one home. The door unlocks, and Margie reaches for the light switch. The space is suddenly illuminated, but nothing stirs inside.

We all enter the shed. Emma and Jason call for their daughter. I don't see anything, and my brief flicker of hope begins to die. The space isn't huge, but it was once used to store farm equipment and holds couches and a closet. I run to the closet and thrust it open. Nothing. Margie joins our search, frantically looking under pillows.

And then I hear a whimper. Time seems to come to a complete stop. The cry comes again. Margie hobbles over to her small bar and looks behind it.

"Oh, thank God," she says, then bends down. "She's here. She's okay."

I race to join her. When I make it around the bar corner, I see Julia. She's cuddled up on a makeshift bed underneath the counter. And she's surrounded by a collection of wild and wonderful things. But I don't pay much attention to them, eager to hold her in my arms. I reach for her, and Julia comes to me. When I stand holding my granddaughter, Emma collapses to the ground in tears. I carry her daughter to her and kneel. "She's okay, Emma. She's okay."

I slide Julia into her mother's arms and then feel Jason move in beside us both.

"Are you okay, Julia?" Officer Jenkins asks.

Julia turns to look at the formidable woman in the dark police uniform. She nods. "I was just hiding," she admits sheepishly.

"Baby, why were you hiding?" Emma asks, desperately wiping the tears from her cheeks.

"Because I don't want to go," Julia says defiantly. "I don't want to move to Dallas away from Papa and Daddy and Miss Margie."

It feels like a knife slides home into my heart, slicing it open and allowing it to bleed out over the floor.

"Oh honey," Emma says. "It's just for a little while."

"I don't want to go!" Julia asserts and then bursts into tears.

"Mr. Campbell," Officer Jenkins says, placing a gentle hand on my shoulder. "If you could give me a quick statement, I'll fill out the paperwork, and we can all get back to Christmas Eve."

"Right, yes," I agree. "Thank you for coming out tonight."

"It's no problem," she says. "I'm just glad this case has a happy ending."

Once I finish my statement, the police officers leave, and I'm overwhelmed by the silence that fills the space around me. The police blocked off the road when they arrived, and there are no cars going by, just occasional owl hooting and the eerie hum of Christmas music playing from my house. Jason and Emma hold Julia close and carry her to their car. They promise to touch base in the morning, but I feel guilty for losing their child and wouldn't blame them if they didn't talk to me for a while.

When they drive off, I turn and look back to the open shed door, the light shining on me like an interrogation bulb. How did I screw this entire evening up so terribly? I turn and walk to the shed, ready to crawl on my knees for Margie if that's what she asks of me. I feel so broken, and all I want is *her*.

The adrenaline ebbs out of my body as I walk until my limbs feel like they have thirty-pound weights tied to them. The post-rush headache slams into me, throbbing and causing my vision to blur.

When I get to the shed, I lean against the door frame and search for my true north, my Margie.

She's standing behind the bar, looking down. "Frank," she says in a way that lets me know she's been crying. "I think you need to see this."

I walk to her, ready for her to shove me out and tell me never to talk to her again. But when I approach her side, I notice that her expression is not one of anger, but of wonder. I turn to look down at where she's staring.

Julia did indeed create a makeshift bed under the bar counter. More than that, a makeshift house.

"My missing blanket," Margie whispers.

"And all my missing Christmas decorations," I say with surprise.

"And my missing jars of peach jam and Amelia's old Simba doll."

"And a photo of Cheryl," I say, kneeling down to study the photo of my late wife.

"It's all here. And by the looks of it, Julia has been building this little dragon hoard for quite some time," Margie says.

I start to reach for Margie and hesitate. I want to touch her. I'm desperate to pull her into my arms and for us to find comfort in one another. But I don't know if she wants that from me. When she turns to look at me, I finally notice what a mess she is. Mascara is spread all over her face, her eyes are red, and her usually wild hair looks like it's been spun in a cotton candy machine.

"Margie, I'm sorry."

"Oh, Frank," she says gently. "I know. And I'm not mad at you. But I think I'm broken. When you weren't home, I lost it. And not just a little tantrum. I mean, I fell into a black hole from my past, and it was ugly. But that's not on you. That's me. And maybe," she sobs. "Maybe I'm destined to be alone."

"Oh baby, no," I say, and then I sit on the concrete floor of the shed and pull her into my arms. Margie chokes on a sob, her whole body convulsing in my arms, and she cries.

I clutch her to me, burying my face in her shoulder. The emotions of the evening finally catch up to me. The fear of losing Julia. The fear of losing Margie. The overwhelming relief of losing neither. And then I begin to quietly cry into Margie's shoulder.

We sit like that for what could be a few minutes or an hour, holding each other, crying, soaking in the other's pain, and sharing the heavy burdens of life we've both carried for so long.

And I know, in this moment, that I will do anything to keep her.

Chapter 43

MARGIE

CHRISTMAS EVE, PRESENT DAY

I'm a disaster. Christmas is a curse. The thoughts run unbidden through my head. *Frank is too good for me. But I don't want to let him go. I need him. Need this.* And selfishly, I'm going to hold onto him for as long as he will let me.

"Come on," Frank whispers into my hair. "It's cold out here. Let's get inside near some heat. I'll pour us a glass of bourbon."

"The good stuff is at your house. I left it on your table," I rasp.

"Let's go to my house then. We'll have a glass, then eat the cookies Julia and I baked for Santa. I think we both deserve a little indulgence after tonight."

He stands and then helps me to my feet. As soon as we step out of the shed, Biscuit greets us, tail wagging slowly. We walk quietly, hand-in-hand, to Frank's house. Just as we cross over his property line, a red fox darts out from behind the bushes at his house and pauses. Frank halts and seems to hold his breath. When the creature bounds away, he releases the air in his lungs and bows his head.

"Are you okay?" I ask.

"Yeah. I think that little fox is a sign from the universe. A good one." He squeezes my hand and then we keep going.

As soon as we get to the front porch, he pulls the plug on all the outside lights. Inside, he turns on the kitchen lights and finds the bottle of bourbon.

"Buffalo Trace, huh? I do feel special." The attempt at humor is weak, but I chuckle anyway, desperate to feel some sort of normalcy tonight.

He pours us each a glass. "Come on. I want to show you something. I know that tonight didn't go exactly as I hoped, but Julia and I put a lot of work into making the place special for you, and you should at least get to see it."

I follow him into his dining room, a space I've only seen in passing when I was running through his house looking for him. The lights are off, but he asks me to wait a moment. He walks over to the wall, rustles around, and then suddenly Christms lights flare to life around the top of the room.

"Oh," I say, surprised and delighted.

Then I look at the table that appears to be set for royalty. A deep, maroon tablecloth covers the table, topped by a Christmas-themed table runner. Tall candlesticks hold candles, and beautiful China adorns the table.

"Frank," I say in wonder. "You did this for me?"

"Of course, baby. I wanted to help you find your joy at Christmas again. I mean, I know tonight turned into the opposite of that and–"

But I don't let him finish, cutting him off with a kiss. "It's perfect," I whisper.

"Any chance you're hungry?" he asks sheepishly.

"It's kind of late," I hedge.

"It's only 7:30. And besides, it's Christmas Eve," he says.

I nod. "Okay."

"Okay."

"Let me run to the restroom first."

I walk away, and when I flip on the bathroom light and look in the mirror, I gasp in horror. It looks like I tried to give myself an emo makeover and failed horribly. Mascara paints my face in tear-streaked paths. My hair looks like it was gnawed on by rats. And my eyes are so puffy that not even ice packs will bring them back down to normal size. I use the restroom, then get to work putting myself back together. This is why I never wear makeup. With the help of hand soap and a small towel, I get the mascara off my face. A quick finger-comb through my hair brings my unruly waves into a semblance of order. Nothing to be done about the puffiness, but at least I don't look like I wandered out of a horror movie anymore.

When I walk back to the dining room, Frank is there mixing up a salad.

"It's nothing fancy," he says. "But it will get the job done."

I follow him to the kitchen and watch as he begins to cook the salmon. He turns the radio on, and "Jolly Old St. Nicholas" comes to life on the speaker. Frank immediately begins to sing along, his rich baritone lending magic to the old carol as he sings: *Jolly old St. Nicholas, lean your ear this way. Don't you tell a single soul what I'm going to say. Christmas Eve is coming soon, now, you dear old man. Whisper what you'll bring to me. Tell me if you can.*

He notices me gaping and winks.

"Frank! I didn't know you could sing!"

"You never asked," he shrugs. Then he turns back to his pan of salmon. "I learned how to make this by watching YouTube," he comments as he cooks. "So if it's terrible, you'll need to go leave a comment on the video because it's definitely not my fault."

"Thank you, Frank," I say sincerely. I've got no bite left in me tonight. "For everything. The dinner, the decorations, the table. This may be the nicest thing anyone has ever done for me."

He glances over his shoulder, his eyes crinkling. "I'm just sorry I wasn't here when you arrived. I can't imagine what you must have thought."

"It doesn't matter. You did the right thing, looking for Julia."

"But I should have let you know what was happening."

"You didn't think. You just reacted, just like a good grandfather should. I would have done the same if Lia was missing."

And I mean it. This I can relate to with my whole heart. I would and did sacrifice everything for my niece, and the fact that Frank would do the same for his granddaughter only endears him to me even more.

He clears his throat. "Interesting thing about searching YouTube for cooking videos," he says slyly. "Is that it also shows you related content you might like. And it turns out that the algorithm has gotten pretty damn good because it showed me something I like a lot." Frank turns to look at me, the twinkle in his eye back. "Did you know there is a YouTube creator right here in our great city who makes jam?"

"Oh, really now?" I say with false innocence.

"Oh, yes. She's quite beautiful and a bit bossy, but I think you'd like her." I lift an eyebrow. "Turns out she's pretty ruthless too. She had a whole episode on her channel dedicated to winning a charity event at her local Christmas Market."

"She sounds cutthroat."

"Positively villainous," he agrees.

He takes the pan off the stovetop and turns off the burner.

"And the plan worked. Or at least it seemed to," he says, walking slowly over to me. "But then she undermined her own game to help someone else win."

"No way she'd do something like that. Not the villain," I say.

"That's the thing, though, isn't it? Maybe she's not the villain. Maybe she's just the morally gray heroine?"

I do laugh, then. "You must have watched a couple of those BookTube episodes while you were clicking around."

"There's all kinds of stuff on there," he says with a chuckle. And then he leans in and kisses me.

THAT NIGHT, AT FRANK'S INSISTENCE, I agree to stay the night at his house. He's determined to still help me find some joy in the evening. So, after we eat, we move to the couch and sit before the fire that kickstarted all of this between us. "Silent Night" plays in the background, and I allow my head to drift to his shoulder. He wraps his arm around me, and we stay like that in perfect silence, listening to the music and enjoying the perfect, comforting company of one another. I allow myself to feel the peace of the moment, to imagine a future where these moments don't have to be few and far between but can happen every night. It scares me a little. But when have I ever backed down from something that scared me?

After we eat our Santa cookies, we wander back to Frank's bedroom. That night, we make love quietly and carefully. It's not the raging inferno of lust, the passion of new touches, or even the tentative exploration of new lovers. It's careful and intentional. Every touch, every kiss, every gentle breath is an "I love you."

We fall asleep in each other's arms, and somehow, despite how terribly this Christmas Eve began, I've managed to find some joy.

Chapter 44

MARGIE

CHRISTMAS DAY 1998

Around 1 a.m., my cocktail of adrenaline and traumatic emotions finally spun itself out, and I crashed, falling asleep almost immediately. Exhaustion took me on an adventure to dreamland in which Santa Claus lectured me on my responsibilities while I frantically made apple ciders for everyone who walked into the hardware store. Just as I started to pour one for a Furby, I was yanked out of sleep by an excited little girl.

"Aunt Margie! Wake up! Wake up! Santa came!"

It takes me a moment to orient myself to reality. *Amelia. Christmas. Right.*

I sit up, head thrumming like the Little Drummer Boy is using it as his personal percussion device.

"Come on, Aunt Margie, come see! Come see!"

Despite my distinct lack of sleep and throbbing headache, Amelia's

Christmas cheer is contagious. I slide my slippers on and follow her bouncing body out into the living room.

"Look, Aunt Margie! Presents! This is the most I've ever gotten. I must have been *very* good this year."

And here I was, thinking it wasn't enough. I ask Amelia to wait just a few minutes while I fix a cup of cinnamon coffee, then I settle in on the couch and watch her rip into her gifts. Simba is an instant favorite, and she is thrilled that "Guess Who" is a game "for just two people." My heart twinges, and I start to fall into melancholy… at least until she opens the ant farm and begins to insist on setting it up in my bedroom. I don't think so.

She's delighted with the small offerings and this moment helps ease my soul just a bit. I can do this.

"Where are your presents, Aunt Margie?"

"Oh," I hedge. "Well, I don't think Santa brings grown-ups presents, baby."

She nods, considering. "That's kind of sad. But it's okay. I have a present for you."

Amelia zips off into the guest room and comes back carrying a drawing. In it, there are two stick figures, who she tells me are the two of us. And we're surrounded by the various animals she's seen walking through my yard: a deer, a raccoon, and an armadillo.

"It's perfect, Amelia. The best Christmas present anyone has ever given me."

"Really?"

"Yes, really. You drew our perfect little family." I realize as I say those words that she truly did. We don't need anyone else: not a man who will abuse and control us, not a man who will love and still leave us. Just us. Perfect and whole.

Chapter 45

MARGIE

CHRISTMAS DAY, PRESENT DAY

"Papa!" A voice cries delightedly through the house. I blink, thinking I'm still lost in a dream. "Papa!" The voice calls again. Biscuit bellows, and I realize that Julia is in the house.

And *I am naked in Frank's bed.*

"Shit!" I whisper and try to scramble out of his bed. But in my haste, I forget my injury. And when I step out of bed and onto my injured foot, I crumple to the ground.

"Papa!" The voice calls more loudly. I realize that Julia is nearly at the door.

I scramble, crawl to Frank's bathroom, and slam the door behind me. Just in time, because I hear Frank's bedroom door swing open. I almost feel bad for leaving him out there naked and at the mercy of his granddaughter.

"Julia," he says huskily. "I'm still in my pajamas. Give Papa just a minute, and I'll meet you out in the living room."

When I hear the bedroom door close, I open the bathroom door and peer out. Frank is sitting up in bed, looking at me, his whole body shaking with laughter. "I felt like an ill-behaved teenager there for a second."

"That was too close. Does she always just come into your house without warning?"

"Pretty much. At least that wasn't Jason and Emma. Though if Julia's here, it means they are here. And if they are here, that means it's nearly lunchtime."

"Oh shit." I crawl back to the bed and scramble for my phone. I have four missed calls from Amelia. "Shit!"

I glance at the time. It's nearly noon.I groan in defeat. I was supposed to put the turkey in the oven three hours ago."

"Dad?" Jason calls out. "Is Margie here? Because Amelia is at the front door looking for her."

"Guess we did get caught," Frank says. But he doesn't sound the least bit ashamed.

I scramble into my clothes, pulling the gold shirt from last night back on as I desperately search for my underwear.

"I'm never going to hear the end of this," I mumble, picturing my niece standing in the doorway and tapping her foot impatiently. Nothing like a walk of shame on Christmas Day.

But when I emerge from Frank's bedroom, rumpled in yesterday's clothes, I'm greeted by warm smiles all around. I dare say Rhett is stifling a laugh.

"Sorry about that," Frank says sheepishly. "Didn't realize it was so late."

"No worries, Dad," Jason says, hugging him. He moves to me and wraps me up in a warm embrace. "Good to see you again, Margie," he says quietly.

Emma and Julia greet me just as warmly. And we're still standing around chatting as I awkwardly try to make my exit when another car pulls up in the driveway. The door slams, and soon, another young man walks through the door. I do a double-take. This man could have been Frank twenty-five years ago, down to the dark brown hair and ice-blue eyes.

"Hey Dad," he says, walking over to hug Frank. Right, he said he had two sons. The other must live out of town. And it *is* Christmas.

"Uncle Drew!" Julia yells, then leaps into his arms.

"Hey there, pipsqueak," he says as he kneels to her level. Biscuit trots up and gives him a welcoming woof.

"I didn't realize we'd have more company than usual," he finally says, taking in the addition of Amelia, Rhett, and me. "I would have brought more pies." He grins.

"We were just leaving," I say. "I don't want to interrupt your family time."

Frank walks up to me, then slides his arm firmly around my waist, pulling me in close. He leans over and presses a gentle kiss to my lips, claiming me in front of both of our families. There can be no room for misinterpretation there.

"Something you want to tell us, Dad?" Drew asks, his tone morphing from joy to incredulity.

"Miss Margie is Papa's girlfriend!" Julia cheers. Leave it to a child to get right to the point.

"Oh," Drew says, brows furrowing. "That's news to me." He looks vaguely hurt and confused.

"It's all very new," I insist. "This is my niece, Amelia, and nephew-in-law, Rhett. We were all just heading back over to my house next door for Christmas celebrations. I have more company showing up any minute, so we'll get out of your hair."

But Frank doesn't let me escape that easily. "It's okay," he says quietly.

"It's not okay," Drew says. "What about Mom? She dies, and you just move on to someone else like you didn't spend decades together?"

I wince as his words hit me like physical blows. But Frank isn't having it.

"Drew, I understand that you're surprised," Frank says firmly. He stands up taller. "But I taught you better than to treat people this way. If you have a problem with me, we will talk about it later. And, in case you forgot, I'm still your father. Besides, I'll never stop loving your mother, but she would have wanted me to be happy."

I want to bolt. I normally thrive on conflict, but being held up in comparison to the memory of Frank's late wife in front of his children is something I can't handle. It's too much.

"Dad, it's Christmas, for God's sake. This was Mom's holiday." Hurt clouds his words, and I can't even be mad at him. He's right.

I feel Amelia's arm slide around my other side, and she clears her throat. "Hi Drew," I glance over to see my niece standing confidently beside me, looking like she's ready to take on a bear… or a man.

Amelia continues, "Look, I know that this is probably a shock to you right now, and you need some time to process it. That's fine. But my aunt is the best person you'll ever meet. She's kind, thoughtful, loyal, and tough as nails. She doesn't warm up to people easily, but your dad has gone out of his way to show her how worthy she is of love and affection. You can chat with your dad more about this later. But you should know that everyone else in this room is very happy for Frank and Margie, and I'm not going to let your dismay ruin her Christmas. My aunt deserves better than that."

Drew has the decency to look slightly abashed.

"I love Miss Margie!" Julia cheers, then runs to give me a hug. She turns and frowns at her uncle. "Those were not nice words, Uncle Drew. Your attitude sucks."

"Julia!" Emma exclaims. "Don't say 'sucks.'"

"But Mommy, sometimes bad situations need bad words. And Uncle Drew is being bad."

I stifle a giggle and glance over to see Frank doing the same.

"It's okay, Julia. I'm going to go to my house with Lia and Rhett. But maybe I can see you later tonight before you go home?"

"Oh yes, please," she says.

"Plus," I whisper. "You left a few things in my shed."

"You can leave them there for me for later," she says.

I raise an eyebrow, then stand. "I'll see you tonight?" I ask Frank.

"As if you'd be able to keep me away," he smiles.

I turn and walk toward the front door. I open it and Amelia and Rhett follow me out. I start to limp back to my house when I hear a noise. It sounds like a high-pitched mewling. I look around, but don't see anything. Biscuit trots out and looks around. The mewl comes again and he lets out a woof, then drops his nose to the ground following a scent. He sniffs furiously, following a trail into the front yard. Suddenly he pauses and his tail begins to wag.

Julia bolts past us to where Biscuit lingers in the yard. "Santa must have gotten my letter!" she says. Then she bends over, and stands back up, holding a tiny ball of black fluff.

"Julia, don't touch wild animals," Emma cries, walking toward her daughter. "You know how easily you get sick."

"It's not a wild animal, Mama. I asked Santa to bring it for Miss Margie."

My brows furrow. Already my brain is spinning through how to keep this tiny creature safe until animal control opens back up tomorrow. I can't tell what it is, exactly. A baby raccoon? A rabbit?

"It's your kitten," Julia says, approaching me.

Goosebumps erupt across my skin, suddenly remembering Julia's declaration that maybe Santa would bring me a cat friend for Christmas.

"It could belong to someone else," I say.

But I know it's a lie as soon as the words cross my lips. There are hardly any houses out here, and the only cats around are strays. This little one must have been abandoned by its mother. I kneel down to

Julia and look at the matted bundle in her arms. Two pale green eyes blink back at me. And then, without ceremony, the little creature leaps at me. I shuffle to catch it, and it settles into the crook of my elbow. My heart melts instantly at this show of affection.

"Looks like this cat chose you, Aunt Margie," Amelia says.

"What am I supposed to do with a cat?" I ask her.

"You needed a friend. Santa brought you one," Julia says simply.

And regardless of what I end up doing with the little thing, I certainly can't toss it back on the ground and reject the gift Julia asked Santa for right in front of her.

"Well, I'll just take it home then. Get it settled," I say.

Julia breaks into a wild grin. "I'll come visit it all the time, just like I promised."

Chapter 46

FRANK

CHRISTMAS DAY, PRESENT DAY

This isn't how I expected Christmas to go. After Margie left, Drew and I walk out to my back patio for a chat. He lays into me immediately, wanting to know if I have lost my mind and if I'm really shacking up with my neighbor. This can't end well, he insists. I let him vent and dump all of his feelings out. It is painful and difficult to stay quiet, but I let him say his piece.

And, when he is done, I look him in the eye and say. "I miss her too, son. Every single day of my life."

"Then why? Is this just filling the void for you or something, Dad?"

"It's filling a void, but not in the way you're implying. I love Margie, Drew. She's brought me back to life in a way I didn't think would be possible ever again. I've dealt with my guilt over this, over your mom. I'm not perfect and don't have it all sorted, but I know that we only get one shot at this life. Your mom knew that and forced me out of my own grumpiness to actually enjoy life with her. She dragged me into celebrating Christmas, despite my own insistence that I would never enjoy it. She taught me a lot. She was a good woman. And now I'm going to carry what she taught me forward," I sigh. "I'm going to allow myself to love again, Drew. And I know that may take you some time to adjust to. But please understand that just because I love Margie, doesn't mean I've replaced your mom, or love her any less. I wouldn't be who I am without her. And I won't be fully myself without Margie."

"And what does Jason think about all this? Or is he giving you a pass just because Julia likes her so much?"

"I don't know what Jason thinks exactly. But he told me he's happy for me. And he's been around Margie several times now. So maybe you should ask him what he thinks. I'll stay back so he can answer honestly."

Drew studies me. "Okay," he says simply.

"Okay, you'll talk to Jason?"

"Okay, I'll back off about all this. I mean, I'm not exactly alright with it, but you're right. What I'm feeling is about me. It will take some time." Drew turns to walk back inside my house, then pauses and turns around. "But Dad, you and Jason are right. I'm glad you're happy. You deserve that."

I walk over to Drew and pull him into a hug. He squeezes me back. And even though things are rocky between us right now, they will be okay. And I know that once he gets to know Margie, he may discover that he actually likes her even more than he likes me.

Chapter 47

MARGIE

CHRISTMAS DAY, PRESENT DAY

As soon as Amelia, Rhett, the kitten, and I make it back to my house, Katie, Jacob, and the Heberts pull up in the driveway. I groan, thinking about my uncooked turkey in the fridge. What a disaster.

Sensing my distress, Amelia leans in and whispers. "Don't stress. Rhett and I will help. It's okay to let someone else help you sometimes, you know."

"Oh my gosh, a kitten!" Katie squeals as soon as she walks in the door and spots the coal-colored dandelion ball in my arms. Rhett's sister is red-headed just like him. But where he's shy and quiet, she's bright and bubbly. She whisks the creature out of my arms and immediately retreats to the bathroom to clean it up.

I head to the sink and scrub my hands, then turn to the crowd. "Hope you don't mind staying for dinner instead of lunch."

DINNER, IT TURNED OUT, WAS JUST FINE. Everyone pitched in to help cook, and never have I been so grateful for the double ovens and the five stovetop burners I invested in for my business. My house fills with warm chatter, flowing wine, and laughter. Katie refuses to put the kitten down, and when I insist she take it with her, she shakes her head solemnly. "No Margie, the cat chooses the owner, and this one chose you."

I huff, but inside I'm relieved. It will be nice to have some company around here.

We eat later than planned, but it's cozy as the sun sets and the Christmas tree twinkles in the living room. It makes me start to love Christmas again. We exchange gifts, and I'm delighted by the new wellies Amelia and Rhett give me. Katie and her mom fight over the jams I gave them, and Amelia and Rhett delight over the cutting board I bought from Frank for their new home.

It all feels cheerful and right, but I can't help but feel like a part of my heart is still missing—a part that's tucked in with his own family next door. I hear a knock at my front door, and my heart stutters with hope. I know my meeting with Frank's son wasn't the best, but I know everyone at my house tonight would love to meet him.

"I'll grab it," Amelia says. She hops up and runs to the front door. She reappears a few moments later with a smile plastered across her face. "You have a special visitor, Aunt Margie."

In walks Frank dressed in that sexy-ass Santa suit. He's carrying a large, wrapped gift. Julia stands beside him in her elf costume.

"Merry Christmas, Miss Margie!" Julia says.

The whole room stands up, delighted at the unexpected visitors.

"Is this one of those Santagrams?" Katie asks.

"Oh, this is much better than that," Amelia responds with a grin.

"Hi there, Margie," Frank booms. "I've heard you've been a very good girl this year." He gives me a wink that makes me blush. Seriously Frank?

"First, you need this," Julia says, holding up a box. I walk over and take it from her, eyeing the kitty litter and cat toys inside.

"Where did Santa find this at such late notice?" I whisper to her.

"There are cats at the farm where Papa works and they had some extra supplies," she whispers back. I nod my head sagely.

"And I have something for you, too," Frank says, holding out the large, wrapped gift to me.

I take it from him and unwrap it, gasping when I reveal what lies beneath the torn paper. It's a beautiful, hand-carved, wooden sign. It has "Margie's Machinations" carved into it. The details are exquisite. There are tiny images carved around the edges, and when I lean in closer to study them, I giggle. They are Christmas ornaments that look very similar to the large ones in Frank's yard.

"Frank, it's perfect," the last word comes out choked. I place the sign gently down on my kitchen table, then throw my arms around him.

He presses a kiss to my forehead and whispers, "Merry Christmas, Margie."

Everyone in the room erupts into applause and whistles. I startle, forgetting there were other people in the room. Amelia fiddles with her phone, and then "I Saw Mommy Kissing Santa Claus" blasts through the wireless speaker. Everyone erupts in laughter, and my cheeks heat a violent shade of red.

"That's one way to introduce you to the rest of my family," I say to him. Then, more loudly, "Well, I guess it's about high time y'all met Frank."

And then everyone descends on him, hugging him and welcoming him into the fold.

It's not long before we're all laughing together in the living room, and I'm thrilled that I get to give Julia her Christmas present: the softest plush fox that caught my eye while I was out shopping. Frank gasps a little when she opens it, but when I look at him, he just nods his head and smiles. A sheen of tears coats his eyes, but he dashes them away quickly.

I also give Julia a batch of cookies just for her. She's delighted, and the sounds of her childish giggles filling my home make this night feel more celebratory than any Christmas has in years.

EVERYONE PACKS UP AND LEAVES at nearly 10 p.m. Jason and Emma stop by to collect their now-sleeping daughter. I'm exhausted, full, and happy. But even with all the guests leaving, Frank stays by my side, holding me close. The sign he made me is beautiful, but his presence in my house is better than any Christmas gift I could have asked for.

A tiny mewl comes from the pillow in the corner. Right, my new companion.

"Thanks for the cat there, Santa," I tease. Then, walk over to scoop up the little fur ball. Katie got her nice and clean for me. Julia set up the litter box and tiny cat food and water bowls.

"What will you name her?" Frank asks.

"Seems like there's only one fitting name," I sigh. "Say hello to Noelle."

"I knew I'd win you over to Christmas," Frank says with a wink.

"I wouldn't say you've won me over, at least not yet."

"What else can I possibly do?" he asks.

I eye him up and down, studying the way his Santa suit clings to his chest and arms. "I can think of a few things."

He chuckles, then lifts his arm above us. I look up to see what in the world he's doing. He's holding mistletoe. "I thought one more gift would be fitting tonight." And then he leans in and kisses me deeply.

I break away. "Frank, I just realized that in the chaos of last night, I never gave you your Christmas gift."

"I don't need anything—"

"Oh, hush, and let me give you your present." I limp to my

bedroom and return, holding a small, wrapped box in one hand while the kitten remains tucked in my other arm. I offer it up and he takes it, studying the wrapping.

"It's so small," he jokes.

"Had to find something to balance out your ego," I say with a chuckle.

He opens it slowly, then peeks inside. Furrowing his brow, he flips it over, dumping the contents into his open palm. "What's this?" he asks, eyeing the enamel pin.

"It's what we are going to give donors to the Juju Bug Scholarship Foundation."

He blinks. "What do you mean?"

"I may have utilized my little YouTube Channel for good," I wink. "There's a fund at the Ruston Community Bank set up to help children who have to travel to receive healthcare. It's under a new nonprofit called Juju Bug. It's still new and has a lot of room to grow. But the Junior League is going to run it and make sure the funds are distributed to those who need it. Believe me, helping them launch this new project for the League went a long way in helping ease their angst over losing the beautification donation."

"Margie, I don't know what to say."

"I know it's an unconventional gift, but I thought–"

Frank's mouth crashes down on mine, his lips moving furiously. I gasp.

"Frank!" I laugh.

"Margie, this is amazing. So thoughtful and just so– I don't know. Did I already say amazing?"

I nod.

"God, I love you," he says on an exhale. I freeze and he winces.

"It's okay. I know you are just excited. It doesn't have to be awkward," I say in one rushed breath.

"I mean it, though," he says slowly. He reaches out and cusps my face, tilting me up to look at him. "I love you, Margie."

"Oh God." I start to cry.

"Hey, hey. Don't cry. And don't feel like you have to say it back, okay? There's no pressure. I just couldn't keep it in any longer and–"

"No, no," I say, shaking my head. "It's not that. It's just. God, Frank. I never thought I'd ever hear those words romantically again. And this just feels, I don't know, *big*. I have a lot of big feelings, and I'm not used to big feelings, well, except for anger, and that never ends well." I'm rambling, so I cut myself off.

"So yeah," I say, lifting my gaze to him. "I'm just surprised and amazed. By you. By love. That I could find this at my age," I whisper.

He presses a gentle kiss to my lips. I inhale his delicious sawdust and pine scent. I feel so comfortable, so cherished, so right.

"Frank," I whisper. I inhale, fortify myself. "I love you, too."

He leans his forehead against mine, and together, we soak up the moment, surrounded by love, the lights from a twinkling Christmas tree, and a small kitten who interrupts our moment with a mewl.

"Yes, yes. We love you too, Noelle," Frank says, scratching the tiny kitten's head.

"Already so demanding," I say to the little furball.

"She'll fit in just fine around here then," he chuckles.

Epilogue

FRANK

FIVE MONTHS LATER
PRESENT DAY

"Nope, it's not over. It's been five months and ten days. You still owe me twenty more mornings of coffee at my house. That was the charity competition bet, and I'm holding you to it," I say firmly to the woman sitting across from me on my back patio.

"If I recall, the bet was coffee on *Saturdays* at your house. Not every day. And I just thought we might try coffee at my house one morning," Margie insists. "Don't get all bent out of shape about it, Frank."

"But I like taking care of you," I say, leaning in to kiss her forehead before sinking back into my patio chair.

"Besides, it's already starting to get too hot to keep sitting outside and drinking coffee."

"We could switch to iced coffee," I say. The corner of my mouth twitches as I try to suppress a grin. When I catch a glance of Margie's scowl though, I lose all control and start laughing.

"You know how I feel about iced coffee," she says, taking a sip from her scalding hot mug.

"Is iced coffee better or worse than Christmas lights?" I ask.

"Depends. Are we talking about the average person's Christmas lights or yours?"

"Mine," I say, and wait.

She slides a look at me and, with intense seriousness, says, "I guess I'll take the iced coffee."

I lose it again, laughing loudly and it's only a moment before Margie is laughing too. It's something I do all the time now. I feel more alive than I have in years, and most of it is thanks to the stunning woman sitting next to me. We will get to celebrate my other joy in just a few hours.

"Regardless of how you take your coffee, make sure you drink it all. We need to finish setting up, and we'll both need the caffeine boost," I say.

"What time do you expect them to come over?" Margie asks.

"Around noon."

Margie checks her watch. "That only gives us a couple of hours. We better get the decorations up."

"And the grill started," I agree.

THE CAR RUMBLES UP THE DRIVEWAY, and I can barely contain my excitement. We've been planning this day since January. Even Biscuit is restless, pacing slowly across my living room. He's missed his pal, Julia.

Everyone has parked their cars behind my house or at Margie's so as not to clue Julia in. When the front door to my house swings open and Julia comes bounding inside, I almost don't recognize her. She's grown at least an inch, and her gaunt cheeks have filled out in both shape and color. She looks hearty, the most healthy I've ever seen her.

I'm so taken aback by her improved appearance that when everyone else in my house shouts, "Surprise!" it startles me.

"Oh!" Julia says.

"Welcome home, Juju Bug," I say.

Margie and I get to Julia first, wrapping her up in hugs. And then Drew dips in next. Amelia and Rhett follow close behind, as do Rhett's parents. Even Margie's friend, Greta, is here. But Julia seems most excited to see Biscuit. She bolts over to him immediately and slides her arms around his neck. His tail wags, acknowledging how much he's missed his best friend.

"I'm cooking your favorite, Juju Bug," I tell her. "We've got hot dogs on the grill."

"And I made chocolate chip cookies," Margie chimes in.

Soon, the house is filled with joyful chatter. It's taken some time, but Drew has finally warmed to having Margie around. As I predicted, he seems to like her more than me. Though much of that probably has to do with how much he laughed when he learned how Margie tried to sabotage me over Christmas. Santa balls will unite even the biggest of Scrooges.

As we celebrate, I hear a knock at the front door. I look around, confused. Everyone is here who should be. When I open the door, I'm greeted by a young woman holding a plate of cookies and looking exceptionally uncomfortable. She has long, blonde hair that she's tied into a low ponytail that lays over one shoulder. Her hazel eyes are wide, and I wonder if she's about to bolt.

"Hi, can I help you with something?" I ask before she can run.

She seems to steady herself. "Um, yes, hi. I'm Kylie. Your new neighbor across the street. Well not that new. I've owned the house for a few months or so but haven't been there much. Anyway, I just wanted to introduce myself. But, I think maybe this is a bad time?"

Julia runs through the house giggling and straight past us through the front door. Biscuit bounds behind her, trying his best to keep up.

"Sorry about that. It's a little chaotic right now, but you're welcome to come in and meet everyone. Margie, my neighbor and girlfriend, is here too. You can meet her as well."

"I wouldn't want to intrude," she hedges.

"Kylie?" Drew steps up to the front door beside me.

The young woman takes a step back and looks dazed. "Drew? What are you doing here?"

"I should ask you the same thing. God, I haven't seen you in what? Two years?"

"Twenty months, actually," she says too quickly.

Drew frowns, then seems to remember himself. "This is my dad, Frank," my son says, patting my shoulder.

"I'm his new neighbor across the street there," she says, looking over her shoulder.

"So you're the one who bought my parents' old house," Kathy, Rhett's mom says.

My doorway is packed now, and this poor woman is being stared down by all three of us. That can't be comfortable. I step outside, ending the bottleneck.

"Kylie, I just pulled hotdogs and hamburgers off the grill. We're celebrating my granddaughter's medical treatment being completed. Please come in and eat with us."

She stares between the three of us, her gaze lingering on Drew, and finally nods. Margie introduces herself as soon as she spots our visitor. I hear her start to warn our new neighbor about my Christmas decorations and the traffic that comes along with it.

"Oh, Kylie, hey," Rhett says.

This just keeps getting stranger. It turns out that Kylie started up a local magazine and knows Rhett through their mutual reporting work. And not only that, but the house across the street that Kylie purchased used to belong to Rhett's grandparents. Small-town living is certainly something. But after Kylie makes the rounds and meets everyone, I watch as she and Drew find a quiet place to chat. I can tell their muffled conversation is serious, and I give them space.

I finally get a moment alone with Margie and Jason, and my son gives us an update on Julia. "It's been miraculous. There's no other word for it," he says, beaming. "The IV infusions combined with weekly hospital visits, physical therapy, and test medications are turning Julia's life around. She'll get to be home most of the time now, but go back to Dallas quarterly for follow-ups. We can do physical therapy at home now, too."

Jason pauses, then looks at Margie. "And I wanted to thank you for setting up that scholarship fund for Jules and other kids like her. It's made a huge financial difference for us already." My son gets choked up, and Margie doesn't hesitate, throwing her arms around him in a tight embrace. He continues, "You too, Dad. Your payment after the Christmas Market took care of the rest of her hospital bills."

"That's the best news," Margie says sincerely.

Watching how my sons have embraced Margie has been one of the best parts of the last six months. She's becoming part of the Campbell clan, forging her own unique place among us.

"Oh, before I forget, I have to give Julia her welcome home gift." The three of us share a knowing smile.

When I finally have everyone in my living room, I begin. "Thank y'all for coming over today to help celebrate Julia's healthy return to her home." Everyone claps, cheers, and whistles. "Julia, darlin', I know it's been hard for you to be away for the past five months. And we have all missed you dearly."

"I missed you too, Papa," Julia says. The room lets out a collective "aww."

"So Miss Margie and I talked to your parents, and we wanted to give you something to show you just how proud we are of how brave you've been."

"I get a present?" she squeals.

Margie steps into my bedroom and comes out carrying a box. It wiggles slightly and makes a noise. Julia's eyes grow as wide as saucers.

She bolts to the box and extends her hands up. Margie kneels, gently placing the box on the ground. Julia rips the lid off… and promptly bursts into tears. My granddaughter reaches inside and pulls out a wriggling basset hound puppy. The puppy's whole body wags as it tries to nibble on Julia's fingers and lick her cheeks. She tucks the puppy in close to her chest and full-body sobs. Not quite the reaction I was expecting, but I can tell the tears come from overwhelming joy. Biscuit approaches, wagging his tail curiously.

"It's time for you to have your own friend, Julia," Margie whispers.

"Can the puppy be friends with Noelle?" Julia asks.

"I don't see why not," Margie says. The cat that found Margie at Christmas has turned out to be the most social, snuggly, outgoing cat I've ever encountered. And she loves Biscuit.

"What are you going to name your new friend?" Margie asks.

"Is it a boy or a girl?" Julia asks, trying to flip the puppy over to see for herself.

"A girl," I say.

"Hmmm," Julia considers for only a moment. "Joy. Her name is Joy."

I glance up and see tears roll down Emma's cheeks. I'm so grateful that my granddaughter is finally healthy enough to have her own dog that I almost forget the next part.

"And there's one more thing," I say, before the crowd dissipates.

"There better not be another puppy back there," Jason says, and the room laughs.

"Not this time."

I turn to look at Margie, noting the tears in her eyes as she watches Julia playing with Joy in front of us. I love her so much that my heart physically aches when I look at her.

"Margie. The past six months have been some of the best of my life," I say.

"Not seven?" she asks mischievously.

"I think that first month was more difficult than fun," I say, chuckling.

"That's fair," she agrees, and her grin is so wide that it makes my knees start to buckle. My heart starts picking up its pace and I tremble.

"And I know six months may seem like a short time to most people. But for the two of us, who have already lived more than fifty years on this earth, I think we both know that we have to make every single moment count. And when you find someone who makes you laugh, supports you when things are difficult, and teaches you how to love and live again, you have to hold onto them."

Her brows knit in confusion, and my knees really do give out then, making the decision on how to proceed easy. I drop to the floor, then pull up one knee and hold the box out in front of me. My arms tremble and the room erupts in surprised gasps. I look up at the woman who showed me how to love again, to fight for who and what you want. Tears slip down her cheeks as she presses her hand over her mouth.

"I think we both know that you and I are the real deal. There's no point in wasting any more time. Margie Murphy, will you marry me?"

Someone squeals. I'm pretty sure it's Amelia.

Margie squeezes her eyes shut, and more tears leak out. For a second I think I've made a huge error in judgment. But when she opens her eyes again, she's nodding her head, "Yes." Margie takes a step toward me and reaches down for my hands. "Stand up, Frank. You know I can't bend down like I used to."

I laugh and stand, and she throws herself into my arms. Then her lips find mine.

"Is that a yes?" I ask.

"Of course it is," she whispers.

"I want to be the flower girl!" Julia shouts.

Biscuit woofs, seconding the notion.

"Now, the only question left is, are we going to move into your house or mine?" I ask, laughing.

"I guess this means we have to go through the new neighbor headache again," she says.

"Don't worry. You'll have me by your side to help you handle them this time," I tell her. And I seal the promise with a kiss.

Acknowledgments

Every book comes with hours of support and love from the people around me. In particular, I've somehow managed to find groups of the most amazing cheerleader friends a writer could ask for. I must have done something right in life to have all of these zesty people surrounding me.

I'm grateful to all of my Salted Caramel Madams, my internet stranger friends turned besties who I once met up with in the Ohio woods. Lindsey, Chandler, Nat, Jacqui, Sarah, Vinsci, Kelsey, Jen, and Cindy, thanks for being there to listen to every gripe and celebration.

Somehow I even managed to join a coven of Cincinnati romance authors who step in to help answer all the questions when the indie writing road gets bumpy. Thank you especially to Delaine, Dani, Chrissy, and Eden. Y'all are the best babes.

I'm especially grateful to my talented and tenacious beta readers: Stephanie, Lucy, Kirsten, Tammy, and Chandler. Y'all always step up to the plate and help me work out the plot holes and help me discern the specifics (and you're right, there are no cicadas in December).

Kristin, my editor, you always make me shine bright like a diamond. Thank you.

To my ARC team, thank you for being there for every stray thought and consideration, and for always hyping my books up to everyone you know. I love y'all.

Jake and Ali, my new audiobook narrators-turned-dear-friends, thanks for not thinking I was too weird when I grabbed you both by the hands and yanked you firmly into my life. I'm grateful that fate brought us together and you both taught me even more about publishing, performance, and tenacity.

To Kellie, I couldn't have survived this past year and every single writing hurdle (especially that gigantic one that almost made me throw it all away), without your guiding light. Thank you.

For every single bookstore who took a chance on my books and helped get them into the hands of readers, I'm forever grateful to you.

To every author who read my books and told the world about them, especially Ellery Adams, who always encourages me to shoot for the sparkly, magical stars: you're my she-ros.

And, most of all, thank you to my number one fans: my mom, my sisters, and my children, who always make me feel like a million bucks every time I write a book. I love you.

About the Author

Jessica is a lifelong reader and writer. She earned a degree in communications and professional writing before making a career in journalism and editing. She has always dreamt of writing books, and her love for novels spurred her into becoming an avid bookstagrammer.

Although she grew up in Louisiana, Jessica now resides in Ohio with her rowdy family and a couple of hounds. When not writing and reading, you can find her browsing the shelves of indie bookstores, or taking her border collie, Rhys, on long walks.

Follow Jessica online:
www.jessicaboothauthor.com
www.instagram.com/jessicaboothauthor
www.tiktok.com/jessicaboothauthor